PRIVATE
BETRAYAL

A Novel By

S.R. Chase

Book and Cover design by Eford Group International LLC

ISBN 978-0-9995276-0-3
EBook ISBN 978-0-9995276-1-0

First edition: October 2017
10 9 8 7 6 5 4 3 2 1

www.srchase.com
@SRChaseauthor

ACKNOWLEDGEMENTS

For the two greatest blessings God sent me, C H A S E ♥.
Thank you for your love and support. We did it!
Remember your dreams are always valid.

To RE. My father. My hero.
Gone, but never forgotten.
Thank you for the gift.

FGM. Salute Marine! Thank you for your service and for the
final push when you said, "You're a writer, so write!"

TW. The world needs more book nerds like you.
Thanks for your support.

RT. Thank you for your editorial push and expertise.
WE. Thanks for listening to the stories locked up my head.

**Last, but not least, to all the women and men, privately
betrayed due to the interruption of others in your love life,
I hope this book brings you comfort. Fret not,
Karma is real.**

CHAPTER 1

Some people are going to hell in a shoe box, Dr. Phillip Andelman thought as he stared out at the grey sky and pouring rain from his office in rural New Jersey.

Earlier he had met someone so evil the devil probably would request he bring him down a pair of shoes when he arrived.

Fifty-six-year-old Terrence Shane, a married father of two, had murdered his mistress of ten years as proof to his wife he had ended their affair. A crime he decided to tell the world by recording it live on social media. Over 100,000 viewers witnessed the woman's bloody slaughter.

As a gift for his wife, he began cutting off the dead woman's breasts. "Look my darling, I'm bringing home a present from her—she doesn't need them anymore."

Before the police broke down his hotel room door, he topped it off by pleading for his wife's forgiveness.

"Reverend Brooks told us at our wedding, let no man, or woman like her, put asunder. Please let me come home," he said staring like a lunatic into the camera.

"She meant nothing to me. To us."

When the judge sentenced him to forty years in prison, Shane decided to shit on the court—literally. He jumped up on the table, took a squat and gassed the place. A dump that rolled down his pants legs onto his defense papers and the courtroom floor.

While the court officers debated who would grab him first, he ran to his wife sitting in the visitor's bench.

Her punch to his jaw knocked him out cold.

"You psycho son of a bitch. You're always embarrassing me. I told you to take your freakin' meds."

After she spat on him, she walked out of the courtroom yelling, "My divorce is final!"

"Granted!" the shocked judge said before adding ten years to Shane's sentence. He also ordered he be sent to the Meadow Banks Psychiatric Hospital. There he would be evaluated to help the judge decide where Shane would use the bathroom for the next fifty years in state custody.

Not even Iyanla Vanzant could fix that life.

**

Dr. Andelman, the CEO of Meadow Banks, enjoyed a moment of solitude after Shanes' police escort and staff had secured him for the night.

A man who could usually control his own emotions, Dr. Andelman now needed his own mental health break he thought while he sipped a steaming cup of English black tea.

With exception of the occasional voice heard over the hospital's PA system, it was rather quiet. Dr. Andelman glanced at the security cameras and saw the glare of Randolph's flashlight.

Thirty-two-year-old Randolph McGuire had been a patient at Meadow Banks since the age of 18. During each employee orientation, Dr. Andelman would click on a projector and present a photo of his favorite patient. He would then explain Randolph's somewhat unorthodox treatment plan for his insomnia.

"Randolph McGuire is one of our security guards. Well not really, he is one of our patients," he would inform them.

"Randolph believes his deceased father, who was a police officer, speaks to him and provides instruction on how to keep everyone here at Meadow Banks safe."

"Has he ever helped with a crime?" Someone asked.

"Yes, once he caught a raccoon with explosives," he said.

"I'm kidding, I just wanted to see who was still awake. Seriously, please do not be alarmed if you see him during his shift which is usually 10 pm to 1 am. His route is the back stairwell from the 10th floor down to the security booth."

"What happens after that?" Another asked.

"Our real security officers escort him back to his room where he sleeps like a baby," Dr. Andelman continued. "Otherwise, Randolph will scream all night forcing us to sedate him. As you are learning here today, our policy at Meadow Banks is to limit the use of prescription medication whenever possible."

Meadow Banks, considered one of the top mental health facilities in the northeast, was located on a 62-acre campus in Meadow, New Jersey--a suburb 16 miles west of New York City.

The hospital's alarm ringing interrupted Dr. Andelman's siesta. There were several distinctive rings depending upon the emergency. This one sounded like a naval ship submarine launch—the alarm for a death.

Dr. Andelman could not recall the last time there had been a death at Meadow Banks. Perhaps it was just an unscheduled emergency drill? That was his hope as he answered his phone.

"The seventh floor? I'll be right there," he said to Nurse Riley, the floor nurse on duty.

Dr. Andelman rushed past staff and noticed their nervous glances. In a world filled with the threat of terrorism, he understood their concerns.

"Everything is alright. There is a situation on the 7th floor, but none of us are in danger," he shouted.

As he rode in the elevator, he heard the hospital's video playing, "Meadow Banks, a place of peace welcomes you."

Not so much today, he thought.

He tried to recall the patients on that floor. Perhaps, it was Mr. Pope. After all, he just turned 90. Maybe he had passed away in his sleep. Death never came at the right time, he sighed.

When the elevator doors opened, Nurse Riley was there. Her gloved hands and uniform were covered in blood.

"Tell me what happened? Are you okay?" He asked.

"Yes, I'm alright. We have a 929 doctor," she said.

A 929 was the code for death by suicide.

"I tried my best to save her," she said.

Her?

CHAPTER 2

Years Earlier

The hot midday sun caught Jeremy Edward Collins by surprise. A burst of hot air took a stab at him as he strolled out of the luxury office building on West 57th Street in Manhattan. Sweat pooled under his armpits. He had underestimated the weather on the unusually hot spring day and had overdressed in a black Giorgio Armani suit and a long sleeve Oxford shirt. The sudden heat went appropriately with the fire he was expecting when he would announce to his father, his boss, that he had just blew another real estate deal.

As he walked to his car parked at the corner, he saw a man taking pictures of his Maserati. *Damn paparazzi.* Just then, a woman stepped up to him. He was about to give her the usual line, "No, I'm not a basketball player. No, I'm not a rapper."

"Jeremy Collins?" She asked, as he looked at the vaguely familiar face attached to a voluptuous figure.

"I thought that was you. How are you doing?" she asked. He noticed her nipples perking through her cranberry silk dress. Her hair was in a nice cropped Afro which accentuated with long hanging silver earrings. Her cranberry Gucci sunglasses fit her face perfectly he thought. The white sweater tied over her shoulders was a classy touch. A little old for his tastes, but he respected the cougars for still having the confidence to even try.

"Elena Harris. Attorney Harris." She said reaching out and squeezing his arm. "I go way back with your father."

He was turned off by the way she had said "attorney" and released himself from her grasp. He resumed walking to his car after a quick hello. He was in no mood for bullshit today.

"Am I being served?" he uttered as she tagged along.

"No, silly, I have process servers for that," she giggled like a schoolgirl as he watched her take a whiff of his Polo cologne.

"Wow you smell really good," she said while seemingly losing her thought for a second.

"Remember we worked on the Horizon Bank deal together?" She said grinning.

"Come on I told your voice sounds like the actor, Dennis Hastert from the Allstate Commercials? Last June. 145th Street."

"I've been told that a time or two," a confident Jeremy replied appreciatively.

"Yes, I remember," he said. "I'm well. Thank you for asking."

Jeremy stared at her skinny legs which glistened in the sunlight. He had to admit, she made him horny. Then again, Jeremy was always horny.

"How old are you now?" She asked.

"Thirty," he said with a look that you can't handle this. He knew he would break her back.

"Well, it's certainly a beautiful day out," she said looking up at the perfect blue sky. She seemed to be open to him making a move. Unfortunately, he did not have the time to flirt.

He pressed the car's remote to unlock the back door while waving the photographer away.

"Is this your car?" Elena pointed. "Nice, it matches the color of my dress. See that?" She giggled again.

She was a silly one, he thought. He took off his suit jacket to place on the empty velvet hanger. *Wrinkled clothes are a no, no.*

As he removed his jacket, he noticed her staring as if she was fantasizing his name was Big Carmel, her private stripper.

Jeremy took the attention all in stride. He was a tall, dark, and handsome bachelor with money and power. As the son of Edward Collins, a wealthy Harlem real estate guru and former Councilman, it seemed he could hardly go anywhere without a random person smiling or trying to talk to him.

"How's your father?" "Can you give him my card?" "Do you have an apartment for rent?" "Can I get a job?" "What's your email?" Jeremy had heard it all. It made him moderately famous and he had grown into it like a B-list celebrity.

"Would you like a ride uptown?" He asked while he sized up her mouth. He was trying to guess how deep he could fit eleven inches of his manhood. It would likely relax him more on the ride.

"No actually, I'm just out on my lunch. Enjoying the sunshine," she said looking up at the picturesque clear blue sky.

"Here's my card. Again. Call me later, she suggested. "I would love to connect Collins Realty with a few real estate deals I have coming up for Harlem."

"I'll do that," Jeremy said and gave her a wink before saying goodbye. She stood at attention for a second before realizing she was standing alone and then disappeared into the crowded street.

Seated comfortably in his car, he turned on the AC to full blast and pulled out a pen. He scribbled the date and a short note on the back of her card.

"Ms. Giggles. Cute rank: 8 Single? Looks like Sheryl Lee Ralph. 50 something. Cougar. Skinny. Good for drinks. Holla if you're thirsty."

He tossed it in the glove compartment with the tons of other cards and notes from admirers before pulling off.

CHAPTER 3

Jeremy used to dream about becoming a model. At six feet, four inches, he had thought his above average height, muscular build and good looks would take him to the runways of Milan or Paris. A stack of modeling agency rejection letters thwarted his plans of becoming one of America's top models.

Jeremy knew he was far from perfect. Age, along with a lot of T-bone steaks, had given him a gut. Instead of a six-pack, he was more like an eight-pack. Yet, that did not stop the women from holding on to what they called his "love handles."

Laser surgery had been an option to correct his poor eyesight, since ophthalmologists advised him against wearing contacts.

"You can't score a three-pointer, if you're blind," said his first and only basketball coach who had humiliated him in front of his 7th grade classmates and killed his NBA dreams. What he lost with his vision, he made up for in his sense of smell.

"Boy, you can smell the breath of an ant," his father joked.

Dark moles on his cheeks, which favored freckles, were the only thing between him and perfect skin.

Although he considered himself African American, people thought he was of mixed ancestry. With his caramel colored skin and deep black curly hair, he would often be asked whether he was from the Mediterranean or South America? Whenever he visited Indian casinos, he enjoyed the hotel comps they gave him because they thought he was Native American.

Jeremy wasn't even sure himself where his looks and stature came from. His parents and sisters were all darker and much shorter. Even his food tastes were different from the family. He preferred Caribbean and Spanish cuisine.

Whenever he would ask his parents about his DNA, they relayed, "Our parents were tall."

End of discussion.

Dressing impeccable was all he knew. While other little boys were wearing cut off shorts and Pro Keds, his mother, whom he called Madam Ernestine, had him in bow ties, linen pants and loafers.

"Your clothes, which cost a pretty penny, must always be pressed and not look like you have slept in them," Madam Ernestine would say.

"Wrinkled clothes are a no-no. They represent laziness or worse, poverty," she would tell her children mainly on Sunday mornings before church.

Jeremy could not count how many times he had gotten popped with a stick if had forgotten his belt or had a button undone. Their mother's note on their refrigerator served as a reminder: "Never embarrass the family with improper grooming. You're a Collins. Remember that."

"First impressions are everlasting," he explained to a group of young men at the Real Estate Society's mentoring day.

"Always remember people will treat you according to how you look. A man's footwear is his calling card. It's not always about wearing Jordan's," he said as he lifted his foot to show a size 15 Brooks Brothers black leather shoe.

"Put on some shoes and not just for a funeral."

Driving uptown, Jeremy listened to the rebroadcast of Steve Harvey's Strawberry Letter. Harvey had just come back from a commercial and was about to give his synopsis on what a woman should do who had caught her husband in bed with her cousin. Jeremy's anticipation of an answer was interrupted when a call came through and knocked the showoff.

It was his pregnant, soon to be wife Dana.

What does she want?

Her call made him even more tense. He was reminded he was overdue for his monthly massage in Chinatown, where Ke Li or Li Ke would give him an erotic "happy ending" on his erogenous zones.

"Hello," he said.

"Hi Sweetheart," Dana said trying to sound sexy with her high-pitched voice that sounded like she had a sinus problem.

"What's up?" he asked annoyed.

"Darling, the moving company called. They said you aren't moving here until next Saturday," she whined. "I thought you were coming this weekend."

"What difference does it make?" He snarled as he swerved away from a yellow cab trying to cut him off.

"This weekend, next weekend? The point is I'll be there soon. Anything else Dana? The traffic out here is crazy."

"Okay then be careful on the road," she said as if he had taken the air out of her balloon, which was his intention.

"Speak with you later," he said before clicking off the call and avoiding her "I love you" ending.

Damn. He thought. *I missed what Steve and Shirley had to say.*

Jeremy had dated all kinds of women. Professional women, women with kids, women without kids, and even a few who had asked him to marry them. All that variety and never once had he come remotely close to marrying any of them. His father forcing him to marry Dana was beyond his comprehension.

Dana Tyler, the 30-year old, socialite debutante and the daughter of the Reverend Oliver and Mamie "snooty as fuck" Tyler was the lucky girl.

Reverend Tyler was the senior pastor of one of Harlem's oldest churches, New Bethel AME. The good reverend branded it, "The number one savior of Harlem's souls."

Everyone knew the only souls he pretended to save were the multitude of women who kept his company after church. The entire Harlem Christian community knew he was a player. Jeremy wasn't mad at him. Get yours was his motto.

This arranged marriage between the Collins' and the Tylers' would take place to help keep "good bloodlines," according to Reverend Tyler.

Born into what could be considered Black privilege, Dana was probably bred to marry someone wealthy since she had been pushed by a nanny in a baby carriage.

Now, after a purposeful delay, Jeremy was moving into her house in Parksdale, an exclusive suburb north of the city where professional women blogged each day and housewives cooked meals for their spoiled kids and wealthy husbands that no one could pronounce.

The contemporary shotgun wedding and pregnancy was weighing him down. Not only was he not in love with Dana—he was not even sure he even liked her. She was a bitch, a cunt and whatever other adjective one could think of to refer to a woman who was conceited beyond her looks. Having money afforded her attention from men who probably would not have given her the time of day otherwise. The leader among the women in her circle, they all kissed her ass hoping she would drop them some crumbs.

Although, he was a fan, Jeremy was mad at Mrs. Beyoncé Carter. She dropped the song about independent women and then went home to her husband.

Today, too many women were using independent personas as a survival tactic. Now men were left with the fall-out and women like Dana with bad attitudes. Jeremy hated those type of women. He either wanted to sock them in the mouth or fuck them into obedience.

"Women don't have bad 'tudes.' Some of us just have to check men, especially when think they are players," she poked at him one day.

13

Dana could send all the subliminal messages she wanted, but Jeremy knew he had pimped her out a long time ago.

During one of his father's annual summer cookouts while everyone partied in the backyard, Jeremy had accidentally walked in on the little 20-year-old prima donna in the guest bathroom. Dana had not seemed to mind as he ushered her to hurry up and finish her business. She rose off the toilet and, instead of wiping herself, she began rubbing in between her legs without shame. Jeremy nudged her out of his way to relieve himself. It's hard for a man to be interested in a porno scene when he must urinate.

Dana leaned casually against the sparkling white porcelain wall and stared at his manhood. He glanced at her to see her moving her tongue in a circular motion around her lips. He almost laughed until he felt his little head say, "Let's get it man."

He grabbed a piece of toilet paper, wiped off his tip and locked the door. He offered his manhood to her like he was handing her lollipop.

"Make it quick."

Without hesitation, she dropped on her knees and added him in her mouth. She started off fast like a madwoman. She was slobbering him, like she was dying of thirst in the middle of the desert. She deep throated him several times giving credence to the belief that church girls are major freaks. Except for a few gags, he was impressed. Just as he was ready to release a mouth full of cum, she halted.

No, don't stop.

She looked up at Jeremy with a sinister smile. She thought she was in control and began sucking on his balls. He heard her whisper, "Come on that's it." Jeremy moaned and bit down on his bottom lip. His groin felt like it was on fire, but he would not give her the satisfaction. Releasing himself would be within his control, not hers.

As if in a trance, she went back to licking and sucking him like he was the last lollipop on Halloween. Jeremy moaned in ecstasy. Then he felt her teeth. She had bit him.

"Damn girl," he said pushing her head off him and knocking her slightly off balance.

She screamed, "I'm so sorry."

"Shhh," he said. "Stand up."

She tried to kiss him, but he turned his head. Then, he turned her around and bent her over. It was time to unlock his own hunger. He pulled up her skirt and stuck his finger between her legs. She was soaking wet and smelled like a mixture of strawberries and shea butter.

Dana gripped the sink as if she was holding on for dear life while little man was introduced to her womanhood. Her young ass had wanted some grown sized man dick, so that is what he gave her. With every moan, he thrust harder. He held the back of her neck so tight; he was making her skin turn red.

She cried out, "Jeremy, you're hurting me."

"Quiet and move those hips," he said.

"Whose pussy is this?"

"Yours," she said submitting.

"Say it again." Bang. He grunted.

"Yours," she screamed.

He looked up and saw they were directly in front of a half-opened window with the shade pulled up. If someone walked past, they would be caught. It added to his excitement.

He was almost done.

He put his left hand over her mouth and wrapped the other around her stomach. He pumped harder until he could feel himself releasing. He quickly pulled out and shot up towards the ceiling. His cum landed all over the mirror and Dana's back. She could hardly stand. Jeremy smiled at her, got a towel and wiped himself off.

"Look at the mess you've made me do," he laughed.

"Clean it up and fix yourself before you come out," he said while walking out the bathroom like he was a superhero.

After that, he tried to avoid Dana at all costs.

A year later, his father had suggested he accompany her to New Bethel's annual awards dinner. Jeremy had stood her up and had honestly forgotten his father was being honored at the event. That stunt had cost him a new car.

Dana returned to college and always stayed in touch. She would send him love notes through emails, texts and left letters at this house. He ignored them and pretended the bathroom incident had never happened.

After graduating, Dana returned to New York and worked as a financial analyst on Wall Street. She threw herself at Jeremy every chance she could and became his first official booty call.

Whenever he stepped through her door with his key, whether day or night, she would open her legs, her mouth and her heart to him.

Some years, he would get with her three or four times, others none.

Then the day came when Jeremy had to pay the piper.

"Jeremy, you are going to have to put that out," Dana said while he was smoked some marijuana at her house.

"Why? I'll just go in the bathroom," he said.

"You can't smoke around the baby," she said.

Jeremy thought he heard the Twilight Zone theme playing.

How high am I? Did she say she was pregnant?

"Look Jeremy, I'm almost 30, unmarried and my biological clock is in warp mode. Most of the women in my circle are already married and have at least one child."

"I don't get a say on this? My circle says I can have kids well into my 60s, maybe my 70s. Hell, who knows maybe my 80s," he said as he grabbed his crotch.

"This is not funny. We have a life coming," she declared. "You make it seem like having a little Jeremy or a little Dana around would be the end of the world."

"Is it even mine?" he asked as he took a final pull and placed the joint in the ashtray.

"Why do men always go there?" Dana asked. "Yes, it's yours. I don't sleep around."

"I'll tell you what," he said as he walked over and towered over her. "I'll give you $20,000 to get an abortion."

The next thing he knew Dana was screaming and calling him names.

"You're really a bastard you know. A real dog," she yelled. "Loser with a capital L. Get out of my house. I don't want your money; I have my own!"

When Father Edward found out Jeremy had offered Dana money for an abortion, he hit the roof.

"Do you think you are going to throw my grandchild down the toilet?" he asked scornfully.

"That's what's wrong with you young cats today. You want to play in the kitty, but don't want to take care of what comes out of the kitty."

Jeremy got an ultimatum.

"Either you marry Dana or get disowned--just like your sister. Period," Father Edward warned him.

Jeremy saw his comfortable lifestyle slowly fading away. He was not willing to sacrifice sleeping all day and working on real estate deals whenever his father could catch him. He knew Father Edward could be ruthless and he did not want to end up like his sister Evelyn. She was now somewhere homeless and addicted to drugs. If Father Edward had his way, he would take her last name back so no one would know she was a Collins.

"Yes, Father Edward. As you wish, is all he could say."

Jeremy had never even taken Dana out on a private date. Now the *New York Times* had just approved a carefully drafted wedding announcement.

All of Harlem buzzed after learning one of their most eligible bachelors had been snagged. Jeremy could not believe people were calling their office offering to pay for a wedding invitation. Their parents were marrying them off like Charles and Diana, when in his mind their life together was more like Bobby and Whitney.

CHAPTER 4

Nurse Riley led Dr. Andelman in a fast sprint down the hallway.

"It's room seven sixteen, sir."

No, it could not be *her* he surmised. She is too young.
The last time they had spoken was less than a week ago and she was happy as a lark.

"What have you got there, young lady?"

"Hey Dr. A," she said excited. "This is my future. It's a college application to Middlesex Community College. I'm going back to school as soon as I get out of here. I'm going to be a nurse and help people just like you!"

She was vibrant and looking forward to celebrating her 30th birthday soon. There were recommendations for her discharge in only a few days.

Suicide?

Six months earlier, she had arrived at Meadow Banks and voluntarily admitted herself. Her psychiatric referral read a diagnosis of "clinical depression" and "homicidal tendencies."

On her paperwork she answered the question, 'Why are you here today? *"I have this persistent feeling of anger. I'm not sure how to shake it. I know it's not healthy. Who knows what I am capable of doing."*

Dr. Andelman had remembered her vividly because he was curious to find out what would fill such an attractive young woman with rage.

Standing at the front desk, even with a tight face and her teeth clenched, he was struck by her wholesome beauty. Her long platinum blonde hair was in two shoulder-length braids and it made her look like she could be a waitress in a mid-western saloon—the kind of place where patrons sang Garth Brooks songs and you could ride on an electronic bull. There was something about her farm girl looks that intrigued him, as he stood staring at what he thought was a younger, taller version of Goldie Hawn.

Even with a simple outfit of ripped jeans, a white T-shirt and cowboy boots, the other women seemed envious. He wished he was thirty years longer.

Perhaps it was her aura of sultry wickedness? Dr. Andelman thought as he felt a sensation he had not felt in a long time.

He remembered when Helen, his wife of forty years, had made him feel that way. Now since they were older, companionship was much more important, he thought. Cheating was not an option, but Helen knew if Jane Fonda ever came calling, she should not wait up.

He thought she looked rather out of place for northern New Jersey. That is until Dr. Andelman heard her speak. Her accent dictated she was either from New York or New Jersey where natives reversed the "er" and "oy" sounds. He heard her say, "I'm from Joysie, not New Yawk."

"Do you even speak English?" She said rudely to the Intake Assistant Lisa Kim, who was Korean.

"Can I get a room or not?" she yelled as if she was checking into a hotel.

"Excuse me young lady, I must ask you to lower your voice," Dr. Andelman said.

"Are you the boss?" She asked.

"I'm tired. I was told you guys would help me. I'm not on a job interview. I need to sleep."

"Yes, we understand. If you have a seat over there with the others who were here first, the nurse on duty will help you shortly," he said while he looked at her glazed eyes. She was high from something.

"Would you like a cup of coffee, tea or perhaps some water?" Dr. Andelman asked trying to be polite.

"No. I'll just go over there and wait," she said as she pranced off stomping her feet.

A few weeks later, Dr. Andelman attended her first anger management class. While all the other patients seemed relaxed, she was tense. Earlier in the day, she had thrown her lunch at the wall. "Don't ever give me any damn Italian food," she screamed.

While she sat with the group, she kept making her hand into an imaginary gun pulling an invisible trigger aiming at the ceiling. When it was her turn to tell the group why she felt she was a patient, she gave a theatrical performance.

"Why am I here? Hmm, that's a good question," she said while standing and patting herself on her chest.

"I'm here, because that strong woman bullshit is a myth. We give our heart and our trust to a man and takes us to the cleaners. The world is just fucked up man. I don't think women are really built for that kind of abuse." Then she kicked her chair and screamed, "I'm here because a cocksucker took my soul and I want it back!"

The noise caught the attention of Hector, a security guard who began walking towards her. Dr. Andelman raised his hand gesturing him to stop. Dr. Andelman had hoped she would finally tell who the cocksucker was that had caused her so much grief.

No such luck as she lowered her voice and apologized. "I'm sorry about that. I must learn to control myself. Seriously though. No bullshit? I'm here because I'm ready to kill somebody."

That was six months ago. Through a combination of medication, talk therapy and family support, she had made great strides. *How could she have committed suicide?* He could not recall her ever mentioning or reading anything about suicide in her case files. She was too tough for that, he thought. She was hurt, but nothing more than a woman scorned. The therapists were more concerned she would commit a homicide rather than suicide.

The fact remained. A patient was dead. Dr. Andelman would need to immediately notify the board of directors. He knew the board president, Helen Diamond who controlled most of the hospital's $300 million dollar a year budget, along with his comfortable salary, would be out for what was left of his 64-year-old balls.

During their last board meeting, she had demanded the hospital install cameras in every patient's room. Dr. Andelman now regretted arguing against it citing the patient's privacy was a priority. They agreed to install cameras in the stairwells only. Hindsight was truly 20-20, he thought as he prepared to open the door to her room.

"Brace yourself doctor, it's not a pretty sight," Nurse Riley said as she handed him a pair of sterilized gloves.

Slowly, he opened the door to an ungodly sight. Blood was everywhere. Her lifeless body was on the bed with her legs opened wide. Her nightgown was pulled up to her chest displaying her naked body from the waist down. He stared a second longer than he should have while he thought about rubbing his finger in between her legs.

Get your mind away from evil.

He pulled down the gown and checked her vitals. Nurse Riley was nervously shaking. He thought talking to her would calm her somewhat.

"Nurse Riley, did you know there are a total of seven places on a human body where you can check for a pulse?" he asked while feeling her femoral artery in one of her thighs.

"No, I did not," Nurse Riley whispered.

"Do you feel a pulse?" she asked optimistically.

"No, she is gone," he said sadly looking down at eyes which stared up at him with a look of defeat.

How did this happen?

"Such a pretty girl," Nurse Riley said quietly weeping. Dr. Andelman made a mental note to recommend all the nurses for crisis management training while he removed his bloody gloves and placed them in his pocket.

"Bailey, come in Bailey." Dr. Andelman relayed over his walkie-talkie.

"Yes, Dr. Andelman, this is Bailey. Go ahead."

"I am in room 716 and have accessed the situation. Please turn off the alarm."

"10-4 Dr. Andelman."

CHAPTER 5

Jeremy turned onto 59th Street and Central Park West. The entrance at New York's most famous park brewed with activity.

A drive on the scenic route uptown would do him good he thought as he watched a man walking a dog on roller skates. That's the New York he loved and the one that always helped his mood swings.

He reminisced about all the great times Father Edward had taken him fishing on the lake and the free concerts they had attended there.

"Did you know each year at least 50 million people will visit Central Park which makes up 842 acres?" he told prospective real estate clients interested in living by the park.

If they were Black, he would add, "Central Park was once the home of Seneca Village. From 1825 until 1857 African Americans lived there in a utopia-type community before it was destroyed for the park's construction."

Hands down the Central Park Zoo was still his favorite place to unwind with an ice cream cone on a beautiful day. Perhaps fatherhood would not be so bad after all as he thought about bringing his own child to visit.

It seemed so much easier to become a father than a husband, Jeremy thought. And from the marriage statistics of Generation X, Y and on, it seemed other men felt the same.

"Hey fella, move along!" A NYPD traffic cop yelled while Jeremy sat idle at green traffic light.

Jeremy searched for a song that would help him keep positive thoughts. His musical tastes were vast. He loved all kinds thanks to the introduction from Father Edward as a child.

"Do not limit yourself to one musical genre, because you can find solace in all types."

He chose Luciano Pavarotti's *Vincero,* his favorite song by the legendary opera singer. Translated it meant, *"I Will Win."*

He turned up the volume and imagined watching Pavarotti at the Teatro La Scala in Italy, the best opera house in the world or so he was told. It was exactly where he wished he was— anywhere would be better than going to see Father Edward, he thought as he turned onto 110th Street and headed into Harlem.

Father Edward was always badgering him about something and letting him know that his real estate skills were below his standards. Jeremy was tired of it but could not think of another way to make a living.

Collins Realty was located on Adam Clayton Powell, Jr. Boulevard at the corner of 133rd Street. Walking into the office was like going on a journey back in time. Although it was 1997, most of the décor spoke to an era long gone. The walls had dark brown paneling matching the brown carpet. Jeremy had always thought it looked like a 1970s living room, minus the plastic couch covers.

Jeremy practically had to fight with his father to get a new couch to replace the dingy orange one in the reception area. He had won the fight but lost the battle. His father plunked down $5,000 for an even older one.

"Hey, it's famous like me," he bragged. "This is the couch Mike Brady used in his home office on the Brady Bunch. Do you remember?"

Jeremy really could not expect much from a man who still pulled phone numbers from a rolodex on his desk.

Father Edward's office décor matched a judge's chambers. He had floor to ceiling bookcases filled with law books. "I was a lawyer in my former life," he would say.

"Knowledge of the law will keep your ass out of jail," is what he preached.

Father Edward was most proud of the law book which featured the *Brown vs. Board of Education* case. It was personally signed by the late Supreme Court Judge Thurgood Marshall.

"He was a great man. Many have sacrificed for young people to go to better schools. Take full advantage," he would tell his children around the dinner table.

Time may have forgotten the office décor and his father may have been old, but there was no doubt, Collins Realty was earning new money—and lots of it.

Last year, the sales volume passed the $200 million-dollar mark making them one of the leading realtors in Harlem, even with a changing demographics. Father Edward's empire stretched from Harlem to Long Island and as far as South Carolina employing a diverse staff of 97 people.

Ms. Enid Brauner, Father Edward's 71-year-old office manager was celebrating her 30th year. A smile with red fire lipstick on a glowing face cheerfully greeted Jeremy.

"Good afternoon Jeremy," she said always so full of life. Jeremy was hoping he would be that happy if he lived that long.

"Ed said to tell you he is running a few minutes behind."

When Mama Ernestine passed away, Ms. Enid became his surrogate mother and taught him Yiddish afterschool. It gave him an edge when working with the Jewish population who dominated the New York real estate market.

It was also because of Ms. Enid's tantrums that Jeremy would never again put pork on his fork. "It's an unholy, vile animal," she would say.

Although Jeremy knew Ms. Enid owned tons of commercial and rental property in New York City, and did not have to work, she still showed up to the office every day. Thirty years and she showed no signs of stopping.

"You will have to take me out of here on a stretcher," she would reply when asked about retirement. "Besides, I can Google and use this new MLS system that you fancy real estate agents use as good as anyone."

Ms. Enid never spoke much about her family. She told everyone her parents had immigrated from Eastern Europe. Each year, during Rosh Hashanah, she would gather the staff and others at her house. Her sons would come with their families.

"They're both bums. They think I don't know they are living off my money," she would whisper to Jeremy. "Wait until I die, I'm leaving everything to the Holocaust Museum," she would say before inviting everyone to sit at her lovely decorated table telling them the Jewish phrase, "Eat and nosh until your heart's content."

Ms. Enid never worried about sometimes being the only White face within miles of the office. The Collins made sure she was protected.

For years, Father Edward would try to move her to an apartment closer and safer to the office, but she would not budge. Even though she was only 5'4', she was both sassy and tough.

"Listen, I love my apartment, Ed. I have a front row seat of the Harlem River and I can see Yankee Stadium across the water. No one bothers me, and I don't bother anyone. It works."

A foolish street hustler had cursed and threatened her one evening. Father Edward found out where he and his family lived and had them all evicted. Then he had the NYPD brass shut down his operation which was feeding crack to the neighborhood. "Spread the word," Father Edward said.

Word got around. No more problems for Ms. Enid. Even the roughest and toughest gangsters sent her birthday gifts and thank you presents for helping their friends or families get housing—it was just the Harlem way.

"Thanks Ms. Enid. Happy Anniversary," he said as he lightly punched one of her gigantic 3-0 balloons tied to her desk.

"Hey, watch that," she chimed. "Those are from my boo."

Shocked, Jeremy asked, "What do you know about a boo Ms. Enid?" He always suspected her, and Father Edward had more than just a working relationship. After all, she was making 70 look like the new 50.

She looked at him and smiled. "A lady never tells."

Jeremy gave out a hearty laugh. "I'm going to my office. Can you buzz me when my father arrives?"

"You got it. Just try and have some patience with him. We are old now; our bark is far worse than our bite."

Two hours later, Father Edward entered Jeremy's office bringing the scent of Ben Gay mixed with Old Spice with him.

"You need to clean this mess up," he said as he removed a box, so he could sit in a chair at Jeremy's desk. *Yeah, and you need to get you a fashion stylist.* Jeremy thought but knew better than to say it aloud.

His father was always so bright with his tailor-made wardrobe choices. Today, Jeremy was in awe at how he was pulling off looking like a big round, swirled rainbow pop you get at an amusement park. He had on a peach, sky blue and yellow plaid blazer with a matching three color bow tie. Under it he wore a sky-blue button-down shirt over some sky-blue pants. On his feet some sky-blue hushpuppies.

"Hey Pop."

"Don't hey pop me. What the hell happened today, and don't you lie? Cecil has already called me from Barkley Development."

"Snitches get stiches," Jeremy said.

"Using street code Mr. Notre Dame?" He jested.

"Boy, how could you let Dan and the Peppermill Group outbid us for the Park Avenue property? Some cats from Brooklyn?" he said. "Do you see any of us from uptown down there buying shit?"

In New York City, the five boroughs may as well be separate cities. Generation after generation, the rivalry will never end. It was likely the reason why residents of New York had to give a two-part answer when someone asked them, "Where are you from?" After they answered, another question came. "What part?"

"Last I heard Brooklyn is not another city and guess what, they have money just like Harlem," Jeremy said.

"Watch your tone before I knock you upside your head. I'm still your father."

Jeremy wanted to laugh—the beatings had stopped long ago. Now he could easily restrain him, or as he daydreamed many times, knock him out.

Jeremy wished he would retire so he become the CEO. But at a youthful 72 years old and no health issues—he would probably outlive them all.

"You know the east side is the future of Harlem—for Harlem people," he rambled.

"I want the Collins name planted all over, from 110th Street to 155th Street! Eastside to the westside. I never had a street named after me, so I'll be damned if I won't own something in every zip code."

"Hold on, let me explain," Jeremy interjected.

"How much money did I pay for that degree? I should have invested that money in a HBCU, at least there I know they would have taught you some common sense."

Jeremy stared blankly but was envisioning picking up his gold, shiny letter opener and stabbing him in his heart.

Jeremy thought about his political science degree and his master's in psychology. He was not using either. Now, to his dismay, he was knee deep in real estate negotiations under his father's dictatorship as the vice president of, "Do what the hell I say," or perish incorporated.

"Well, what happened?" He said glancing at his watch.

"Speak up. I'm meeting the Mayor for drinks in a bit."

"Their bid was $100,000 more than ours. I didn't think all those extra zeros were worth the investment," Jeremy answered calmly.

His father stood up, barely taller than the desk and slammed his hands down. Boom! "THAT'S THE GODDAMN PROBLEM, YOU DIDN'T THINK!" He said looking at Jeremy so hard he felt he could see through him. "I SENT YOU DOWN THERE TO CLOSE THE DEAL," he said as he pulled out a silver flask from his pocket likely filled some expensive Scotch.

"Son, all you had to do was call. You know like call and ASK me if I would be willing to put up the extra capital."

"Would you have paid that amount?" Jeremy asked.

"That's a lot of money. $740,000, probably not?" he said and then took a long gulp.

"Ahhh. You want some?"

"No, I'm good" Jeremy said.

"I'll tell you this, I will make sure Dan doesn't get any building permits to move forward with the renovations they need. We'll have them wasting money by the second. Then in about a year, or two," he shrugged. "We'll make them a low-ball offer, he said as he drank so more.

"They know better than to think we going to have some damn Brooklyn cats uptown—they better go get some property in Bed Stuy or East New York."

For some reason Jeremy started sweating. His father always made him nervous, especially when he was angry.

"Let me get out of here." *Yes, why don't you get out of here.*

Father Edward then calmly, almost serenely said, "Listen, let's go to dinner tonight. I'll have Milton circle back around with the car to pick you up. It will be a few hours though because you know the Mayor is long-winded."

Jeremy thought he is so bi-polar.

"Also, I have Dana's ring for you."

"Can't. I'm meeting up with Chad tonight to 'celebrate,' he said dryly while throwing up quotation signs.

"Well, drop by the house and get the damn ring. It's in the safe in my study. Do you remember the combination?"

"Yes," Jeremy answered.

The ring that I'm giving to the woman YOU want me to marry. The woman that I don't even love--the ring you spent $75,000 on."

Jeremy just shook his head.

"Yeah, that was kind of cheap, you think?" Father Edward asked seriously.

"Anyway, you have had more than enough time to get it yourself. So, I got it done. What have I told you about procrastination?"

Jeremy recited the line he been saying since the 4th grade: "It makes easy things hard and hard things harder."

"Listen, Jeremy," his father said while he walked over and placed his hand on his shoulder. "Dana is a good wholesome girl from good stock. An only child, she is probably lonely as hell. Damn, these are the times in which I wish my Ernestine, may she rest in peace, was here to guide us," he said sadly.

"I'll admit Dana is not the prettiest woman I've ever seen you with. With a little exercise, better diet, maybe a piece of wig and some makeup, I think she could be more attractive—but not much because you know her mama is only about a seven herself," he laughed.

With her average looks, Dana would be considered cute to those who liked light skinned women with reddish brown hair. The type of person people in the Black community called a redbone. She was about 5'7" and she was overweight.

Everything about her style was business. She always dressed as if she was on her way to a corporate meeting. She never wore makeup and her hair was always pulled back in a bun. The only time she let her hair down was when she had sex.

For God's sakes, she still wears pantyhose.

No, the woman Jeremy envisioned himself with would be like him—she would walk like a runway model and heads would turn when she walked into a room.

"It's not the way she looks. That's not the problem here pop," Jeremy said thinking about Dana's knocked knees which touched when she walked. It was her demeanor.

"She has the angry Black woman syndrome," he said. "She stays bitching about everything. If it's nothing there, trust me she will find a reason to complain."

"Make her happy son. A happy wife is a happy life," Father Edward said from experience.

Jeremy thought Dana needed a street ass whipping with her cocky privileged attitude. She was also the queen of self-satisfaction.

"Why shouldn't I post on Facebook the good things in my life?" She asked one night when Jeremy had complained about her posting a picture showing them on a church retreat in Ghana.

"Do people need to see your suite? I mean you even posted a picture of the complimentary slippers with the hashtag #myvacationisbetterthanyours," he said. "That annoys people. Not everyone can vacation in Africa."

"Well, it's all true. Besides don't you think our people should see some of Africa? I just let them know it's not all jungle. And the resort should pay me for the free advertisement. You know I have 5,000 friends on the book," she answered not understanding his point at all.

"I don't love her. That should count for something," Jeremy relayed to his father.

"Love will come. But you should count your lucky stars that Jerimiah Hyde's ugly ass daughter got married off first. I almost lost you to her in a poker game," Father Edward joked.

"Do you see her kids? Excuse me Whoopi Goldberg, but my grandkids would have probably looked like Celie from *The Color Purple*."

Love ain't no where around here, Jeremy thought. He had never been in love with anyone. In fact, he could not even admit he knew what love felt like. He only loved money.

"You have spent your whole twenties bullshitting. Right now, you have no wife, and no steady girlfriend from what I can see. People are starting to talk. They think you're gay. You're not gay are you son? Of course, you're not," he answered himself.

"So now it's time to make you an honorable man and carry on my legacy. Don't tell me her getting pregnant was a one-time hit and run?" He asked with a look of intrigue.

Jeremy laughed and realized that he really loved the old man.

"What's so funny?" he asked Jeremy.

"I've been hitting that for years."

"Even better." He replied. "A cootie cat you already know."

"Cootie cat?" Jeremy asked curiously.

"Pussy, boy pussy. You know what I'm saying. Cootie cat, now that's the real old school," he said letting out a hearty laugh which shifted his dentures.

"Seriously, you will marry her because we are good Christian folk. Both her father and I are from down south. Abortion and abandonment are out of the question. "Real men take care of their babies and the women who have them," he told him.

"Besides," he continued. "I can't wait to see my new grandchild. A boy at that!" He clapped his hands and broke out in a happy dance.

"Enjoy your night kid," he said before skipping out reciting, "It's a boy! You hear that Ernestine? Ha! A boy!"

That evening before heading out to celebrate, Jeremy left the blue box from Tiffany's on Dana's night table with a note that read, "Enjoy. See you soon."

CHAPTER 6

Edward Alfred Brooks was born in 1925 in Eve's Run, South Carolina. He was the sixth of ten children, three girls and seven boys born to his father, Walter, a barber and his mother, Eloise, a homemaker.

"I'm from the moonshine and outhouse capital of America. A place where you can get drunk and shit all in the same yard," he once told Rochelle Robinson, a Pulitzer Prize winning journalist from *Ebony* magazine.

Robinson had somehow managed to convince Edward, and his wife Ernestine, to grant her their only public interview.

Ernestine was a short and stoutly woman. She spoke as softly as a frail flower, but her words were as harsh as a tsunami. With her there was no gray area in life.

"Everything is black or white," she would say. Life does not give extra hours for confusion," she told Robinson.

Her face held the wrinkles of a life unfulfilled. When she rarely smiled, it showed a weathered face. Makeup allowed her to cover up years of unspoken indiscretions.

She let Robinson know, "I'm only doing this interview with him because I wear Fashion Fair," the legendary cosmetic brand created by Ebony Publisher John H. Johnson's wife Eunice and the first specifically for Black skin. "You will be sure to let her know that for me."

Ms. Robinson's stared at the Confucius quote painted in large gold letters on the wall behind Edward's desk.

"Before you embark on a journey of revenge, dig two graves."

"You have that quote so prominently featured Mr. Collins. What does it mean to you?" Robinson inquired.

"That quote was inspired by my late Uncle Henry Jackson. May he rest in peace," Edward said.

"When we first came to New York in 1949, I worked for his real estate company. He also had a quote behind his desk and told me, "A man should always set the tone for guests when they enter your door."

"Is that right?" Ms. Robinson continued intrigued. "But why is this particular quote important?"

"Revenge is important for one's dignity. Digging two graves means when you do someone dirty, you should be prepared to take the payback for your mistake," Edward stated while staring at Ernestine.

"In other words," Robinson said. "Don't start none, won't be none."

"Yes!" Edward exclaimed and clapped his hands one time. "Something like that."

"How about this one? Don't write a check your ass can't cash."

"Yes, I know that one, my parents used to tell us that all the time," Robinson said laughing.

Edward and Ernestine did not crack a smile.

"Would you two like anything to drink?" Ernestine asked. Edward's remark had made her uncomfortable.

"Yes, something cold, if you have it," Robinson said.

"Yes, thank you dear." Edward said faking a smile. She winked at him before walking out.

"When your wife comes back, let's talk about how you two met," Robinson requested.

"We don't have to wait for her. Time is short," he said.

"We met at the annual Chester County, SC Sadie Hawkins dance. Back then it was the biggest event in town," he said telling her Cab Calloway had performed that night and the women went crazy.

Ernestine returned and said, "Yes, that dance. I'll have to admit, he was a little short for my taste," she explained taking a poke at Edward who was 5'8".

Edward gave her a smirk. She knew he hated anyone discussing his height.

"But what he lacked in height, he made up for in charm. With his fine clothing, he could easily pass for a boy who grew up on our side of the tracks," she said making a reference to the rich side of town she grew up on.

Edward folded his hands on his desk. Ernestine continued cautiously, "But most of all, he always treated me like I was a princess and he was my knight in shining armor," she said as she went to sit on his lap.

Robinson had not noticed the tension.

"Mrs. Collins you're a pretty fine dresser yourself. I mean look at you today. You look stunning. "Is that real fur on your collar?"

"Yes, it is. A white fox. Thank you so much for the compliment," she said while stroking it.

She was right. Ernestine was one of the finest dressers in all of Harlem and some could argue in all of New York City. For the interview she wore a Periwinkle colored two-piece skirt suit. The white pin box hat covering her short haircut gave her look of elegance. Short herself at 5'5", she always wore at least three-inch heels when she could.

Edward played along while he pinched the back of her arm causing her to get up off his lap.

"She was the prettiest girl at the party and boy, could she dance," Edward said. "Before I even knew her really, I knew she was going to be the woman I was going to marry," he said with regret.

Robinson thought about her own pending divorce. It was good to see a couple who had been married for so long who were still very much in love.

The Collins always pretended well.

**

By 1960, at the start of the Civil Rights Movement, the Collins' were a household name in Harlem. A powerhouse couple, who had grace and charm, they were known for mentoring and providing jobs for others who were interested in real estate careers. They were equally generous with their money and gave graciously to many charitable causes.

Each year, the Collins scholarship helped young people who needed money for school, and they tithed generously at several churches.

When people were jailed for rioting in 1964, Edward and Ernestine bailed out at least forty people. That, along with all their other civic contributions, including large donations to the police and civil rights organizations helped propel Edward as a formidable community leader.

In 1965, Edward celebrated his 40th birthday by winning a seat on the New York City Council. As one of the Councilmen, Edward was among the first to learn of the city's plan to revitalize Harlem through lottery sales of brownstones. Sharing that information with the right people made him a millionaire overnight.

By night, they dined and entertained some of New York's elite, of all ethnicities, in their beautiful Victorian mansion called the Le Maison Rounde. It was located off Mount Morris Park, a landmark designated neighborhood known for its stately homes.

Their house was not the most expensive, but it was Harlem's only round house with eight bedrooms, four baths and a maids' quarters. It was built like a fortress with a huge black fence and a wall which totally blocked any street level views. The home's best feature was the grand foyer which had bright white marble tiles and a stunning two-story chandelier.

Ernestine spent warm days tending to her backyard garden filled with a host of vegetables and her favorite flower lilacs which surrounded the house.

Edward had everything a man could ever want. Yet, there was one thing he longed for.

With each birth of his four daughters, he would anxiously wait to hear the words, "It's a boy!" Much to his dismay the words never came. He lived in a house full of debutante girls who left hairbrushes, barrettes, and dolls everywhere. He grew tired of ballet lessons and etiquette classes.

He secretly envied men who had sons.

"Let's try again for another child," he urged Ernestine one day while he that sat poolside under the warm Acapulco sun. "We'll name him Ernest after you."

"Darling, the only way I'm having another baby is if Jesus himself gets me pregnant," she responded much to his dismay.

That was the final straw and the day he his heart grew cold for Ernestine and the girls.

CHAPTER 7

J eremy dialed Chad Eisen, a retired superstar quarterback for the New York Heat who now coached the team. Jeremy knew Chad was probably his only real friend. Of course, there were always stragglers hanging around.

People like Orrin and Mark who Jeremy had given jobs to. Yet, they did not have the decency to even wish him a Happy Birthday or a Merry Christmas each year. Or the other one, Paul, who stayed in Jeremy's office so much, away from his own job, Jeremy was beginning to think he was a spy sent to steal real estate information for the competition.

No, Chad was the closest thing to a brother he had ever known.

Jeremy found that out three years prior when he needed a ride home after having a biopsy procedure. Jeremy was nervous, scared and alone. The medication had left him woozy. The clinic refused to release him unless someone picked him up. Requests to his so-called friends went unanswered.

Just as Jeremy was about to press the app for a car service, Chad arrived leaving football practice at MetLife Stadium the second he heard Jeremy needed someone.

When Father Edward, or anyone else questioned why he hung with a White guy, he told them to get lost. Sometimes a person's color didn't matter.

When Chad answered, he heard his wife Brooke yelling in the background.

"What is she yelling about now?" Jeremy asked about Brooke, Chad's certified Georgia Peach from the Pittsburgh section of Atlanta.

Brooke was something else. A true Aries, she spoke her mind. She once told an ESPN reporter who inquired about their 10th wedding anniversary celebration, "I'm so fly, I got the White guy, even White girls couldn't get. Me and the rapper Eve should start a club."

"Hi Jeremy," she yelled into the phone.

Tell her I said hi," Jeremy said.

"Miss loudmouth is around here talking about how good she cooks. Then she went racial on me," Chad said. "Telling me Black people cook better than White people."

"How did she know it's me?" Jeremy asked.

"Because she probably has an app on my phone that alerts her whenever I get a call," he said jokingly. "You know they have all kinds of surveillance equipment these days."

"Don't nobody call you but Jeremy," she yelled.

""I was just about to tell her what White people cook better than Black people, or any other people for that matter," Chad said luring them into his joke.

"What do White people cook better than Black people?" Jeremy and Brooke asked simultaneously.

"Probably alligator or some shit like a swan," Brooke said.

"Wrong," Chad laughed.

"White people cook Meth better than anyone else," he said cracking up. "But I have to admit that's not mines. I just saw it on YouTube, but it's funny as shit, right?'

"Yeah, that's a good one," Jeremy said laughing.

"Now be quiet woman and fix me something to eat," Chad said and there was dead silence.

"Man, I'm sorry about that. Just another friendly game of ebony and ivory living together in harmony," he said.

"I'm in awe that she actually shuts up when you tell her. It's hard for some women to do that, especially the sisters."

"That's because she knows White men are serial killers. I'll have her ass tied up at our cabin and no one will ever find her," he joked. "I'm just kidding in case anyone is listening in on the line."

Jeremy knew Chad and Brooke had the relationship dreams were made of. Or so he guessed that what it looked like.

"I love that woman," Chad said. "And it's about mutual respect and this good Irish sausage I lay on her." Jeremy pictured him grabbing his crotch.

"You know studies show when a woman gets a good fuck, something in her chromosomes humble her or some shit like that. I got her around here cooking corned beef and cabbage on a regular just like my Irish mother used to make," Chad said laughing.

"You two are funny." Jeremy could not remember the last time he laughed with, instead of at, a woman.

"Are we still meeting tonight at A Soulful Affair?" Jeremy asked which was the reason for his call.

"Yes, sir, it's celebration time for you! Seven o'clock. Which I know is seven thirty for you colored people."

"I see you got a lot of jokes today blarney man," Jeremy shot back.

"Just happy to be alive man," he said.

"Dress up a little, no khakis," Jeremy suggested.

"Cool beans." Chad said.

"You know only dudes from Pittsburgh or Boston say cool beans, right?" Jeremy asked.

"I rep my city all day. Go Red Sox. By the way, we're taking your Yankees out this year!"

"Yeah okay, see you later. 7 o'clock." Jeremy said. He heard Chad say, "Later. Come here foxy mama, come give big daddy some."

Jeremy hung around the office returning messages and scheduling appointments. Mainly he spent the rest of the afternoon on the dating site, American Singles. It had become one of his favorite hobbies. Marriage or no marriage, there were still some willing sexual participants from across the nation waiting for screenname winkforyou740 to log-on.

CHAPTER 8

With the alarm off, the room was eerily quiet. Dr. Andelman could hear were the raindrops hitting the windowsill. They grew louder by the second.

He looked around the room. Something did not feel right. He grabbed a bed sheet, tore it in half and began wrapping her bloody wrists. An empty pill bottle was on the bed. When he picked it up, one pill fell out. It was likely an over the counter sleeping pill. He placed it in his pocket.

How odd he thought. Someone would take their own life by taking pills and slitting *both* of their wrists. *Why was that familiar?*

Her corpse made a sound and echoed in the room.

"Oh my God, she's alive!" Nurse Riley screamed.

"Likely air from her lungs," Dr. Andelman calmly said. "Keep your voice down."

Then without warning, her body expelled her bladder. The scent of her stomach's contents releasing a powerful smell into the air. Nurse Riley turned pale before she ran out.

Dr. Andelman thought he felt a chill that arrived as soon as it left. A spiritual man, he wondered whether that was her soul leaving her body. The rain began to pounce, and thunder roared.

Standing over her body, he recited the Yizkor, the Jewish prayer mourning of the dead. *May your soul rest in peace.*

Dr. Andelman called out for Nurse Riley. "Has anyone else been in this room?"

"No, doctor, just me. I came in because I saw her light was still on. I checked her pulse to see if she was still alive which is how I got all this blood on me. I'm sorry, but I panicked."

What did she use to cut herself? Dr. Andelman asked himself while grabbing the blanket between her body and the wall.

Nurse Riley pointed to the wall and said. "Doctor, look!"

On the wall, written in blood, was one word, "WINK."

Dr. Andelman knew exactly what it meant.

"Bailey, come in Bailey."

"Yes, Dr. Andelman."

"Please call the police."

CHAPTER 9

Facts. I am powerful. I am fine. That was Jeremy's attitude as he strolled past the long line of people waiting to enter A Soulful Affair. The bouncer recognized him and pulled back the black velvet rope which separated the have from the have nots.

"Good to see you Mr. Collins," he said.

"It's good to be seen."

Jeremy wore a navy linen blazer, with a bright white Ralph Lauren T-shirt, some jeans and navy butter soft leather loafers. For a final touch, he threw on some Chanel for Men.

He nudged his way through the after-work crowd in the popular nightspot on New York City's Upper West Side. Patrons hoping to spot a celebrity or two glanced his way. A live band played smooth jazz which set off a nice vibe amidst the loud chatter and the sound of clinking glasses and plates.

Jeremy approached Chad who was standing as the center of attention among a group of men.

"Hey everyone, this is my good friend Jeremy Collins, he's a realtor," he announced while giving Jeremy their college handshake.

"Jeremy, this is, I can't pronounce. What's your name again?" He asked a guy with long locs and a dashiki.

"Hey, I'm Rashod," he said while extending his hand.

"Good to meet you," Jeremy said while shaking his hand that Rashod would not let go of.

"Where do you get your shoes from?" he asked Jeremy staring at his feet.

"Friedman's in Atlanta. I've been buying from him for years," Jeremy said retrieving his hand.

The others were wishing Chad well on the upcoming football season. Chad reached into his pocket and handed each of them two tickets.

"What? No tickets for your man Jeremy?" Rashod asked like a groupie.

Chad ignored him. Jeremy just smiled.

"Sir, can you follow me?" A hostess asked Chad.

Right on time, Jeremy thought.

"See you at the game fellas," Chad said.

With that they were off to the VIP lounge. Chad was always so generous.

"It's a tax-write off and good PR," he had once said. "And since my family never comes to the games, even when I used to play, I just give them away."

A Soulful Affair was the perfect backdrop for single women who were willing to do a lot for a little. They exchanged petty conversations, cleavage and lustful beginnings to obtain free drinks, appetizers and hopefully a donor for their next month of bills.

The lucky ones got invited to a table for a full meal or into the VIP section to partake in some complimentary drugs and/or the unlimited top shelf liquor. Men used their credit cards like auctioneers seeing who would grant them the most for their black and platinum card swipes.

"Look at them scheming," Chad said. "Sometimes I think women can actually smell your bank account."

"No, they smell the hope of access to that bank account. That's the way you reel them in," Jeremy responded surveying the VIP room. "Give them hope and they turn into dreamers."

"Is it that easy?" Chad asked.

"Listen, women will fantasize an entire life with you in ten minutes," Jeremy said. "Especially when you look this good."

Chad laughed. "Dude, it's time to celebrate!" Chad pulled out two Cuban cigars and handed one to Jeremy.

"What else you got in those pockets? "You're pulling out tickets, cigars and shit," Jeremy joked.

"Shut up man. Congratulations!" Chad said and meant it. He was happy his friend was finally tying the knot.

"Yeah, I guess," Jeremy said as he lit the cigar. "This cigar is about to be like my life. Up in smoke."

"Look at you. What is this linen?" Chad asked as he pulled Jeremy's sleeve. "Still dressing like a model." His touch gave Jeremy a shiver.

"No just good cotton. Ralph Lauren," Jeremy laughed. "Forget the clothes, let's what we can get into tonight," he said.

"Sowing wild oats, are we?" Chad asked.

"Trust me it's out of necessity because Dana is pregnant."

"Yes, I'm looking forward to becoming a Godfather!" Chad exclaimed. "I'm gonna be like Al Pacino."

"But seriously if you're dry down there," he pointed to Jeremy's groin. "I can get you some extra lotion from one of the Heat's sponsors," Chad laughed.

"Shit ain't funny. Dana and I haven't had sex in months. I had to ask her whether her mouth worked. Suck a brother off or something," he said secretly hoping Chad, with his sexy thin lips and broad shoulders, would one-day volunteer for the job.

"Well no worries," Chad said. "The ladies look hot tonight! Let's have some fun."

Jeremy admired Chad. In college, every White guy was looking for a wife. They all wanted the wife, picket fence house, two-car garage, two kids, and a dog.

"Listen, that's the real American dream." Chad said. "It's the key to economic empowerment. Marriage is honorable. "Besides who wants to really walk alone in this world?"

"Me," Jeremy said raising his hand.

"Being a husband is equal to king of the jungle. And as the king, you can still go out into the kingdom and get your feel of the land. Just be discrete," Chad said.

Even with their wives, White men cheated as much as Black men. Women in the movies like *Fatal Attraction* and the *Hand That Rocks the Cradle* were the exception, not the rule, in White adultery. Or at least that's what Jeremy thought.

Chad sipped his drink and glanced to the main room. He summoned the waitress whose face was filled with too many Botox shots. She eerily looked like a plastic doll.

"We need a bottle of Grand Marnier, a pitcher of water, and a platter of finger foods, something with some dip," he requested as she smiled from ear to ear.

"Yes, sir. Right away, by the way my name is Chelsea and I'll be your hostess tonight," she said before she pretended to drop some napkins. Then as if she was on an audition, she slowly bent down to pick them up allowing them a view of her white lace panties under the black leather miniskirt.

"Nice," Chad said as he smacked her on her ass.

"Yeah, waitresses can get it too," Jeremy said as she walked away holding her back arched and her ass out.

"I don't see why not," Chad said staring at what he thought was a nice vanilla milkshake.

"You know damn well you're in the wrong time zone to even give a woman a kiss on the cheek," Jeremy joked. Brooke was crazy enough to kill him, the woman, and her whole family if she ever caught him cheating.

"Jay, do you see those women over there?" He asked, ignoring his warning. "Those women over there by the bar. Wink at them for me," Chad said while waving hello to them.

Chad made that request every time they were out. Jeremy would wink at a woman and, like magic, she would stand at attention like a robot.

A therapist once described Jeremy's seemingly charming ways as, "either a symbol of an unfathomable charmer or a narcissistic sexual predator."

Jeremy knew pulling women for Chad could be dangerous. Chad was a closet sadomasochistic who enjoyed having sex with women who wanted to get beat. The kind of beating that left a black eye. Women who loved being choked until they almost passed out. The kind of sex you had to pick a safe word before you began.

The type of sex a man would never do with his wife.

"I would never ask my precious Brooke to participate in something like that. My alter ego fucks those women, like a hobby; while the real me makes love to my wife," Chad confided.

During his off season, Chad traveled all over the world to places like Columbia, Brazil, the Dominican Republic and Thailand to feed his guilty pleasures with willing strangers. Jeremy was seriously thinking about joining him on the next trip.

Jeremy fantasized about women who would attempt to fight back. He would overpower them with a roughness until their screams and cries turned into orgasms. He had yet to find a woman who he could trust to go to that dark place, and it frustrated him.

When the waitress returned Chad asked, "Do me a favor darling, send over two glasses of champagne to those women over there."

"Which ones?" She asked seemingly disappointed that her peep show seemed forgotten.

"The two over there at the bar, the Asian and the Black one." Chad said as he nudged Jeremy. "Are you down?"

"No thanks, I see something else. But if you can't handle them," he said smiling. "I'll gladly stay."

"No, I got this," Chad said waving him off. "It's going to be a *Rush Hour* type of night. Chan and Tucker man!"

Jeremy exited the VIP and went to the bar.

He sat four seats from two women who were drinking and chatting. When he caught the eye of one of them, he winked. She then tapped her friend who turned around to look Jeremy's way.

He could tell by their attire; they were not from Harlem. Their badly coordinated clothes gave them away. They looked like they had purchased them in a store that made you check your bag at the door.

Jeremy also knew no uptown woman would be caught dead with those fake designer bags they were holding. Growing up in a house with five women, who dressed in the best designer clothes, had given him an edge on women's clothing.

It was her body and her cute face that appealed to him.

She stood up and pretended as if she wanted to stretch her legs. *How strategic.* She was about 5'8" and thick. A true BBW with oversized breasts that probably gave her back pains. Her thick hips were attached to an ass that made Jeremy wonder whether it was real or full of silicon.

Jeremy eased up on them at the bar.

"Please get these lovely ladies another round," he summoned to the bartender.

"Thank you. I'll have a glass of Moet," she said.

"Make it a bottle and a glass of cherries," Jeremy requested while the women expressed their excitement.

"A glass of cherries?" her friend asked.

"Yes, I like to pop them," Jeremy said with sly look.

"What's your name?" Jeremy asked as he got close enough to sniff her cheap perfume. He had to hold back a sneeze.

She stuttered with a slight Caribbean accent, "Um, I'm Sha—Shanice Harris and this is Myra. My friends call me Sha."

"Jamaican?" Jeremy said slowly with an accent.

"Ya, you got it mon!" Sha responded jokingly tilting her head back and moving her long braids from her face. *Damn she is sexy. I want to name her sexy chocolate.*

"Nice to meet you both. I'm Jeremy," he said staring at her cleavage. He wanted to drop a cherry down there and suck it out.

"Oh snap, I know who you are," Myra said.

"You're that realtor guy," Myra blurted out after sneaking a peek at this groin area. "I saw you featured in some magazine in the 40 under 40 because you closed a $5 million-dollar deal on a Harlem brownstone, or something like that. You were standing on a rooftop with your father?" Myra said disappointed he liked Sha more than her.

"Right you are, little lady," Jeremy said while he drank down a glass of champagne in one gulp.

"What magazine was it?"

"*Black Elite*," he answered.

Sha gave her friend a look that read, "Please go somewhere cockblocker."

Myra got the hint. "Nice meeting you. Have fun you two," she said before walking off.

Jeremy sat down next to Sha. Drink. Eat. Dance. Talk. Smile. Laugh and repeat.

Sha was from the Walt Whitman projects in Brooklyn. Jeremy didn't even know where that was, but he knew Whitman was a famous poet.

He thought she had given him her whole life story. Ironically, he enjoyed listening.

She was 34 years old and attended night vocational school while she worked as an unlicensed hair stylist. She had been a single mother since the age of 16 and her son had just left for the Army. Her parents lived in Flatbush, a place she called the "Little Caribbean." She was allergic to grass and cats.

When Jeremy went to say goodbye to Chad, he was in the middle of lap dance from one of his *Rush Hour* women, while the Busta Rhymes hit bellowed over the speakers, *"Put Your Hands Where My Eyes Can See."*

Jeremy thought it was quite a sight while Chad threw him a salute.

Jeremy walked out of the club with Sha on one arm and Myra on the other. They headed up the West Side Highway to a New Jersey hotel with a glass of cherries.

The next morning, Jeremy awoke from a freaky ménage trois. Myra, who had put in work on his body, snored loudly. Jeremy thought she had "done a little something strange for a piece of change," as comedian Mike Epps said in *Friday After Next*.

One thing he knew for sure, two women felt better.

Sometimes she would leave chocolate candies wrapped in gold foil that looked like coins on his bed. Other times it was real money. That was the silent signal to come. One time he visited; Carl was there with nothing on but his underwear.

Carl was the strange boy who lived next door. He looked like a grown man, but he acted like he was eight years old. They said he liked to eat paint as a child. He was always carrying a bucket of something: pennies, paper clips, soap, matches, anything he could fit in there.

She had ice cream for them. There were bowls of ice cream.

She told Jeremy to take off his clothes. Then she pointed to his groin. "Put some ice cream down there. Carl wants some ice cream. Vanilla is his favorite."

Carl was clapping and smiling. "Ice cream. Lick. Yes."

Carl go get your ice cream Jeremy has for you."

Then she would join them.

**

Jeremy checked his voicemail.

"Jeremy, this is my fifth call. What kind of man goes missing when his baby is due? Get your ass to Mt. Sinai Hospital before I call Ed," Dana's mother yelled.

For some reason, Jeremy thought he would be feel more excited about the birth of his first child. Like how the soon to be dads on TV or in the movies acted. Excited, nervous, happy. Instead, he was on the edge of the bed feeling paralyzed.

Sha awoke and began rubbing his back.

"Good morning baby. How are you feeling?" she said with morning breath that hit Jeremy like a ton of bricks.

"Good morning," he said holding his breath before getting up to dress. He wanted to take a shower, but there was no time. Yet, he did not want to greet his new child with the scent of two women on him.

"Come back to bed baby," Sha requested. Ignoring her, he went into the bathroom. His phone vibrated again, so he sent a text to Mrs. Tyler.

"I'm in Queens and on my way. I will be at the hospital as soon as possible. I'm rushing. J.C."

"Where are you going?" Sha asked, as came out of the bathroom and watched him put on his clothes.

"I had a good time last night. Thanks for the fun," he said staring at Myra's ass under the sheets.

"Take this," he said handing Sha $200.

Sha was surprised and felt like a cheap prostitute.

"It's for you both to get some breakfast and take a cab back to the city," he said. "I have to go. I have your number and will be in touch. Tell your girl I said later."

Sha faked a smile.

"Thank you. Drive carefully," is all she could say because she felt dirty and cheap.

CHAPTER 10

On Saturday, April 11, 1998 Dana gave birth to Jeremy Edward Collins, Jr. at 2:24 pm. Junior was a healthy baby who weighed eight pounds and six ounces and was 19 inches long.

"He's going to be a tall one like you," the nurse said as she handed Jeremy the baby. For the first time he felt a sense of purpose in his life and swore he would be the best father.

Father Edwards and the Tylers' wasted little time. Wedding invitations were mailed out the following week.

Two months later, on a picture-perfect day in June at an extravagant ceremony, Jeremy took Dana as his bride in front of hundreds.

Jeremy had to admit Dana made a beautiful bride in a designer dress so expensive Rev. Tyler would not tell the cost.

"Let's just say we had to get insurance on it," he told a reporter.

At the reception, before leaving for their honeymoon in Bermuda, their parents bestowed their wedding gifts.

Father Edward gave them both matching Bulgari watches. Dana's parents gave them a lifetime membership to the exclusive Parksdale Yacht Club.

"You have to wait for someone to die, before they accept new members," Rev. Tyler said proudly.

Jeremy was not impressed. He would have preferred an invitation to fellow Harlemite Sean "Diddy" Combs' annual All

White Hampton Party. It was an event Jeremy had wanted to attend for years.

Rev. Tyler handed him a set of keys. Keys which would turn on the engine of a forty-seven-foot Hatteras yacht.

"You can't be a member of a yacht club without a yacht," Rev Tyler joked. "But you two are still young, so it's a lease that me and Ed will use anytime we like."

Dana jumped for joy so much her tiara fell, and she broke a
heel on her shoe. "Thank you, daddy, thank you so much. Can we name her Destiny?"

Jeremy's thought about the amount of fun he would have throwing parties for his clients and how much he would save on hotel costs. Now he could bring women to his boat. They would surely be impressed.

Yes, I could get used to this married he thought while smiling and thanking the good reverend.

CHAPTER 11

Yacht aside, Jeremy found it difficult to settle into married life. He loved his son, but he felt trapped.

Dana nagged him about everything.

"Tomorrow, we're going here." "Next week, we absolutely must go here." "Do you think we should get red or black leather for the seats in the theatre room?" "Do you like your ketchup in the fridge or the pantry?"

It was the first time he had ever shared living space with anyone but his family or his college roommates. Dana was driving him crazy and he was restless.

On her social media she posted their every move. If someone one wanted to kidnap them or burglarize them, she made it easy.

"Here we are just waking up." "Here I am brushing my teeth while Jeremy is making steaks on the grill." "Here we are on the Tappan Zee Bridge." She finished them all with hashtag #marriedlife #Blacklove #Destiny.

Yet, Miss wife overdose thought he was the only one with the problem.

"Maybe you should go and see a therapist to help," Dana suggested one night as she sifted through Fourth of July invitations to Martha's Vineyard at their 10-seat glass dining room table.

"Maybe *I* should go to therapy? Not *us*?" He asked curiously as he thought about having a small BBQ instead of going to Massachusetts.

"Well you're the one having problems sleeping. You think I don't notice you're struggling with something?"

"If I needed to sleep, I would take some sleeping pills."

"Let me ask you something Dana. Have you ever been forced into something you did not want to do?"

"Not really," she replied seemingly without a care in the world.

"Okay, let me put it another way. What type of therapy do women need who trap men by getting pregnant?" He continued, "I mean that has to be some type of mental illness, right?"

Dana could feel herself getting a little angry, but she was determined to be a loving wife at all costs. She had remembered a quote she memorized from a social media post. She silently recited it to herself.

"Neurologists claim that every time you resist acting on your anger, you're actually rewiring your brain to be calmer and more loving."

She chose kindness and walked up to the love of her life and wrapped her arms around his waist.

"Listen, we have everything. A fabulous home, a happy son and more money than we could ever need. We can grow a nice family. Why is that so hard? This all is a blessing." She squeezed a little and he responded in kind holding her. His touch comforted her and made her feel protected.

"Am I that bad? I love you. I love this family more than anything," she said.

When she spoke with a soft tone it melted Jeremy. That is what a lady should sound like he thought.

He looked down into her hungry eyes. Eyes, he knew, were yearning for him. He put his hands on her shoulder and kissed her forehead.

He picked her up and gently placed her atop the kitchen island. She smiled and took her hair out of her ponytail as he pulled down her panties with his mouth. He opened her legs and began gently licking her clit. She put her head back and moaned, "Yes. Oh yes," she said. "Right there baby. Yes. That's so good," she said rubbing his head.

He squeezed both her breasts together with one of his large hands. She placed her hand on top of his and gently rubbed them. His love was uncontrollable, as she began a slow grind feeling the cold marble under her ass.

"Please don't stop," she whispered.

"I'm not," he whispered back.

"I'm gonna lick my name on your pussy. Can daddy, do that?"

"Yes," she purred, while his tongue licked a J and then an E, and then she joined him, "R", oh my "E", yes "M." She had to catch her breath while she trembled.

"Damn," she screamed and tried to back her ass up.

He grabbed her thighs.

"Don't run, I'm not done," he said.

She breathed harder and started screaming,

"Oh my God; Yes, Jeremy! Yes, I love you!"

He started sucking on her clit like his mouth was a vacuum. The suction made her scream out, "I'm cumming, Oh God, I'm cumming."

She shivered as if she had been given an electric shock.

Jeremy stood up and stared at her.

She had a soft look on her face—almost angelic. Jeremy put himself inside of her and stroked slowly until he came. *She needs to be like this every day.*

"Baby, thank you. That was so good," she said as she sat up on the island and accepted a passionate kiss from Jeremy. He stood in front of her and whispered, "Always remember, I care for you and Junior, but it's going to take me a while to understand this life that was chosen for me by you and our parents," he said while gently licking and kissing her neck.

"I will be the best father I can be, because Junior didn't ask to be here. I take full responsibility for him."

Dana pushed him back. "Same ole Jeremy."

"Be still woman, listen to what I'm saying," he grabbed her and held her to his chest.

"What are you saying?" She asked as she pretended to break free but submitted to his will at the same time.

"I'm saying to kill that I need to go to therapy crap." He leaned in, surprising her with his hard penis on her thigh and she smiled.

Then bam! He grabbed her throat and squeezed it. She broke free and jumped down holding her neck.

"Are you crazy?"

Jeremy got pissed because he lost his erection.

"I'm playing." He lied. He was trying to give Dana a chance to be that woman he needed, and she had failed.

"What's to eat around here? I've seemed to have worked up quite an appetite," he said while stepping away and opening the refrigerator.

"All of this food in here and a man can't even get a meal," he said while grabbing some pastrami.

For the first time Jeremy had really scared her. There was something about the way he looked at her. But he was not going to punk her.

"You just tried to choke me, and you think you don't need a therapist?" she asked while watching him casually spread mustard on a piece of rye bread.

"Do you hear me speaking to you?" She asked standing out of his reach.

"Can you get me a soda please?" He asked.

"Do you choke those sluts?" Dana asked.

"It wasn't me," Jeremy said casually.

"You're Shaggy now?" Dana asked. "Well, mister it wasn't me, let's agree to have our asses home by the time the sun comes up each day. I'm tired of all your little sleepovers wherever you are. Our son should get a good morning from his father every day.

Dana continued releasing her inner vixen. "You may be out there messing around with those ungodly women, but they won't be waking up eating breakfast with MY husband."

"Let the church say Amen," Jeremy said.

"I promise you, I'm not joking," Dana said.

"Woman, I just gave you some good loving and you're still bitching? Go wash your ass or something," he said.

Dana used to read the classics. Now everywhere he turned in the house, there books with names like *"Ratchet Chicks Win" and "Life as a Thug's Wife."* Maybe he would start reading some and turn into the gangster dude she must be fantasizing about.

She had not been back to work since she had Junior and was addicted to reality TV shows. Dana was changing from Claire Huxtable into some mouth almighty hood queen. He already had a Sha. He did not want to come home to another one.

"Yeah, I'm going. You just remember what I said. "Respect," as she flounced her way out of the kitchen.

Bye Felicia.

"Got it. Hashtag #Team Marriage," Jeremy said wondering what Sha was making for dinner while he devoured his sandwich.

CHAPTER 12

What does a woman do when the man she is with has not defined their relationship? She makes one up in her head and then calls another woman for a free therapy.

"Polygamy: When a man is married to more than one woman at a time. See girl, I told you," Sha read aloud to Myra over the phone.

"I also read that in many places in Africa, and even in Utah, men have more than one wife."

"Did I miss the wedding ceremony?" Myra asked sounding salty. "Although I hope to visit one day, right now we don't live in Africa and you two are not Mormons."

"Well, he's treating me like a wife," Sha said. "We're getting ready to celebrate our third anniversary. How about that?"

"Girl, I love you, but miss me with that."

"A weh yuh a seh?" Sha said in the Jamaican Patois dialect.

"How many times have I told you when in America, speak English?" Myra laughed.

"What did you say?" Sha inquired. "Your phone faded for a second and I couldn't hear you."

"Anyway," Myra said in between popping her chewing gum. "Seriously, he is never going to leave his wife. Three years and he ain't left yet."

"He told me give him five years, just two more to go," Sha said with conviction.

"Listen, when men want you, they capture you sooner than later. They are hunters and don't want anyone else to get their prize. Go ask a guy," Myra said. "And three years is a long time to be with someone else's husband, you better watch out for his wife."

"Well I believe him," Sha said. "He is the one is coming to my house. I'm not going to his," Sha tried to reason. "You know Jamaican women don't care nothing bout de wife. Especially some Yankee wife," Sha laughed. "We can share de money."

Yes, it was about the money somewhat. In her mind she was already Jeremy's wife--at least one of them.

Sha felt one day, if she was patient and obedient, she would have the number one spot. Her family would be so proud she got a rich American man.

Why doesn't Dana just die already?

Sha was tired of struggling. It was time for her to rest.

During her teen years, when she should have been having fun hanging out with other young people, she was warming up bottles and changing diapers on her son David. The monthly strolls to the welfare office were the worse.

His father, Daryn, had dreams of a rap career. He fed her the story they were going to live in a big house in Ochos Rios.

One night while they were on the Coney Island boardwalk, he proposed and married her. Their honeymoon was a blanket on the sand while they feasted on Nathan's famous hot dogs.

"This is how our parents did it back home in Jamaica," he said with the wisdom of a twenty-two-year-old.

She believed him and let him have her virginity.

Nine months later, at 16 years old, she become a mother.

By the time David started kindergarten, Daryn had a hit record that made it to the Billboard 100.

By the time David finished kindergarten, Daryn was walking down an aisle at a real wedding with a Latina girl from the Bronx. They had two more children and moved to Florida.

Jeremy was the first man in almost twenty years Sha had ever loved. Raising David on her own taught her a lot about motherhood. Having a big ass, bit tits and being able to cook well taught her lot about men.

Loneliness called her name for years. Before Jeremy, her life consisted of the hair shop, school, home and an occasional trip to Jamaica--mainly to attend funerals of family members. Now Jeremy was filling some nights. If she had to share him with some other woman, then so be it—the heart wants what the heart wants.

"Did I tell you we are going up to the Foxwoods Resort in Connecticut soon for his birthday?" Sha said.

"Really now. Well, that should be nice," Myra said rolling her eyes up in her head.

Sha left out the part she was paying to take him. She was yearning to wake up in his arms instead of him always leaving like a thief in the night.

So whatever Ms. Myra from Queens was trying to say was not resonating. Sha grew up in Brooklyn, and what Brooklyn wanted, Brooklyn took.

Three years with two women and Jeremy was not in love with either of them. They were so different. One wanted to know all about his day, while the other wanted to know about his night.

Jeremy found himself thinking too much about Sha. He reasoned that was because she gave him the most attention. Dana was neglectful. Her only form of communications seemed to be a to-do list or instructions for something.

Sha was good company, could cook, kept a clean house and was a lot cheaper than call girls. Thanks to Sha, Jeremy could not remember the last time he had even been in a strip club. When Sha put on some dancehall music, she become a lap dance queen. Sexually, there was nothing she would not do for him.

Three years had flown by. Sha was now too clingy and was not helping him make money. He needed someone to help add to his bottom line. Women came easy. What he needed was his own money to get from under Father Edward's stronghold.

Dana was getting suspicious and snooping around. He did not want to hurt Sha, but he knew it time to let her go.

Sha ended up making it easy for him.

Jeremy felt a man could have more than woman, but never the two shall meet.

Dana threw him a birthday party at the yacht club for his 33rd birthday.

Sha decided to crash and show up with seven friends. A group that large were noticeable. Forget bad and bougie, they were sad and trashy. It did not help a few of them had blue and burgundy colored hair. Their tight-fitting outfits were tacky. They were out of place among the other guests who were all dressed properly for a party at such a nice place.

Something had told him to ask Sha to leave, but he did not want her to cause a scene.

"Why didn't you at least tell me you were coming?" he asked her after he pulled her into a maintenance closet.

"Because you would have told me no," she said as she tried to kiss him.

"Are you crazy, we don't have time for that right now," he said pushing her arms down. "Besides it smells like bleach in here."

"What's up with your clothes? You look like you're on next at Antwan's Strip Palace."

"Come on baby," she said feeling on his crotch.

"My father is out there. You're tripping."

"Come on, you know you want some. Really quick, let me hit daddy off," she said giving him surreal sensations, but he controlled himself.

"Listen up. You can stay but you and the Real Housewives of Brooklyn better behave."

Sha loved him calling her a housewife.

"Alright, am I going to see you after?"

"Maybe, we'll see," he lied.

"Wait five minutes before you come out," he instructed before giving her a wet sloppy tongue kiss leaving her wanting more.

"Honey where have you been? Your guests have been looking for you," Dana asked with a sly look on her face. "It's time to cut the cake."

Jeremy stood before the smiling faces. Half of the people were friends and family of Dana. The other were his father's friends. Nevertheless, he appreciated they were there to wish him a happy birthday.

"Thank you all for coming and for the gifts," he said addressing the crowd.

"Dana has put together a splendid event. Can we all give my wife a hand?" Dana stood waving and smiling as if she had just won the title of Miss America.

"Dana, I don't think you know this," he said gesturing her to come and join him by his side. "This is the first birthday party I've ever had." Everyone began clapping.

They hugged and kissed. Their colored coordinated clothing matched their admiration for one another.

"I love you baby."

"I love you more." She said acting giddy and raising her left hand over her mouth showing off her massive 3.5 carats wedding ring.

While Dana basked in her spotlight, Sha stood in the back of the crowd frowning. In her mind, she knew their little performance was a fraud. Last night, her and Jeremy had a five-hour sex marathon.

The DJ put on Stevie Wonder's tribute to Dr. King's birthday. That was the cue for the crowd to sing Happy Birthday. When the song stopped, Jeremy started to make his wish and blow out the candles.

Sha yelled out, "Happy Birthday Jay," as she pushed her way through the crowd.

There she stood with her seductive outfit in front of Jeremy, as if Dana was not standing next to him. The crowd watched in anticipation of what was coming next.

Sha began singing the sultry version of Happy Birthday like Marilyn Monroe had sang to President John F. Kennedy. She was off-key and clearly drunk.

Jeremy was embarrassed. He suddenly pictured his yacht sailing right down the Everglades swamp with Dana having him tied on the stern.

Sha was making a fool of herself, but he never moved his arm from around Dana. She tensed up and made a fist. He pulled her closer to him.

When Sha was done, she winked at Jeremy and giggled as one of her friends escorted her away.

Dana stepped aside from Jeremy and began clapping.

"Everyone please give tonight's surprise entertainment a big round of applause. Chad did you do this?" She looked over to him for support.

Chad played along and put his hands up and said, "Guilty." The crowd laughed while they clapped.

Jeremy watched Brooke walk over and whisper something to Sha. Then Sha and her entourage walked to the exit.

The party continued as if she was never there.

"Who was that woman?" Dana asked as they were undressing at home after the party.

"How am I supposed to know? I thought you said Chad hired her."

Dana sucked her teeth. "You better get your hoes in check. I'm warning you."

Jeremy was so angry at Sha. That was her final straw. Disrespecting his wife was not a part of the game.

The fact was, at the end of the day, Sha lived in an alternative universe in his world. Although he missed screwing her, their time was over.

Instead of Sha taking the hint and bowing out of the extramarital affair gracefully, she became a stalker. So, he ignored her. She obviously had no shame. Her communications after the party were of a desperate, irrational woman.

One time she had left a twenty-three-minute voicemail saying she had booked some package for them to go out of town. She had to know that never was going to happen he thought. Besides going out to eat in Brooklyn, they had not been anywhere else together except the hotel in New Jersey when they had first met.

Her other attempts at seduction were a turn off.

For weeks, she was relentless. When he changed his phone number, she started sending him emails and then started calling his office demanding to know why he was not coming over. "You owe me an explanation," she texted one day. The only person he owed any explanation was to his wife, and even then, she would barely get the truth.

The last message Ms. Enid handed him from her was, "If I don't hear from you by tomorrow, I am coming to your house."

No problem, if she wanted a goodbye in person, then that is what she would get. He texted to let her know he would see her that night.

When Jeremy arrived at Sha's apartment, he was surprised to find his key still worked. He walked into the smell of sage she was burning.

"It's to keep the bad spirits away," she would say. It smelled good and immediately relaxed him while he poured himself a drink.

Sha was in the bedroom laid across the bed listening to John Legend's song, *She Don't Have to Know.*

I've never really listened to the words. Damn that Legend went deep. Just tell Sha what you need to say and get out of here.

"Hey baby, I'm so happy to see you," she said. Jeremy thought she looked cute in her T-shirt and cut-off shorts.

"How are you doing Sha?" Jeremy said standing in the doorway looking around the immaculately clean bedroom. Everything was so neat. Dana was so sloppy in their bedroom.

"I've missed you. I'm so sorry about what I did."

"Turn off the music," Jeremy requested.

"Why would you come to my party and act a fool?" Jeremy said as he felt his phone vibrating in his pocket. He knew it was Dana looking for him.

"I thought we had an understanding," he said.

"Have you ever heard of King Solomon?" She asked but he was not following the relevance.

"Yes, of course," he replied taking a sip of the vodka.

"Well you know King Solomon had 700 wives. There is no way only one woman could fulfill all your desires. A big, strong man like you."

"King Solomon also lost his entire kingdom because of women," he said.

"I know you have a wife and son," she said as she sipped a glass of orange juice. "Obviously, I don't mind sharing, but do not disrespect me by ignoring me Jeremy."

"Stop lying," he said.

"I'm not lying. You're a Scorpio and I'm a Cancer. The stars say we are compatible. Dana is a Leo and she is not better than me. She is too bossy for you. Look at Halle Berry, Jennifer Lopez. Angela Bassett. All Leos. You don't like women like that. Our stars are aligned."

She's a liar. All three of those women are fine and I would not mind spending some time with any one of them.

How the hell did she know Dana's sign? Why is she comparing herself to my wife? There was no comparison. Sha had no idea what him and Dana had, or why.

79

Marry Sha? That was never going to happen for a whole lot of reasons. The most important one was he met her in a club and on the first night, he had sex not only with her, but her friend as well. If she did it once, she would likely do it again. At least he knew with Dana he was the only one touching her.

"I'm already very much married," he said. "And I have no plans to marry anyone else Sha. That's just reality."

Sha stood up off the bed and walked over to look out of the window.

Jeremy went and sat on the bed.

"You're looking kind of bloated, is that why you've been acting so crazy?" *Yeah that's it, she's on her period.*

"No, I'm pregnant."

Jeremy spit out his drink and it splashed all over her dresser. Fear was not something he was accustomed to feeling, but at that moment staring at her stomach it scared the hell out of him.

Damn it, she was just like Dana. Were they reading the same playbook on trapping a man with a baby? Who was the author?

"I know you don't love Dana," she said her name again with familiarity as if they were both long lost friends.

"I am going to need you to keep my wife's name out of your mouth," Jeremy said with an attitude.

"Look who is on hashtag #teamwifey," she yelled.

"Let me ask you something?" *You can tell me all her business, but when I say her name you trip? Where were those* protective thoughts when I was licking your ass, giving you de batty wash," she yelled.

"What a sewer mouth," he said ready to slap her. "Lower your voice."

"This is my house. Fuck the neighbors."

"You're pregnant. Congratulations," he said sarcastically. "What do you want from me Sha?"

"I want you to leave her and come and be a family with me and our child. Shit, I love you, can't you see that?"

"Let me ask you something. If my name was John Doe, the broke musician living in a room somewhere with a 1985 Toyota, would you still love me then? Would you have used birth control?"

"But you're not a John Doe, are you?" She retaliated.

"If you didn't love me, why didn't you use condoms?" She clapped back.

"You are too old to be having a baby and what about David?"

She came over to him and reached up for his neck and began kissing him. He could taste her tears on his lips. He was telling her to stop and pushing down her hands. She put his hand on her ass which felt like a soft pillow and he squeezed it.

Fuck it.

He whispered while he licked her neck and said, "Lay down, you're going to do exactly as I say?"

He sat next to her on the bed and summoned her to take off her shorts. With every touch, her legs opened wider to allow him full access. As she laid there spread eagle, he stood up and took off his pants and underwear.

He summoned her to put his penis in her mouth. She began slowly licking his shaft up and down. *One, two, three licks.* Then he turned around and bent over while her tongue went along his thigh to his ass. She was softly kissing his thigh while holding his penis. Ahhhh, Jeremy thought while he anticipated the next place her tongue would explore. When he felt her hot wet tongue circling his asshole, his blood rushed to his penis. He had missed her hot mouth. He would need to find someone else to do this for him. When he was as hard as he could get, he turned over and put himself deep inside her wet vagina. It felt hotter than usual. *Pregnant pussy he thought.*

"Welcome home," she whispered between her moans.

Goodbye Sha.

When they were done, Sha laid on his chest.

"Please stay the night with me," she spoke softly.

"You know I can't do that Sha."

"It's nearly three am. Are you really going to leave me and drive all the way up to Westchester this time of night?"

"Just enjoy the moment. I'm not leaving yet."

"See that's what I mean, you're over here sleeping with me and you can't even spend the night?"

"First of all," he said, "We don't *sleep* together. "Second, you've heard my phone vibrating for hours. You know who it is." He grew impatient because she was messing up his mood with foolish pillow talk. He just wanted to lay there while he thought of a way to convince her to get an abortion.

Sha sprung up and wrapped the sheet around her naked body. "So, you think because you buy me gifts, help with a few bills and groceries, I'm just your whore?"

"Sha I've never treated you like a whore. Whores are quiet," he laughed.

"I'm not laughing," she said.

"Listen, don't go getting brand new on me like with this baby stunt you are pulling."

"A stunt?"

"Yes, a stunt," he said as he rose to get dressed.

"Now you're pregnant. Houston, we have a problem."

"I thought you would be happy."

"Happy? Trust me, I'm far from happy. What is my wife going to say? "

"She doesn't have to know."

"You think life is that song you were playing earlier? You're too old to be having a baby. I'm a Collins. A baby mama would be uncivilized."

"Then divorce her and marry ME."

"You're not serious, are you? He asked as he glanced at her modest furnishings. Dana would likely have furnished the basement with her stuff.

"You think you're better than me? That's fucked up," she paused and looked down at the floor.

"Well I'm having this baby."

"No, you need to get an abortion. We CANNOT have a child together. How much do you need?"

"You mean money?"

"Yes, sweetheart I mean money, how much do you want to have an abortion?"

His offer stunned her, but a payoff did not sound like such a bad idea.

"A million dollars," she said looking at him for the yes. Fuck love. Get money.

"Woman, that's not even realistic, but I knew there was a price," he said shaking his head.

"Suit yourself. If you want to take care of a baby by yourself, go for it. But what you will not do is break up my marriage. That I can promise you."

"I was joking about the money. Have I ever asked you for a quarter?" She said crushed.

"You stand here in my home and insult me. A home that always welcomed you. That's messed up."

"You're on your own Sha. I came here to say goodbye. You're going down a lonely road. Be sensible," he said. "Get an abortion and move on with your life. I'm married."

"Fuck you blood clot ras. I'm having this baby."

"Suit yourself, but don't call me and definitely don't come to my house," he said as threw his keys on the bed and walked out slamming the front door.

CHAPTER 13

Sha kept Jeremy abreast of the details of her pregnancy in the hopes he would come back to her.

"Jeremy guess what?" Her voice message stated, "The baby is kicking. I'm making oxtails tonight; you should come through."

Every doctor's appointment she sent a text: "Today, *we* are five months. Guess what? We're having twins!"

A week later, she called to say she had a stillbirth and one of the fetus' was gone. Her cries made Jeremy feel a touch of sadness and he planned to go visit her.

The next day, she sent a message that changed his mind. "You're a bastard and I hope you die just like our other baby."

Two weeks later another text: "Jeremy please call me; I beg of you. I miss you so much."

Then that text came—the one that let him know that for the next 18 years, he would be intertwined with Sha.

"I had the baby. Her name is Christina Collins Harris. I'm at Brooklyn Hospital on DeKalb, near Junior's the cheesecake place."

Even Jeremy knew he couldn't be MIA any longer and he went to see his daughter.

Hospitals always made Jeremy feel sick. The scent was too much for him. The mixture of disinfectant with germs shot up his nostrils like rockets. He wanted to ask for a mask.

When he arrived in Sha's room, he was surprised to see an older woman who resembled her. If looks could kill, Jeremy would have been dead and cremated.

"Jeremy this is my mom, Claudia." Sha said laying in the bed holding their daughter.

"You're a wicked man. Cursed before you were even born. When you get old, you will be lost at sea," her mother said before she grabbed her purse and left.

"How are you feeling?" Jeremy asked Sha ignoring Mama Bitch.

"Why does she look like that?" Jeremy asking about the baby's face.

"She has Down's Syndrome." Sha with watery eyes. "But I have accepted my sin and I'm asking God for forgiveness," she said softly while looking at Christina.

"I warned you not to do this," Jeremy said as he noticed the Bible on her side table.

"Hold your child, let her know her daddy is here," Sha said as she invited Jeremy to take Christina out of her arms.

"Jeremy, I need to know if you are going to be a good father. Just like you are to Jeremy Junior," Sha asked. "You see our baby needs special care."

"Listen, the only thing I can offer you is money," he said as he looked down at Christina in his arms. She smelled so good, like lilacs he thought.

"I'm so sorry little one. So sorry. We will get you the best of care," Jeremy said as he handed Christina back to Sha while telling he had to go. Dana was outside of a movie theatre waiting for him.

"Already you leave us? Just like that? Like you did us a favor by dropping by?" Sha said with tears flowing. "My mother is right you're so lost."

**

Sha had not wasted any time. By the time Christina was two weeks old, Jeremy was served a subpoena to appear at a child support hearing.

Father Edward's accountant would conveniently fix his income. Sha should have come to him for money instead of going to the court. It was spiteful and so now she would get less than what she may have received from him directly.

For weeks he had stalled telling Dana. He knew she would hit the roof, probably blow it off with a shotgun. Chad suggested he come hang out and they could talk about it more in person.

Chad's get together was a boy's night with his friends Terri and Ruben, Terri was the only female Chad would allow in the man cave. Terri had self-proclaimed and proven herself to be "harder than most men."

"I can't believe you have a baby with that woman from A Soulful Affair," Chad said while they played a game of pool and took shots of White Hennessey.

"Dang man, you've been messing with her all of this time? I guess I should have known after that little stunt her ass pulled at your party—red ball corner pocket," Chad called out.

"Do me a favor and turn that volume up some," Chad said to Terri who was watching a Knicks game.

"Don't you know you have to hit it and quit it?" He said lowering his voice because Brooke was upstairs. "The longer you stay, the harder it is to get rid of them."

"Hoes get 90 days. A super hoe, maybe 120. Any longer, the probationary period is over. Now, she's on the payroll. Then you should get a tax deduction and shit," Ruben chimed in.

Ruben was an overweight 52-year-old with a big stomach and a gap in his top teeth. He had been married for 14 years. Him and his wife Regina had three children which added to the other four he had by four other women. Jeremy wanted to know what he had told all those women to get so many babies. What a master manipulator. Seven kids? He could only imagine how much he was shelling out every month in child support on an accountant's salary.

"Listen, the grass is always greener on the other side, because that shit is fake," he said while stuffing his face with some hot wings.

"Ten years ago, my side chick had to take out a restraining order against my wife. The two policewomen laughed at her and she was scared shitless," he said recalling the visual.

"Are you saying, you've never cheated in 10 years?" Chad asked.

"No," he laughed. "I'm a cheater, that's what I do. There are too many flowers in the garden. What I'm saying are hoes get 90 days," he said. "The key is to remember any woman dropping her panties who knows you're married, is a hoe. Men, and society are tossing them too much respect these days. They are starting to act like a wife."

"Man, you brought your wife the drama. I'm surprised she didn't fuck you up for real?" Terri chimed in with her Newark, NJ tough attitude which matched her oversized baggy jeans, a wife-beater T-shirt, and bandana headband.

"Don't think I didn't get it. Now every year, I pay for her to go on some luxury trip called *LadyScape* where her and some other women travel all over the world to celebrate themselves. Shit, sometimes I have to work overtime just so she can have spending money," he said remembering she asked for her deposit last week. "I know this, had I not been messing with ole girl for so long, it probably would have not gotten that far," Ruben added.

"She's a smart one, I need to look up *LadyScape* online," Terri said while laughing. "I got someone who owes me too."

Jeremy just listened. He was glad to be around others with similar struggles. Dating and love was tricky.

"Well, all I know, us White boys, as you call us, don't go through all these problems," Chad said.

"Please explain, I want to hear this," Terri said.

"Me too," both Jeremy and Ruben said.

"I'm going to hip you all to something. Pay attention because I'm only going to say it once," Chad said.

"White women are called mistresses and cheating husband are having affairs. Shit sounds so proper," he laughed. In exchange for secret sexual encounters in which we rarely, if ever get caught, we give the women, average cock. Well mine is a little different. They get a big cock over here. Then money, an apartment I pay for, so I can save on hotels. Maybe, for Christmas, she'll get a fur or some nice jewelry." Chad stood as if he was teaching a workshop on how to be successful on a job interview.

"If she gets pregnant, and that's a big if, we got a nice private doctor on standby cause shit happens. When we're done, they go away quietly, or we kill their ass. Simple," he laughed.

"Are you following me?" He asked like a schoolteacher.

Everyone nodded affirmatively like judges in a pageant.

"White women respect the wife's position who is probably screwing her husband and the pool guy, her exercise trainer or somebody else. She never is going to get caught because we would kill them. NEVER. Besides she keeps it short, maybe once or twice she opens her legs. Her husband probably has more money?" He shrugged. "She is too scared to get cut off. A mistress never, ever bothers their children or tries to turn a man against his own kids."

"Keep going," Terri said.

"Now on the flip side. Black women are known as side chicks. Men who fuck with them are cheating. They have absolutely no respect for your wife, your children or your village."

Ruben interjected. "He's right, they are hoping every day your wife finds out."

"Exactly," Chad said. "Now, your wife is sitting at home sexless because you are giving all your energy to a?"

He stopped to listen.

"A hoe," Terri said.

"Right," Chad continued. "Now your wife is searching for the reason you're not giving her the boner and she is turning into a private investigator."

"Yeah, I think Dana is better than an FBI agent, for real." Jeremy said.

"Now in exchange for all this, the Black side chick gets a big cock, or so I've been told," Chad said laughing. "Maybe a few dinners out here and there, some cheap jewelry and maybe a few dollars. Her goal is to get pregnant, so you can pay her child support for eighteen years. She wants you to forget about your other kids and may be jealous of time you're spending with them instead of her. You're so pussy whipped you forgot who runs the world. We do. Men, not women and certainly not," he stopped to listen again.

They all said in unison, "Hoes."

"Damn, you went deep on us," Jeremy said.

"I'm speechless man, we need to get you on Oprah or some shit like that," Ruben said thinking how almost everything in America was based upon something racial—even infidelity.

"Shit is true," Chad said. "I got some women actually thinking Valentine's Day is February 13th," he laughed. "The only woman who has even the slightest chance of running me is my dear ole mother and I had that attitude before the money."

"You're right," Jeremy said. "Sha was intoxicating. Like if she had a spell on me for real. Her and all that incense."

"Yeah, I bet she was feeding you too," Terri said while Chad looked at the tray of hot wings. "You have to watch out for that. Women put shit in food to trap you."

"I believe it," Ruben said. "Have you all ever heard the one that if a woman buries your underwear in her yard, you will never want to leave?"

"Damn, nope I don't know about that one," Chad said. "I know the one about women putting their period blood in spaghetti sauce to make a man stay with them."

"That's just nasty," Jeremy said.

"Nasty, but effective," Terri said. "It works on women too," she laughed. But you don't want to mess with that kind of stuff. It always backfires. You could end up getting the person, but they may get paralyzed or some shit. Then you're stuck taking care of them."

"Be careful of what you wish for," Ruben said.

"Well right now Jay, Dana, as your wife has a right to know that you have another child in this world," Chad said.

"Yeah, that's the same thing my pops said before he read me the riot act for having the family's first baby mama," he laughed.

CHAPTER 14

Dana sat at her dining room table drifting off into space. She had lost track of time. Listening to Luther Vandross and his slow love songs were making her feel worse so she clicked off the Bose system. Junior was down for the night and the house was quiet.

Her laptop was opened to an email, sent so casually by a stranger, sexyms1700@gmail.com. Communications that would likely change her life forever.

Hi Dana, you don't know me, but as a woman and a mother, I thought you should know the pics attached are of Jeremy's new baby Christina and her mother Shanice Harris. Their daughter has Down's Syndrome. BTW, that carrot cake at his birthday party was good. Can you tell me where you got it? Anyway, that is all. Have a good day.

Dana tracked the email address to someone named Myra Simpson who worked at a law firm in Brooklyn. Yeah, a simp, that name suited her she thought.

Dana enlarged and stared at the picture of the Miss Marilyn Monroe impersonator holding a newborn baby wrapped in a pink blanket. A baby who looked more like Jeremy than even Junior.

Anger would not let Dana grieve the sadness she felt. Junior was practically still a baby himself and the fool of a husband of hers had gotten someone else knocked up.

This charlatan of a woman who wore a copper-looking wedding band. Was she married? Was Jeremy a polygamist? She counted back ninth months to remember what was happening in their own lives.

Dana had been thinking about having their second child. Perhaps their own little girl. Now this.

Dana was anxious to see how Jeremy was going to explain. It was bad enough, she kept having recurring bouts of Chlamydia with an awful discharge. Now she had confirmation he was likely having unprotected sex with that nasty looking woman.

"What time will you be home tonight?" She asked him after calling and trying to remain calm.

"I'm on my way now. I should be there by nine."

"We need to talk," she said before hanging up on him.

Jeremy knew when a woman said she needed to talk that was a heads up for an argument. He braced himself for another night of Dana's bullshit.

The house was pitch black when he walked in. Before he could turn on the light, he felt a slight wind past his ear and then heard glass shatter. He jumped causing his glasses to fly off. He thought it was a home invasion.

"Dana!" he yelled.

She switched on the light. He looked down and squinted to see broken glass on the floor at his feet and the roses he had given her yesterday. *This must be serious for her to give up a $1,000 Waterford crystal vase.*

"Yeah, you blind motherfucker," she roared like a WWE wrestler. She lost all sense of poise and grace when she was in the same space with him. It was as if his spirit bought out the worst in her.

"A baby, a freakin' baby! It's not enough you are out there giving up all your goodies, but you have the nerve to have a baby? Laying up with a tramp raw? Then you don't even tell me. Nine whole months?"

Jeremy was stunned, but not surprised. He would give her time to release her anger, but if she threw something else, he knew he would slap her ass to the floor.

"I have put up with all of your cheating ways," she said shaking her head from side to side while pointing her finger at him.

"Your lies, the way your mouth moves differently when we kiss. I know you. Everything. I can tell what you ate just from smell of your farts."

Okay she is certified crazy now.

"I've even put up with you coming home smelling like cheap ass perfume and now I'm always itching down there," she said pointing to her pelvic area. "Dammit Jeremy."

"You need to calm down Dana. Where is Junior?"

"He's fuckin' sleep upstairs. Where do you think he is this time of night?"

"Keep your voice down before you wake him," he warned.

"I knew you were never in love with me, but I had least thought you cared enough not to violate me with a baby from some whore."

"It's not like that," Jeremy said getting a word in.

"Confirm it. You have a daughter?"

"Christina is her name," He said aloud for the first time.

"As in Christ?" Dana said. "That's blasphemous."

"Listen Dana, the woman tricked me."

"The woman? You sound like she's a stranger?" Dana sat down on the sofa and put her head back as if she had to rest. Jeremy just stared trying to figure out what to say next.

Then Dana sprang up.

"What happened? Did she just accidentally fall on your dick? No wait, these hoes out here now stealing sperm. Tell me asshole, did she steal your sperm and freeze it?" She asked.

"Then I have to find out through some email from some bitch named Myra. A fuckin' email to tell me that my husband, Lord, my husband, the father of my son, has a baby from some chick named Shanice. I should have beat her ass at your party."

Dana pointed to the laptop. "Yeah, you're busted. It's over there, go look."

"Not before you calm down."

Sweat poured down Dana's face. She pulled off her Korean store-bought wig and threw it at him.

"This fool got me out here wearing these itchy, hot ass wigs, when you know I'm about that perm life."

Jeremy walked backwards to the table, still facing Dana. She was looking for something else to throw.

"Now, I'm going back to get tested again. I need to start putting co-pays in my monthly budget like I'm the one out here screwing the whole city."

Dana threw a lamp while yelling, "This is so not the life I wanted for us."

"Dana, if you throw something else, you will need to worry about more than a baby. Calm the fuck down," he said as he caught the lamp and placed it on the table.

"When were you going to tell me Jeremy? That's what I don't get. Betrayal is real. Are you going to be that man whose hidden family shows up at his funeral?"

Shit, Jeremy thought as he read the email. He felt a migraine coming on and started rubbing his temple. Why would Myra do this? Brooklyn chicks. They took grimy to another level, but they had no clue what Miss Harlem, a woman from America's first Black ghetto, were capable of. They were calculating predators when provoked. Jeremy was scared for Sha and Myra.

"Go pack your shit and get out. I'm tired of you," Dana demanded while pulling out luggage from the hall closet.

"Don't act innocent. You know this was a forced marriage by our parents," he said walking over to her and kicking the suitcase down the hall.

"Did I ask to get married? Did I ask to have a baby with you or her?"

"Arranged, not forced," she said.

97

"That's semantics," he said.

"You stood in front of my parents, our family and friends and what did you do? You said I do. No one had a gun to your head."

"Listen this is something that happened. We can work through it," he said casually.

"You had better get out of here before I do something I will regret," she said backing up down the hall.

"Be a man for once in your life. We are done. Go raise your love child. Get out. You never deserved me or Junior," she said throwing his coats out on the floor from the closet.

"I am not going anywhere. You started this sham of marriage and we are going to finish it," he said stepping in her face and pulling on his leather jacket she held in her hand.

She thought about going to get their gun.

He winked at her. She reached up on her tippy-toes and slapped him cross the face.

"Save that wink bullshit," was the last thing she said before she fell to her knees after he backhanded her.

"Keep your hands to yourself. I'm no bitch Dana!"

Dana was terrified as she sat on the floor holding her face. *Maybe I should call the cops.*

"You both tricked me. I didn't want a baby with either of your dumbasses. Now that they are here, I'm responsible for them," he said thinking he should have knocked her ass out.

"I feel sorry for MY children."

He waved his arms around their magazine inspired home and said, "You did all of this for status. Admit that shit. Sha did what she did for money."

Dana was speechless. She wanted Jeremy dead.

"I'm going upstairs to go to bed, and I suggest you do the same. Or you can stay right down there on the floor," he said caring less than three fucks.

"Something is seriously wrong with you," Dana yelled at him walking to the stairs.

"It's like you have no soul. You're a soul snatcher."

He ignored her and took two steps at a time to go upstairs to their bedroom.

Jeremy knew Dana was angry and even hurt, but he was not leaving. He was a man and still the king of the castle. How many times did he have to tell her, "I run this house, it doesn't run me?" She was drinking more than the Kool Aid those books and TV shows were serving her if she thought she was putting him out.

On the other hand, whatever, little scheme Sha was playing, it was dead. When he got upstairs, he retrieved their gun from the safe and tucked it under his side of the mattress. Then he went into the bathroom, locked the door and called Sha.

CHAPTER 15

Sha felt as if she had won the lottery when she saw Jeremy's name on her screen.

"Hello."

"What have you and Myra done?" He said as he flushed the toilet and turned on the shower to drown out the sound of his voice.

"What are you talking about?"

"Myra sent Dana an email telling her about you and Christina." *This was her chance to come clean.*

"What! I can't believe she did that. I had nothing to do with that Jeremy, believe me." *An email, I told her ass to call.*

"When did she send it?"

"Today."

"Don't you want to know how the baby is? You should come and see us."

"Did you hear what I just said? Dana knows about Christina."

"Yeah, I heard exactly what you said. I guess what I'm saying is that you should come and see your daughter."

"I'm getting ready to go to bed." He said as he searched for some aspirin for his throbbing headache.

"Are you at your condo?" She inquired.

"No, I'm at my house. I probably won't be down to the city for a few more days," he said.

Sha was surprised and dismayed. She thought Dana would have put him out. That's what she would have done. She was so sure Jeremy was going to leave and drive over to her and Christina.

"You're staying there?" she asked curiously.

"I live here?"

"Where is Dana?"

None of your damn business he wanted to say. Instead, since she wanted to play games fine with him. She was lucky he didn't circle back and fuck Myra. Her ass was always more appealing than Sha's, but he wanted to respect her. Then they pull this shit on him.

"My wife is getting ready to come to bed, so I'm jumping in the shower. We're good," he added on purpose.

Sha felt her heart sink as walked over and stared at Christina asleep in her crib.

She hung up and waited for him to call back.

He didn't.

Jeremy was not dumb. He knew Sha had that done that shit on purpose. That call was to let her know he was not leaving his wife. Now if Dana wanted to leave him that was another story.

**

Dana put a bag of ice on her throbbing, swollen cheek before downing a large glass of Merlot with pain killers, in one gulp. She was hoping they reached her bloodstream fast. Add domestic violence to Jeremy's list of marital sins. She poured another glass and let out a heavy sigh.

"Woosa," she said as she stared at the open email.

Fuck it, she thought and hit reply.

Hello Myra Simpson. *Yeah simp, I know who you are.*

Thanks for the message. I remember you all at my husband's birthday party. I really thought you all were the hired help, because you all were dressed like prostitutes.

Do me a favor, send me Shanice's number or ask her to call me: (914) 555-1218.

Sincerely, Mrs. Dana Tyler-Collins

P.S. We got the cake from the Little Pie Company on 43rd Street. Enjoy.

Send. *Hi Bitch.*

Myra never responded and getting Sha's number was as easy as logging into their online cell phone account.

Dana could hardly walk up the stairs after drinking the entire bottle of wine. For some reason her tears just flowed automatically as if she had no control. She went to check on Junior before crashing in the guestroom.

He was so handsome and so innocent. She sighed as she thought he would be another statistic of a broken home.

Jeremy had not even apologized for breaking his vows, let alone making another baby. Dana knew it would only get worse. It was time to cut her losses before he gave her something that a pill couldn't cure, or worse, she was a featured story on the television show *Killer Wives*.

Regardless, she would make sure Junior still had a good life without his father.

For nearly a week, Dana thought about contacting Sha. Under normal circumstances, Dana would not even dignify speaking to another woman about her husband. When a man cheats, women should confront their man, not another woman, were her thoughts.

For years, she had watched her own mother remain quiet at her father's infidelity.

"Listen Dana, your father and I have been together for longer than I can remember. He is handsome and wealthy. Of course, there are going to be women at his beck and call. How does that affect me?" She asked when Dana inquired about her father's cheating ways as they put together care packages for homeless youth at the church.

"You don't think it's disrespectful?" She whispered making sure none of the others could hear them.

"Daddy and these women around here look right in your face like nothing. Some are even members of your woman's leadership program. I just don't know how you won't speak on it."

Her mother started touching her $10,000 diamond bracelet Oliver had purchased at a Sotheby's auction.

"If I would have left your father when I first learned he slept with someone else, I would not be sitting where I am today. It would have easily been another woman in my place," she said looking at her wrinkled hands.

"I have ignored them all and chose a life of luxury. And to be honest with you, I'm not innocent either," she laughed.

"It's unrealistic to think a man, or a woman for that matter is only going to sleep with one person their entire life," she paused and smirked. "And I say that as a preacher's wife."

"Well, Jeremy is the only man I have been with since I have been grown, so it is possible."

"Possible yes and that's your choice. And I don't mean to sound harsh daughter, but where has that unwavering loyalty gotten you? You know your father and Ed made that boy marry you," she said.

Dana appreciated her honesty.

Ignoring a cheating man was one thing. Ignoring a woman who had a baby with your husband was another story. Perhaps if Dana would have stepped to her sooner, she would not have felt so comfortable with her husband. No, if she could go this far, Dana had something to say to her.

"Just ignore it and let a man, be a man. That woman and that baby are his problems," her mother advised. "No one can touch your inheritance."

She would take care of Jeremy in her own way, Dana thought as she called the homewrecker.

"Hello," a woman said.

"This is Dana Tyler-Collins, I'm looking for Shanice Harris."

"This is she."

"I'm calling to discuss how we can support Christina."

"Is that so?" Sha said knowing she was lying.

"What can I do for you?"

"What can you do for me is the wrong question I believe. You have been carrying on an affair with my husband."

Sha got defensive. "Why are you speaking to me like I'm a child. An affair? Jeremy is as much my man as he is yours," she said with conviction. "I got three years in, what about you?"

"Is that so?" Dana asked. Clearly, she is delusional, Dana thought.

"Now, from that affair, you have a daughter that my husband I would like to know how we can help. Is she okay?"

"My baby is fine, and she will stay fine," Sha said sarcastically. "As for YOUR husband. A husband you should have kept on a leash. I know women like you. So high and mighty in your fancy house with your fancy car, degrees and sex twice a month. You sit at home acting so entitled to YOUR husband barely doing what a man needs. I heard you don't even fuck him right."

Dana was beyond pissed as she stared at her wedding photo on top of the fireplace mantel and thought about setting in on fire.

"Your baby has special needs. How is she fine?" She asked thinking trying to remember she was raised in the church as she spoke to the demon woman.

"I called you woman to woman and you are giving me attitude. You know you wish you were in my shoes. You wish you had my life. So, let me tell you this miss three years in. I bet you a million-dollars, even if I left Jeremy today, or he left me, he ain't coming to you."

"You don't know what he would do. I bet you never thought he would be with someone else having a baby," Sha said.

She was right about that Dana thought.

"Let me ask you something? How many times have you pretended to be me? Wrote Shanice Collins down on paper? Dreamed he was with you and your child standing over her crib? How does it feel to be the baby mama and never a wife with not one, but two children?"

"Be you? Girl bye." Sha sucked her teeth loudly. "My children are blessings and will always be taken care of and that's all that matters."

"You keep telling yourself that honey. God don't bless no mess. Sideshicks always settling for a piece of a man. You can't get your own? Jeremy is not taking care of that baby, his father is. The estate is. Jeremy probably doesn't even know how much you get or when you get it."

I hope she is feeling this in her soul.

"You were looking for the come up. Now see, women like me know women like you too. Let me guess, you grew up poor, met a rich guy, a little power, and saw dollar signs. He's stupid and you're stupid. Fell for the crisscross."

"You think you know so much?" Sha said thinking she was a bitch just like Jeremy had said.

"I hope you spend every waking moment looking at your daughter and are reminded of the sin you volunteered for."

"Fuck you Dana Collins. You don't know me? I'll come and whip your ass."

"Wait, you had a baby with my husband, and you think you're gonna whip my ass?" She let out a hearty laugh.

"When your ass is feeling froggy, leap. I'm sure you know where our fancy house is. Which is by the way where Jeremy, MY HUSBAND, sleeps EVERY NIGHT. Not only will I whip that ass, but then I'll have your whole family deported."

The fuckin' nerve.

"Real talk. You WERE Jeremy's H-O-E—Had any dick lately?" She yelled.

"You should have aborted that baby just like he's doing you now. Bye bitch."

Sha stood motionless. She had to brace herself as she broke down and cried. Dana was right. She should have never messed with and certainly not have had a child with a married man.

CHAPTER 16

Jeremy's attempt to salvage his marriage had not worked and he worried about the financial impact of a divorce.

"Marriage is easy to get into, hard to get out of—especially when children are involved. Prepare to spend a pretty penny," the family attorney advised.

Father Edward showed his disappointment by stiffing him on commissions. "That's repayment for Dana's ring," he said. A ring Dana kept and probably pawned to buy that new baby blue Jaguar.

Before he could even think properly about the technicalities of divorce, Dana laid out the terms.

"Junior will have the absolute best upbringing afforded to him for being a Collins and a Tyler," she let him know. There were no court hearings or any other discussions between them except Dana telling him she was swearing off Black men forever.

"There might be some good and loving Black men somewhere, but you certainly were not their representative. Black women have options now and I'm willing to risk it again."

Father Edwards set up a trust fund for Junior who would receive a million dollars on his 25th birthday. Between now and his 18th birthday, the family would pay Dana $25,000 per month in support, if she did not have another child. If she did, the amount would be reduced to $10,000 per month. She also received a lump sum of $150,000 in alimony. Dana kept her house; Jeremy kept the boat lease and moved back into his condo.

Three years after they had said "I do" and 13 years since the bathroom, it was over.

Jeremy had not planned on fatherhood this way. There would be no more sharing his money with another child. For his own private divorce party, he got a vasectomy.

**

An entire year had passed since Jeremy had left Sha and Christina in the hospital. He missed her first Christmas and her first birthday. The $2,500 direct deposit she received every month, from a Collins subsidiary in South Carolina, was her only link to him.

No texts, no calls, nothing.

Sha was surprised when she found out him and Dana were divorced.

One day, while she lurked on Dana's Facebook page, she saw her in the arms of a White man she referred to as her fiancé.

Lucky her, Sha thought.

Would Jeremy ever be interested in Christina? Sha was thinking about giving her up for adoption.

"You're crazy," Myra said one day while Sha was blow drying her hair. "You've got a daughter by a rich man and his daddy is even richer. Now he's single and you're still doing hair at this same ole' shop."

109

Myra thought about reaching out to Jeremy herself. She knew they had connected that night in the hotel. Sex was his weakness. Something was up with him.

"Around here visiting the March of Dimes and adoption agencies, while he is off somewhere living his nice life. Your car is busted and you're behind in rent. Wake up."

"I'm not trying to bother those people. He doesn't want Christina and he sure doesn't want me."

"See that's the problem, you're thinking emotionally. It's not what Jeremy wants, it's what is. The State of New York says you are entitled to 17% of his income."

"Seventeen percent?" Sha repeated.

"Yes, seventeen. In that article it said they were pulling in millions a year. I bet you Jeremy getting' at least one. If it were me, I would be in front of Judge Judy with that article."

Sha thought it was time to readjust some things.

CHAPTER 17

Sha sat nervously in the reception area of Collins Realty. Myra had a point. It was time to appeal to a higher authority. She was ready for negotiations and had dropped a pretty penny on a Calvin Klein suit she wore from Macy's. She felt awkward wearing business attire, but her future was at stake.

Mr. Collins had sounded pleasant enough on the phone, even thanking her for reaching out. He confirmed Christina was a Collins and he was willing to listen to her despite the circumstances. In Sha's mind she knew the mother, and the child of a Collins should be properly cared for, no matter how she was conceived.

Father Edwards arrived and looked at Sha and sighed. *The Marilyn Monroe woman.* Great. Another woman had snuck in a Collins baby. It was de ja vu all over again.

"I've heard so much about you Ms. Harris. Let's go to my office," he said as he allowed her to walk in front of him. Eyeing her backside, he understood Jeremy's attraction.

Sha had not realized he was such an old man. He had aged a lot since Jeremy's party. He looked stressed as well.

"Please have a seat," he gestured. "Jeremy should be here any second."

"Thank you," she said as she sat in the freezing office where her fingertips were cold.

"Where are you from?" he asked.

"Brooklyn."

"No, I mean where were you born? You have an accent," he said.

"I was born in St. Ann's Parish. In Jamaica."

"Home of Bob Marley? Correct. I remember visiting once."

"Yes, it is," she answered.

Father Collins knew she was there for money and not some reunion. She had not even bothered to bring her child with her. Because of her antics, Reverend Tyler, his longtime friend, would not return his calls.

Sha tried to make small talk about the weather.

Where the hell is Jeremy?

"They say it's going to rain tonight."

"Yes, that's what they say," he replied while reading over some mail.

"How old is the baby?" He asked.

"Christina is one years old already. Time flies. You have four daughters yourself, right?"

"Three, well two now. Two of them have passed on," he said sadly. Life was too short he thought.

"I'm sorry to hear that. May they rest in peace," Sha said sincerely.

"Thank you." Edward said wondering how many zeroes he would have to put on a check for her.

"Listen, Mr. Collins. I'm sorry it's gotten to this. I know Jeremy and I are adults, but I didn't know what else to do. I need help," she said nervously.

"It's alright. I understand," he said.

"I mean don't you think a decent man would visit his child?"

Edward let her know she should not get comfortable.

"Decency is in the eye of the beholder," he said tartly. "Some would argue a decent woman would not sleep with and then get pregnant from a married man."

Sha had not expected that response. *Just be quiet until Jeremy comes. Use your phone. Check your email or something.*

"I see you have on a wedding band," Edward inquired. "Are you married?" If she was, he would offer her less.

"No, I'm not married," she said looking at the ring. "Jeremy gave me this."

"I see," Edward said. What a pitiful, desperate woman, he thought. He hated his son was playing with her emotions like that. I'm too old to understand these young people, he thought.

Sitting alone with her was a mistake. Edward buzzed the intercom.

"Enid, can you come and escort Ms. Harris into the conference room?"

Whatever. Sha thought. Rude ass. Like father, like son.

"Right this way," Enid said as she led her out of the office. Memories are oftentimes easily triggered. Edward opened his desk drawer and stared down at the woman's picture. He still missed her.

Twenty minutes later, when Sha walked back into Mr. Collin's office, Jeremy was sitting in one of the chairs facing his father's desk.

"Hello Jeremy," she said thinking he was still fine.

He ignored her. Mr. Collins' entire mood had changed. He was subtler, more subdued. It was as if he was speaking to her for the first time. They were both crazy, she thought.

"How is your daughter doing?" Mr. Collins asked.

"She is okay."

"Do you have a picture of her?" Sha showed him Christina's face on her phone's home screen.

"She's cute," Mr. Collins remarked.

Jeremy showed no interest and sat there pouting like a little boy on punishment.

"We are all here today because you have informed me of your financial situation Ms. Harris," Mr. Collins said.

"That is correct," she answered. Sha felt like she was in court speaking to a judge.

"Christina needs a lot of help. She needs therapists, and stuff like that. It's also better if she goes to a private school," she said while pulling out the admissions packet for the Stone Mountain School for Special Needs.

"This school is in Georgia?" He asked as he looked through the brochure.

"Yes," she replied. "Most of my family is down there living in Snellville. I'm having problems paying my bills and my car is on its last leg. Then there are her medical expenses."

"You want to take our daughter all the way to Georgia?" Jeremy finally spoke. It had been a long time since Sha heard his voice.

"You have not seen her since the day she was born. I think I should be able to take her anywhere I want," Sha stated.

"The law says you need my permission to take her out of the state and I want a paternity test," Jeremy blurted sounding more like he was in a store begging a parent for candy.

"No disrespect to you sir," Sha said to Mr. Collins. "I've been receiving child support for years now. Do you think we are on fuckin" Maury Jeremy? But if you want to take a paternity test, let me know where I can sign up."

"You hoe. I told you not to have no baby from me," Jeremy said angrily. "You sit here and talk with that sewer mouth in front of my father like that? No respect having ass."

"You want to bring up the law? The law states I'm entitled to 17% of your income. I don't think you need to bring up the law," she responded.

Jeremy wanted to slap her, but he just gave his father the look like, do something about this please before I do.

"Enough," Mr. Collins interrupted. "You two can argue on your own time. Christina is a Collins, so I'm here to make sure is taken care of. Jeremy if you wanted a paternity test, you should have done that a year ago."

"How much do you need for the school?"

"Tuition is right there," she said pointing to the packet. She was tired of them both and ready to leave. I'll just go to court, she thought.

"Where will you live in Georgia?"

"Well I have to find a job and an apartment."

"Come back tomorrow at the same time and I will have an answer for you? And Ms. Harris, please bring my granddaughter with you," Mr. Collins said.

"Mr. Collins, I don't want to play any games."

"Save your threats. I am here to help," he said while he rose from his chair and went to open the door.

"Have a good day, Ms. Harris."

"Thank you." She said as she walked out ignoring Jeremy.

Father Edward gave Sha $5,000 a month in child support, paid the school's tuition for two years, and gave her a deed to 3-bedroom house in Snellville. He threw in a used Toyota Camry for good measure.

"Shit, it would be cheaper to just kill her," Jeremy joked when his father gave him the details.

"No, son, it's cheaper to keep her, that's how the saying goes," he said looking at his son wondering where he had gone wrong with him.

"Always remember son, one should never leave a good deed unturned," he said as he drifted off into a daydream.

"I was just joking. Why are you looking at me like that?" Jeremy asked curiously.

"Nothing son. I was thinking about something else," he said before getting back to the issue at hand.

"Oh yes, Christina. That little girl did not ask to come into this crazy world. May God watch over her life," he said trying to control the sudden sadness that overcame him.

CHAPTER 18

It was a freezing November morning in 1968. Colder than usual. Winter had arrived early as a punishment for a long hot and rambunctious summer in New York City.

Father Edward awoke to the sounds of the CBS trademark teletype. "1010 WINS time: Eight am. The temperature is 18 degrees."

Father Edward had never gotten used to the northern winters—very few southern people ever did.

He had dreaded going to the office, but he knew Saturday were busy days for realtors. It also gave him a chance to see people in the neighborhood who were gone all week working downtown. He had no idea it was going to be one of his luckiest days.

He rushed inside his office and was greeted by a Latino woman seated and holding a crying baby. He knew the sound. It was the cry of an empty stomach.

"I'm sorry sir, she does not have an appointment," Enid said as she came out to greet him and take his coat.

"It's okay, I'll handle it."

The woman must have been desperate to have a child outside this early in this cold, he thought. She was about 30 years old. The thin jacket and sandals she wore were no match for the outside temperature. The baby was wrapped warmly, but the blanket was dirty.

"Good morning, Can I help you?" Edward asked.

She pulled out an empty bottle from a dirty paper bag and said, "My baby needs some milk and food. Can you help us please?"

Mr. Collins called for Enid and handed her twenty dollars.

"Can you run to see if Ms. Gurdy is open and get this child some milk and some food please?"

The young woman smiled and stared at the money.

"Very good, thank you," she said softly while rocking the child who had quieted down a little. She kept the child close to her. *Food is coming soon my little prince.*

"What's your name?" Edward asked.

"My name is Sophia Montrell," she said looking at him with hypnotic brown eyes.

"What brings you here today?" Edward asked.

"My son and I really need a place to live," she said. "The people say you can get a place for people in need?"

"We get housing for people. Do you have any money?"

"No, I don't have anything," she answered.

Edward felt compelled to help.

"Would you like anything to drink?" he asked smelling the pot of coffee Enid had made.

"Coffee please?" She said.

"I'll be right back."

Edward returned with their cups and her son was sitting in his stroller trying to put himself to sleep, likely trying to fight off his hunger.

"Shhh now little one, yours is coming," she said gently.

"What's his name?" Edward asked.

"Gabriel Montrell."

"How old is he?"

"He will be one on November 18th."

"Wow, that's a few more days. Happy Birthday little fella," Edward said beaming. *A baby boy right here in my office that needs a home.*

"Where's his daddy?"

"In the war, I guess. They say he's dead," she said sadly.

"He is in Vietnam?"

"Yes," she said.

"I know a few men over there. I'm praying for them and their families."

Enid came back in the with the milk and a bagel.

"Give me one second to heat this up. Do you have his bottle?" She asked. Sophia who handed the bottle to her.

"Where do you live?" He asked her.

"Nowhere now. I'm from Florida. I came up to New York City two weeks ago looking for his father. We've been staying at a rooming house until I ran out of money," she told him.

"Do you have family here? Friends you can say with?"

"No, I was an orphan. No family. All I have is Gabriel and he has me," she said as she kissed him and gave him his bottle and started breaking him off some of the bread.

Edward watched quietly. Gabriel was a handsome little fella. He was big for his age and looked like he was already two or three. He drank the bottle quickly and wanted more. When he finished eating the bagel, he fell right off to sleep. The whole scene pulled at Edward's heartstrings. No child should be hungry in this world, he thought.

Enid interrupted his thoughts, "I have Mrs. Anderson on the line, she is at 2341 St. Nicholas and the realtor has not showed."

"Call Jeremy or Orrin, let one of them handle it please," he said without taking his eyes off Sophia.

"And Enid, no more calls today. Clear my schedule."

"Is that so?" She said giving Sophia the evil eye.

"Are you hungry?" He asked Sophia who nodded yes.

"Come on let's go."

Sophia was the same height as Edward, and he liked looking at her eye to eye.

Edward loved her walk. Even in the cold with tattered clothing she was gorgeous. Her slim body did not have an ounce of fat. She was so feminine too. Her mocha skin looked so soft. Edward was strongly attracted to her.

Sophia hesitated before getting into the car.

"It's okay, that's just Milton. He's my driver. Come on get in, it's cold out here," he said holding the door open for her while Milton folded up the carriage.

Edward took her to breakfast at Twenty-Two West on 135th Street, a popular restaurant and night spot where the who's who in Harlem and New York came to hob nob with politicians, celebrities and others. People like journalist Jimmy Breslin, former Mayor Abraham Beam, and ex NBA player Walt Frazer had all dined on their fabulous cuisine while others came to build their political careers.

"My, my look who's here. It's been a long time, Councilman," Miss Lillian, the hostess greeted them.

"Lil, you're looking lovely as ever," Edward said to her. Lillian and Ernestine had been good friends for so long, they named one of their daughters after her.

"And what do we have here?" she asked looking down at the baby. "Ed, what have you been doing?" she joked. "I'm going to have to call Ern."

"No, she needs a place to stay. I just thought I would bring her to get something to eat," he said.

"Well go on, sit wherever you like. We'll take good care you all," she said faking a smile at Sophia.

As they walked to their seats, people said their usual hellos and Edward greeted them back. Some had peculiar looks on their faces as they looked at Sophia. It was rare to see a Latina woman in West Harlem and she was dressed shabbily. Because she was with Councilman Edwards, they knew to keep their voices down if they were discussing her.

The food at 22 West reminded Edward of his mother's down-home cooking in South Carolina. He missed it. Ernestine had long stopped cooking southern food.

"People of our pedigree should eat better now. It's better for our diets. All that grease will kill you," she said one afternoon amidst a kitchen full of dirty pots attempting to make escargot, a recipe she got from a woman during their trip to France. So much for French fare. Two of the girls ended up getting food poisoning.

Sophia ate her food as if she had missed a few meals.

"Slowdown, there's no rush," Edward said.

As she leaned down to take a spoonful of soup, he could see the shape of her small breasts. He felt the blood rushing to his groin.

"Is there anything else you need Ed?" Lillian asked interrupting him staring at Sophia's breasts.

"No, we're good Lil. Just trying to figure out where she is going to stay."

"You know I have a basement studio, but Clarence and Shark, are painting it and doing some repairs."

Yeah, Clarence owes me $50 he thought.

"It should be move-in ready in a couple of days." She said. "You know I keep it off the books, if you know what I mean?"

Sophia's eyes lit up.

"It will be fine for her and this here adorable baby—quiet and clean she said looking down at the sleeping young man.

"You remember where I live right? Your wife has been there many times. 51 Edgecombe, right next to St. Francis' church."

"Yes, I know it," Edward said between bites of his fried fish and buttery grits. He had caught her little slip referring to his wife. Women stick together he thought. Sophia acted oblivious and she sipped her coffee.

"How much is the rent?"

"For you, and to help someone, let's say $15 a week," she laughed.

She had made it cheap on purpose, so she would come. She would have to keep an eye on this one, she thought. She could not wait for her break, so she could call Ern and report this little mealtime.

"It's just temporary. Until she can get on her feet and find an apartment," she said as she walked off to greet another patron.

"See? That worked out well. I'm sure it's a nice place."

"Yes, I cannot believe it. I'm so happy. Thank you so much," Sophia said.

After breakfast Edward took them shopping to Blumstein's on 125th Street and bought them some warm clothes.

"Is this the store Dr. King was stabbed in the chest by some crazy woman?" She asked looking around in amazement at the Thanksgiving decorations.

"Why yes it was. That was in 1958. I'm impressed."

"They have been talking about it on the radio, since he died this past April. He was a good man," she said.

"Yes, he was," Edward replied.

After shopping, they walked down the street to the Teresa Hotel where he booked them a room.

"You can stay here for a few days, until Ms. Lil is finished with her place for you," he said watching Gabriel playing with his new toys on the bed.

"You did all of this for us for nothing in return," she said admired the fancy hotel room. She was looking forward to taking a long hot bath. It had been a long time since she had been in a place with a bathtub.

"One rarely does anything for nothing," he said.

"I understand," she said as she took off her top.

"No, no, please don't, I'm a married elected official," Edward said as he turned his head away. "That's not what I meant. You can pay me back later, when you get a job and such."

Sophia was relieved. She had not told him that she was no stranger to prostitution.

"Right now, you guys are safe. Here's a little cash. For now, stay warm, and get some rest. Here's my number and you have Lils'. I'll check on you guys tomorrow. And with that he was off. Edward felt brand new.

**

One day, you're casually riding home from the theatre with your husband, enjoying the quality time. Then out of the blue he requests you put together a birthday party for some kid of some woman you don't even know.

A woman Lillian told Ernestine showed up with him at 22 West. A woman and her child having breakfast with her husband.

It was times like these when Ernestine truly wondered if Edward thought she a complete fool.

After meeting Sophia and her son, Ernestine let him know, "I'll do this little party, but I pray to God that is not your son."

"You're crazy. Do you think I would do something like that you? What kind of man do take me for?"

"All I know is she is a stranger. I don't trust her," Ernestine said firmly.

"She's a kid in trouble with a baby, that's all. Besides we could use a little party around here."

"I guess you're right," Ernestine agreed. It had been a long time since she had given a party for one of the girls.

"We will keep it small. No outsiders," she said.

Sophia and Gabriel became a permanent fixture in the Collins' house. For the first time in her life Sophia felt like she was in a real family.

Gabriel took his first steps in their foyer. Edward rejoiced when Gabriel started calling him, 'Da-da.'

Edward enjoyed hearing the sounds his hard-bottomed shoes running on their parquet floors.

"Ernestine, we have more than enough to share," he would say when she complained and accused him of spending his free time with Gabriel and Sophia.

"I'm old enough to be her father."

"Only if you had her at 12 years old," she responded. "That ain't hardly a kid," she said watching Sophia standing at her kitchen sink rinsing off some apples.

Sophia must have gotten Ernestine's vibe when she was around. One day, out of the blue, while they walked home after church, Sophia gave Ernestine a hug.

"Thank you for everything you have done for me and my son. These last three years have been the best days of my life. I never had a mother or a big sister. I look up to you. May God continue to bless you Ms. Ernestine."

Ernestine felt the fakeness. Sophia had gotten way too comfortable in her home. When Edward had suggested she get a set of keys she hired someone to pack all his clothes and left them by the front door.

That ended that crazy talk.

She knew the woman wanted her husband. She saw how Sophia looked at Edward with starry eyes. Ern had also warned her, "Mama, she rolls her eyes at you when your back is turned."

The jury had convicted her. Ernestine was raised to know there could only be one queen per household.

Ernestine pretended not to see the glances of women at church who mumbled as she walked by.

It was time for them to go.

"The women at church are all calling me a fool. They say that I'm allowing your mistress and baby to live in our house. They are saying we are a polygamist family."

"Village gossipers strike again," Edward laughed.

"Listen she has her own place, why does she need to be over here so much? It's time for her to find her own husband for that boy who is now three years old," Ernestine argued.

"Listen woman, everything is fine. Let people talk. You and I, and this family know the truth."

That night, Edward came home and found two twin beds had replaced their king-sized one. He was not confused by any means. Ernestine was sending him another warning.

CHAPTER 19

Ernestine was having a restless night. The summer heat was taking its toll on her. Usually she slept as if she was in a coma.

The breeze barely moved the window curtains. It was too hot to sleep. She missed the girls who were down south for the summer.

It was after 2 am and Edward's bed was still empty. She pictured him downstairs in his office working on some deal that would make their lives even more comfortable. The midnight oil was not foreign to him.

Perhaps he was up for a little company, she thought. It had seemed so long since they had spoken without arguing—so very long since they had touched. She began to regret the two beds. Perhaps she had been too stubborn, she thought.

Maybe she should talk to Sophia herself. It was her house and she no longer wanted her around. So that should be enough.

What she knew is that she loved Edward and missed her husband. She needed the man she had fallen in love with back. Going downstairs, surprising him and having a cold drink with him would likely do them both good.

As she entered the kitchen, she heard the faint sound of music. The moonlight shined through the window on the door leading to his office. It was a full moon and made her feel even more naughty. She tiptoed and quietly opened the door leading down to his office.

She heard music. A man singing in Spanish. He had been listening to a lot of that lately. In fact, everyone in the house was learning Spanish from Sophia, whose mother was Puerto Rican.

It was that moment she decided she would try and give Edward a son. The son he dreamed about. Although she knew at her age, the pregnancy would be risky. It was a chance she was willing to take to save her marriage and make her husband happy.

Her blue camisole made her feel sexy and she knew it was Edward's favorite color. She was so ready and tingled at the thought of him kissing and holding her like he used to.

Slowly she tipped down the staircase. Candlelight flickered off the walls. Edward loves candles, she thought.

She heard Edward panting. *Is he exercising?*

Then she heard him say, "Yes, yes, yes."

Her eyes felt like they were burning. Rage engulfed and overtook her, but she remained quiet.

He is holding her.

Sophia's naked body was on top Edward facing him. She saw the sweat dripping down her back. She moved in sync with him. Up and down. Down and up. She was holding up her hair with her hands. They moved in a familiar unison while their spirits rearranged Ernestine's heart and soul.

Edward said, "I love you."

Ernestine thought back to the first time he had ever said those words to her in the field of lilacs on Mr. Johnnie's farm. It had seemed like yesterday. Tonight, his look was different.

He was enjoying her.

Sophia responded with, "Forever?"

Edward replied, "Yes, forever."

Ernestine placed her hand over her mouth to prevent herself from screaming. She stood quietly and still. Long enough to watch them finish their lustful betrayal.

They had invaded a sacred space without any regard for the sanctity of their home. Ernestine needed to retreat. She tiptoed back upstairs as silently as she had come down. She went to the room where Gabriel was sound asleep and peeked in. *Is this Edward's bastard child?*

The next morning, Ernestine opened her eyes and stared up at the ceiling. A spider in the corner making a web let her know she was not dead. Death seemed more satisfying than the pain she felt in every piece of her body.

It was a nightmare she had convinced herself. Edward had not come upstairs all night.

It's a new day, or was it? She asked herself. Her husband had not been downstairs last night having sex with another woman. A woman she had treated like a little sister. A woman she welcomed as a member of her family.

He had been holding her. He had been enjoying her.

She sat up and tried to put one of her feet on the floor. *She moved in slow motion.* Her throat felt tight and dry. It would take every ounce of strength for her to get up.

Yesterday morning at church, Reverend Tyler had ironically spoken about adultery. *"Remember God hates the sin, not the sinner."*

"God please give me strength today. My heart is wounded, and I need you," she prayed as she tasted her salty tears. She sat on the side of the bed and wept for a few minutes before taking a warm shower. As she baptized herself, the water lifted her spirits somewhat.

She retraced her steps. His office was empty. The emptiness was supposed to pretend the night away. No music, no whispers, no candles, no Edward, no Sophia. Standing in the middle of the room, she knew she was not alone. Her husband and his whore had left a present.

Their gift of a private betrayal.

A musty fragrance.

It was the lingering scent of sex.

Ernestine knew facing Edward would not be easy. Would she forgive him? Would she forget? Her thoughts confused her.

She knew whenever he came back, he would need to decide whether it was her or Sophia. If he chose wrong, it would be the end of the Collins' empire and she would send him to the soup line.

CHAPTER 20

Ernestine had finished a soothing plate of collard greens and cornbread for lunch. "Healing food" her mother called it. She used it as a bandage for the bruises she received from Ernestine's father.

"Something about the greens touching the side of a good piece of cornbread makes me feel better," she told her one day staring at Earnestine with a black eye. "Go ahead, eat, you will feel better too."

Ernestine ate her lunch and then went to escape into her garden. Neither her heart nor her mind was clear as she anxiously waited for Edward to return home.

The doorbell rang. It was not a pleasant surprise. She knew she would be awful company. Ignore it.

Another ring. Maybe it was a package, she thought as she put down her flowers and went to answer.

She peered through the stained-glass window and saw Sophia standing on the other side.

How many times had she come over after screwing my husband?

Are those horns coming out of her head? She really is a demon.

Ernestine opened the door and Sophia casually walked in, just as she had done hundreds of times before. Strolling in like she had not a care in the world.

"Something smells good," Sophia said standing there with the glow of love all over her.

"Where's Gabriel? Not attached to your hip I see," Ernestine said as she walked back into the garden.

"He's at his day care over at the Milford Center," she said following her.

"Ed," I mean Mr. Edward put him in it. It's part of a program President Lyndon B. Johnson started. It's really good for Gabriel to be with other children his own age."

Ernestine could have cared less about some program. She was getting ready to put her out, when Sophia said, "I came by because I wanted to speak with you alone."

"Is that right?" Ernestine said noticing for the first time she had on a short snug blue dress. *Are you wearing that for Edward? His favorite color. I have a dress that color.*

"I'll be right back, off to the bathroom," Sophia said leaving Ernestine to drift off into a daydream.

"What cha doing Mama Ernestine?" Anna inquired.

"Making a nice bouquet of roses for Ms. Agnes from the church. She's in the hospital again. I thought I would take her a bouquet to cheer her up."

"I'm in the middle of writing a school report about our family history, but I can help you take off some of the dirt." Anna said.

"Wait, grab an apron or you will get dirt all over that pretty dress."

"I was wondering Mama Ernestine. I have read magazine and newspaper articles on you and Father Edward, but I don't see anything about your parents."

"Is that so?" Mama Ernestine said knowing it was on purpose. "Well there is a reason for that," she paused before continuing.

"My daddy was a mean man. A drunk who would come home from a night of partying and beat us. Beat me and Mama for no reason."

She left out the part, it usually happened after her mother would yell about him keeping company with Ms. Bernice down on Hanover Street. It was like he was angry he had to go home to them.

"We never told a soul about daddy's beating. Those are private things."

"That's just terrible," Anna said.

"It was," Mama Ernestine shook her head.

"He had all the money in the world but was still evil and miserable."

Anna listened intently.

"Wait, I'll be right back."

Mama Ernestine returned carrying a shoebox filled with old pictures.

"Look, here is daddy and mama."

"Whatever happened to them? I mean how did they die?" Anna asked looking through the photos. "Can we put their photo on the piano with all the other family pictures?"

Ernestine reached for the box and began putting the pictures back.

"Child, are you listening? Did you hear what I just told you? I surely do not want to look at that man's face every day. Her voice went almost faint as she picked up her mother's photo, "Mama I miss you."

"Mama thought his beatings somehow hurt her insides," she said. "She used to say that was why she could not carry any more babies. I was the lucky one who got through," Ernestine recalled with solace and heartbreak.

"My daddy ended up beating my poor sweet mother to death. But I was long gone by that time. Your daddy probably saved my life."

And then those thoughts seemed to get suppressed right back into the vault she had kept them in all those years as she casually said to Anna, "Hand me those roses over there, but be careful they have sharp thorns."

Sophia's presence returning to the garden brought her back to the present. It was better to live in the present. Right now, she was trying to understand why she had allowed this woman to cross her doorstep again.

"I've been trying to tell you something for a long time," she said.

"Edward and I are in love," she said as casually as telling someone the time. "I think it's time for you to know because I feel guilty."

Was she for real? One does not just walk up to a wife and casually say their husband is in love with them. My husband is not allowed to love another woman.

"Ernestine, can you hear me?"

"Sophia, I am going to count to three. IT is time for you to go," she yelled as she stomped her foot.

"One."

"Ms. Ernestine, I'm sorry but it's the truth," she said standing there with her hand on her hips.

"I saw you two last night. Is that what you're calling the truth? Sex with a married man while his wife sleeps upstairs? You must be really proud of yourself," she said while walking over to the table with her garden tools.

"Two."

Sophia was surprised, but relieved. At least she would no longer have to hide her feelings, she thought.

"I will leave, but I thought I should be the one to tell you he is planning to divorce you," Sophia said brazenly.

Did she say they are going to kill me?

Three.

As Sophia turned to leave, Ernestine slammed the metal in the back of her head.

"Look a hoe for a hoe," Ernestine said as the blood spurted out of Sophia's head, knocking her off balance.

Sophia did not understand what was happening to her. She was dizzy. Blood streamed down the side of her face blinding her in one eye.

Ernestine struck again. This time on her face.

"You think you're so pretty, don't you? Think you are so bold," Ernestine yelled as Sophia grabbed her mouth and spit out a tooth.

"Oh my God, what are you doing? You're loco," Sophia cried out in agony.

Sophia tried to crawl to the door. She could not understand why she was moving in the opposite direction? Then she realized Ernestine was dragging her by her hair.

"Help me, somebody help me." Sophia screamed.

"Shut up or I'll go pick up Gabriel and kill him."

Sophia stopped moving and began quietly weeping.

Ernestine leaned over her and whispered, "How much do you love my husband now? Tell me again. Wait, I can't hear you."

"Please I'm sorry. Please call for help, I'm bleeding," she said quietly holding her head trying to stop the blood.

Ernestine sat down next to her on the ground and started rambling, "Daddy's whore. Why did daddy have to beat us because of you? All those nights Mama and I got beat because of you. Why couldn't you find your own husband?"

"I don't know what you're talking about, please help me. I am sorry. Oh God, I'm bleeding."

"Look at your little blue dress. Your blood is making it turn purple. Edward hates purple. Always telling me he hates my lilacs. Aren't they beautiful?" She said while picking up one and smelling it.

Edward pulled up in the driveway. His stomach growled. It reminded him he had missed breakfast. He had lost his appetite and guilt had taken over him.

For so long he had shared an innocent friendship with Sophia. Never as much as an awkward glance the countless times they were in each other's company.

Then last year, something came over him when he went by her house. She had just exited the shower with nothing on but a towel. Her skin was radiant. She offered him a back rub and one thing had led to another. They were discrete as possible, getting together a few times when they knew Lil was at work.

Last night was a huge mistake. Her enticing eyes and three glasses of distilled scotch were the predators. In his own home, while Ernestine slept upstairs made him shameful. Never again, he thought.

As he exited the car, he heard Ernestine screaming from the backyard. He ran to the back. The sight of Sophia on the ground bleeding shocked him. Seeing Ernestine sitting by her yelling about her father overtook him.

"Oh no. What happened? Ernestine! Ernestine! Do you hear me as he reached down for Sophia? Where's Gabriel?"

"Don't touch her."

"She needs help. We have to call for help."

"The only help she is going to get is from the grim reaper. He should be on his way."

"Woman, have you totally lost your mind?" He said while looking around the backyard. If they had not built such a high fence someone could have easily saw what was going on.

"Edward, do you think I'm stupid? I know no one can see in here. Even the trees block all the people's windows. I could have killed her in the house, but who wants all that blood inside?" She said looking like a deranged mad woman.

"This is my private space in this busy city. Feels like we're back home doesn't it?" With trees and bees and good air," she said while taking a deep breath.

Sophia, barely breathing said, "Ed please mi amor, please call for help. I, I, I can't breathe."

"Still with the mi amor? Do you see this? Bleeding and all. She loves you so much, she will still disrespect me, your wife, in my face."

"Sophia, what did you do?"

"She let me know you two are in love, and you are divorcing me," Ernestine said laughing.

"Why would you come here and tell her those lies Sophia?" Ernest said using his handkerchief to try and stop the blood coming out of the side of her face.

"You expect a whore to be honest? You think she really loved your little stubby ass? All she wanted was your money—our money! She used to be a prostitute. Did you know that? You're such a fool."

Ernestine handed Edward a shovel.

A look of horror came over Sophia's face. She tried to run. "No, no, please," she pleaded.

Ernestine picked up the hoe and bashed her again. This time practically knocking her out.

"I saw you two last night," she said with scorn at Edward who was speechless and hung his head in shame. *A prostitute?*

"Tell her that you will love her forever now. Today is her judgement day. It's either her or me," Ernestine said.

"No, no, no," he said horrified at the thought of what Ernestine was requesting. "You want to slaughter her?"

"Slaughter?" Is she a pig? Can we eat her?"

"No, I'm getting rid of a demon. My mama would be alive today if wasn't for her. Start digging. Look let me show you how it's done," as she snatched the shovel from him.

Ernestine pranced around singing, "To have and to hold from this day forward. La, la, la. Forsaking all others. La, la, la. Until death do you part. Can you hear that Edward?"

"And even you, you down there getting blood all over my good dirt in this yard. Can you hear those vows?"

Hours later when the sky darkened the hole was ready for Sophia. Edward and Ernestine rolled her over and pushed her down. She fell in on her stomach. Sophia used the little strength she had left to turn herself over, so she could get some air, although she knew it would be brief.

Sophia focused on staring at a star in the sky and could not believe this was her fate. She recited the Lord's Prayer in Spanish.

As Edward was about to fill up the makeshift grave with dirt, the doorbell rang terrifying him.

"Honey could you get that? I have blood on my clothes," Ernestine asked.

Edward just knew it was the police. Thoughts of prison entered his mind. He could say the women had gotten into a fight. It was self-defense or something. How would they explain the hole in the backyard? How could he explain Sophia, who was dying in a ditch in his backyard?

"Well, what are you going to do lover boy?" Ernestine asked looking down at Sophia who was quietly mumbling.

Edward ran to wash his hands in the kitchen sink and took off his bloody shirt before answering the door.

"Good evening Councilman Collins. I'm sorry to bother you this evening. I'm Edna from the day care center. My family, the Daniels are members of New Bethel."

"Yes, I know you. You're Sonny and Catherine's daughter," he said trying to rush.

"Yes, sir. I have Gabriel here as you can see. His mother has not picked him up and there is no one at her home. You are listed as his emergency contact. Do you know where his mother is?"

"Yes, she went on a job interview. It probably just went longer than expected. He can certainly stay here. I'll take him home later." Gabriel ran inside the house and was greeted by Ernestine.

"Thanks," she said relieved. "I'm really sorry to have bothered you. You looked like you were building something?" She said as she stared at the dirt on his pants. Edward thought she could hear his heart racing. He looked down and saw the blood on his shoes. He quickly kicked them off and pushed them into the vestibule.

"No, it's no bother. We got him. Thanks for bringing him."

"Thanks again Councilman," she said as he closed the door.

"Come Gabriel," Ernestine called out to him and took him to the dining room table. "Sit down for Mama Ernestine, eat your snack and play with your toys until we come back."

"Where's my mommy?" He asked innocently.

"She went away. She will be back soon okay?"

Yes, ma'am," he said.

Ernestine and Edward went back outside.

"We need to hurry up," she warned.

Ern, I can't do this. Not with Gabriel sitting right inside. Where is your humanity?"

"You're right, we should put him in there with her. The bastard child."

Edward was hoping he would not have to kill Ernestine. He would not allow her to hurt a child. Edward walked over and looked down at Sophia.

"Ern she is still alive. No, we can't."

"Do you want me to go to jail for this whore? Throw in the dirt and hurry up."

Edward was tired. He leaned on the shovel. "Ern, this is a crime of passion. You will not go to jail."

Ernestine picked up the hoe and held it over his head ready to strike him.

"I'll dig two graves if you don't finish. I mean it Edward."

"Can you hear me you witch?" Ernestine said looking down at Sophia's body. "When you get to hell make sure you don't bother anybody's husband."

"Keep your damn voice down woman," he said as she threw the murder weapon down on her body and casually walked in the house.

Sadly, it was either her or his wife.

Edward scooped up the fresh dirt and closed his eyes while tossing it in. He purposely covered Sophia's face first.

He would never forget the horrific look she had.

It was a face of terror.

**

The next day Edward filed a missing person's report with the NYPD and personally called the police commissioner.

"You will have all the help we can provide Ed. An officer from our missing person's unit is on the way to get all the particulars."

"This is not like Sophia. I'm not sure what happened. She was here yesterday morning, but was rushing to a job interview," Ernestine tearfully explained to the aloof officer who was checking out their home and likely daydreaming about living that grand one day himself.

Edward interjected, "I guess we should tell you."

"No, Edward, I don't know if you should. We can't."

"Tell me what Councilman?" the officer asked.

"Well, $20,000 is also missing," Edwards stated. "I came home and found the money gone. It was my fault. It was in a bank bag on my desk. I forgot to put it in the safe. Thankfully, we have insurance."

"We do not want to press any charges, Sophia is like a daughter to us," Ernestine said while holding Gabriel on her lap.

"We have a description and an APB will go out when I leave. This is a priority case from high up, so I will be in touch. Please give me a call if you hear from her," the officer said while handing him a business card.

"We will. Thank you, officer," Edward said while leading him out of the house much to his relief.

The next step was to contact NYC's child welfare agency. One of their social workers planned to place Gabriel in an orphanage until they could find Sophia or a relative willing to care for him.

In the meantime, he stayed with the Collins'.

At first the social worker visited to check on Gabriel once a week. Then twice a month. Six months after Sophia went missing, Edward handed her an envelope with $20,000. That visit was her last. Shortly after, she recommended the Collins' be allowed to legally adopt him.

A year later, in 1972, just in time to start regular school, Gabriel Montrell, son of a murdered Sophia Montrell and an alleged dead solider, became Jeremy Edward Collins.

Word on the street was the Collins' paid Sophia and had purchased Gabriel. Others speculated, she had stolen their money and left him with Edward who was his real father.

The Collins never told anyone Jeremy was adopted and as time went on, no one cared.

The police searched for Sophia for a year. No one else ever came to look for her or Gabriel. Her cold case sits in a warehouse file with the NYPD missing persons unit.

**

Edward and Ernestine sat in their parlor designed like an English sitting room full of mahogany fixtures. He sipped on a glass of cognac, while Ernestine stared blankly at the orange flicker in the fireplace.

"Ernestine, what we did was so wrong. So very wrong." Edward said full of remorse. Ernestine sat still, ready as a cat to attack a mouse. "I am so sorry I hurt you," he said.

"Are you listening to me woman?"

"Yes, I hear you," she said. She had not expected Gabriel would be a part of the deal.

"We should have killed him too," she said nonchalantly.

"I need to know that you will not hurt Gabriel. Promise me that Ern," he pleaded.

"If that child is staying in this house, I'm moving to the fourth floor," she announced.

"As you wish, Ernestine. Just please don't hurt him."

Edward knew his wife's mind and soul were gone never to return. Things had not turned out like he planned, but he was grateful for a son.

**

Sophia's murder would not be the only tragedy at Le Maison Rounde.

Years later, while taking a mid-day nap, a candle caught fire in Ernestine's bedroom. A jammed door trapped her inside.

People on the street reported they would never forget the sounds of her horrific screams as she stood burning at the window, yelling out the name "Sophia."

The news reported: *"Fifty-one-year-old socialite Ernestine Collins, the wife of Harlem businessman Edward Collins, and their 13-year-old daughter Ern Collins died today from an accidental fire in their Harlem home. Mr. Collins could not be reached for comment."*

The fire investigators speculated their daughter went up to try and rescue her mother but also found herself trapped. Rather than burn to death, she jumped out of a window. Her body landed on top of one of the metal spikes surrounding the house. She died instantly.

A motherless house bred contempt and dysfunction for their family.

When the crack era of the 1980s hit Harlem, it captured Evelyn with a vengeance.

Father Edward pretended she no longer existed. She died in 1998 at the age of 36 from complications due to AIDS.

Father Edward, out of shame, had not even attended her funeral. No one outside of the funeral parlor staff knew, he sat weeping for hours with her body each day until her service.

**

Anna, who was 19 at the time of her mother and sister's death, went on to Harvard and law school in Chicago. She married and uses her husband's last name. They comfortably reside in an Illinois suburb. She barely visits or speaks to Father Edward.

**

Lillian, who was 15 years old at the time of her mother and sister's death, left the house at midnight the day she turned eighteen. She later married a doctor and they spend their lives traveling to remote parts of the world on medical humanitarian missions.

Lillian rarely has any family contact except to pick up wire transfers of money from Father Edward. Sometimes they get returned.

**

Father Edward never remarried. In 2002, at the age of 77 while eating dinner and watching his favorite TV show, Law & Order, he went into cardiac arrest and died alone.

When Jeremy found him, he was clutching a dirty blue dress with dried up blood stains.

CHAPTER 21

Neither Anna, nor Lillian stayed after Father's Edward's funeral service. Jeremy's limousine led a caravan of about 30 cars to the cemetery, but he rode alone. So many people bought food, gave cards and their sympathy. They were showing respect to a man they felt had lived a great life and gave so much to the Harlem community.

Jeremy was disappointed his sisters left before they even laid Father Edward to rest. They came alone without their families and left New York as if a hurricane was on the way.

"You're lucky Lillian and I even came," his older sister Anna said as they sat in the front pew of the church in front of Father Edward's casket. They both wore all red.

"For our mother's blood," Lillian said.

"This is quite a show you put on here," Anna whispered while watching mourners pay their final respects.

"You should have cremated his ass and been done with it," Lillian said. "Mama Ernestine didn't even have half of this. The bastard didn't even come to Evelyn's service. I hope he rots in hell."

"Lil, you know you must not speak ill of the dead," Anna told her. Lillian just rolled her eyes.

A frail looking Reverend Tyler, came out of retirement to eulogize Father Collins. He spoke to the congregation about forgiveness and regret.

"I'm telling you all right now if you have a friend or family and ya'll ain't right, make it right today. I want you to fix it," he said wiping his forehead with his handkerchief.

"Tomorrow is not promised to any of us, but God gave us today," he said looking down at Father Edward's casket.

Neither Anna, nor Lillian must have heard Reverend Tyler's message. While walking out behind the casket, Anna said, "You know mommy died of a broken heart."

"How come he got to live to be old? He should have been the one in the fire," Lillian said as she burst into tears and a few people came over to console her.

"Just so we're clear baby brother. Neither of us want anything to do with Le Maison Rounde or the company. You can have everything," Anna said speaking on Lillian's behalf.

Shortly after laying Father Edward to rest, Jeremy found himself at a bank to open Father Edward's safe deposit box.

The bank manager led him to box number 317. Jeremy smiled as he remembered that was the number Father Edward had always used for the lottery, and probably before that, illegal numbers.

After the manager left him alone Jeremy stared at the gold-plated box for a second wondering what he would find.

Inside there were stacks of bills, some Chinese Yen and stock certificates.

As expected, there were deeds to several properties and some other papers. Jeremy was surprised to see a 1949 dated Pullman train receipt and a charred wedding band.

Curiosity got the best of him when he found a picture of a little boy with Father Edward and a Latino woman sitting on a beach—they were holding each other and smiling. He stared at the little boy and saw his own reflection.

This is me as a baby? Who is the woman? Father Ernestine stepped out on Mama Ernestine and had me?

At the bottom of the box were some headphones, a mini tape recorder, a cassette and batteries. The tape had the words, "Confidential. To Jeremy, my only son" written across it. He put everything together and hit play.

Father Edwards's voice sounded calm and sullen. He spoke slower than usual.

"The evil that men do often lives after them; the good is oft interred with their bones."

William Shakespeare, Jeremy thought to himself.

"Hello Jeremy. By the time you hear this, I will have likely gone home to be with the Lord, my dear Ernestine, Ern and Evelyn. Hopefully, He has forgiven me for my humanly indiscretions. What I am about to tell you is something I have kept hidden your entire life."

Jeremy leaned back in the chair. The only thing louder than the air coming out of the vents was the sound of Jeremy's racing heartbeat.

"Let me get right to it. Mama Ernestine and I were not your biological parents."

Jeremy hit the rewind button. *Not your biological parents?*

He took a deep breath.

"Your real mother's name was Sophia Montrell and your father's name was Alfonso Washington. Sophia was from Miami. She came to New York in 1968, just before your first birthday.

She is the woman in the pictures with you.

Sophia came to New York to look for your father, an Army solider. She said he had been killed in the Vietnam War. Sadly, I could not find any record of him. He may be buried at the Tomb of the Unknown Solider or in an unmarked grave in a memorial cemetery. He likely did not even know you were born. We adopted you."

No wonder she treated me like she did, he thought. I was not her blood and she hated my real mother. This shit is surreal.

"I loved Sophia, as much as a man can love a woman. Her and I had an affair for about a year. Ernestine found out. By then Sophia had fallen in love with me and made the fatal mistake of telling Ernestine. It was a mistake that cost Sophia her young life. She died when she only 33 years old.

Ernestine did something horrible. Something terribly wrong. We cleaned it up.

You should know Sophia's body is in the backyard

151

under the tree near the shed. I imagine Ernestine paid her own retribution in the fire."

Who are we?

Jeremy hit stop.

Sophia's body. Ernestine did something terribly wrong. They killed her? Buried her in our backyard?

Jeremy was awaiting the part where Father Edward was going to say this was all a sick joke.

Was he referring to the tree where each winter Jeremy spoke about the branches? *"Look at this everyone,"* he would say to the family. *"The branches look like they are reaching out for a hug? Mama Ernestine can trees hug?"*

"Jeremy get away from that tree," she would answer.

The tree that never grew leaves.

My real mother was with me all along?

Right in the backyard.

Jeremy hung his head.

**

It was the darkest space in the house. No light ever shined from the outside. The fourth floor where Mama Ernestine would disappear to every night. Father Edwards had instructed the children never to interrupt her time alone up there.

A game of hide and seek had led 12-year-old Jeremy beyond the boundaries of the dark hallway leading to the steps that would take him to her private alcove.

The music he heard was unfamiliar. Slow music with a woman's sad voice, "Honey I get oh so lonely..."

Jeremy tiptoed quietly up the stairs. On the last step, with the push of a foot, it creaked, and the door would open. He could see the flicker of candlelight.

Mama Ernestine was naked and sipping on a colorful drink with cherries in the glass. Lots of cherries.

She slowly swayed her body to the music. She saw Jeremy at the door. She winked and led him inside. Mama Ernestine pushed the door closed and Jeremy entered another world.

"Dance with me Jeremy," Mama Ernestine said before she hiccupped. "I'm not going to bite you," she said. He was a lot taller than her. She pulled him close and put her head near his chest.

Another body felt so unfamiliar to him. She was warm and smelled like candy.

The music stopped ending their dance. She motioned him over to the bed and handed him a magazine.

"Look at this."

He opened the pages and looked at the pictures of naked women smiling at him.

Mama Ernestine grinned and sipped her drink. Then she handed him another magazine. One with naked men.

"Do you like these too? she asked curiously while putting her hand where he knew she was not supposed to touch. Jeremy jumped and said, "I don't know."

She instructed him to take off his clothes.

"Make it quick," she said.

There he stood naked in front of Mama Ernestine. He tried to cover his private parts. Then she handed him a glass of liquid with lots of cherries in it.

"Here drink this, it's magic and it will make you feel good," she said while she started rubbing on his penis. It felt good. Then Jeremy felt dizzy. He followed along to what she wanted him to do.

"You're going to do as I say," she said as she captured his virginity.

Jeremy awoke and was alone. He felt sticky around his penis and his hand smelled funny. Where is Mama Ernestine?

He put on his clothes and bolted downstairs. The family were all in the dining room.

"We were going to wake you for dinner, but you must have been very tired son," Father Edward said giving him a curious look.

As he got ready to sit down, Mama Ernestine, who seemed to be back to her normal self, said, "Go wash your hands before you eat."

He looked at her. She smiled and winked.

Jeremy winked back.

Mama Ernestine and Jeremy had a secret they would they promised to take to their graves.

Jeremy visited with Mama Ernestine on the fourth floor many times and he loved those magical cherry drinks.

Then suddenly, Father Edward barely let Jeremy out of his sight, and he was never able to visit the fourth floor again.

The next year, Jeremy left to start high school at a Connecticut boarding school. Mama Ernestine died in the tragic fire a few months after.

"Jeremy, I know you may have a lot of questions, but no one will be able to answer them for you.

Every family has their secrets. I really do not think we would be human without them. Always remember, you are my son. A son I prayed for. A son I raised and loved.

I am so sorry about what we did. I'm sorry about everything.

The Collins' name is precious. I implore you not to share this recording, or information with anyone.

Do right by our legacy. It was almost your destiny when your mother walked into my office that cold winter morning.

What I have left, you will be able to survive comfortably, but not for long.

The Collins name still stands strong. Use it to your advantage.

We were already rich before I was elected, but after I won, well, that is when I became wealthy beyond my dreams.

I love you son. Forgive me."

As the recording went dead, the only thing that prevented Jeremy from turning over the table, is that he vomited.

A light knock at the door and a voice on the other side startled him.

"Sir, are you okay in there?"

Clearing his throat, Jeremy said, "Yes, I'm fine. Can you get me a drink of water please?"

He pulled out his handkerchief to wipe his tears and his mouth. He wondered whether his sisters knew. Hell, they were not even his real sisters, he thought. His head was spinning. Anger was not the proper word for what Jeremy felt. He was broken and damaged.

An orphan? That one was hard to believe but it had made so much sense to him now.

He opened the envelope and there it was, the birth certificate of Gabriel Montrell, along with his adoption papers.

My real name is Gabriel? The angel in the Bible who Lot tricked and Gabriel ended up carving up the body of his wife into pieces?

Jeremy grabbed everything out of the box making sure he had not even left a paperclip behind. He opened the door and a concerned looking bank employee handed him a glass of water which he drank fast.

"I'm sorry about the accident," he said as the employee looked inside perplexed.

"Is it possible to open my own box today?" Jeremy asked.

"Yes. If you would follow me but you look like you've seen a ghost. "Are you sure you're okay?" He asked.

Jeremy knew he would never be okay ever again, but he answered, "Yes, I'm fine. Thank you for asking."

CHAPTER 22

The For Sale sign in the front lawn of Le Maison Rounde was the talk of real estate agents across the city. Jeremy had listed the home, easily worth millions, for $1,971—the year Sophia took her last breath there.

Attorneys were hired to dissolve Collins Realty and to sell off its holdings to the highest bidder.

Jeremy found correspondence from the IRS where he learned Father Edward was on a payment plan for hundreds of thousands of dollars. The rest of his estate was distributed equally among him, his sisters, and their children which did not leave him much.

Sha's payments were stopped. It was collateral damage for selling the house so cheap. Let her get a real job. If she was smart, she had been saving, he thought.

Jeremy knew he would use his name to his advantage, and he would be ruthless. He would never trust anyone again, nor would he ever tell his real story to anyone.

Yet, he knew, to know where a man is going, he must know where he has been.

That was Jeremy's last thought as he walked away from the tree where his mother had laid dead for decades and shut door to their house for the last time.

CHAPTER 23

NYPD Detective Klowsky moved the phone away from his ear. The loud voice yelling in his ear was giving him a migraine.

Dr. Adelman was on the other end. Again.

"Listen detective, I can assure you her death was not a suicide," he yelled. Klowsky had designated him his chief pain in the ass.

Every week for the past three months he had called faithfully to find out whether a suspect had been arrested in a death the coroner had ruled a suicide. Case closed.

Besides, Klowsky thought who would want to kill someone who was already in a mental institution? Was that not punishment enough?

On the other hand, Klowsky knew many more incidences where someone inside of a mental institution had committed suicide.

Each year in the United States, about 1,800 people commit suicide while hospitalized, he heard once on some investigative television show.

"I'm telling you she was vibrant and happy," Dr. Andelman continued frustrated. "It doesn't add up."

"Why don't you stick to helping patients and let us stick to the police work," Klowsky told him, for what had seemed like the 100th time.

"Find her killer. I've promised her mother justice."

"Doc, the case is closed. It was a suicide. Some things you must let go. There's nothing new here. We are sorry for her mother and family's loss."

"One of our nurses said another woman died the exact same way about fifteen years ago. Wrists slashed and sleeping pills. That is not a coincidence."

Now that was interesting, he thought.

"Did you say 15 years ago?" The same way?"

"Yes, I have the file in front of me," Dr. Andelman said.

"Now you're talking my language," he said.

"Tell you what, I'll come back out there. Is it possible I can speak to the nurse tomorrow?"

"Absolutely," Dr. Andelman said. "We'll see you then."

Dr. Andelman knew she had been seeing a man. A powerful man. One who had manipulated her mind and left her reeling in pain.

"I know it was wrong of me to be with married men. Especially that one. His wink led me astray. It was as if I signed up with the devil," She told Dr. Andelman.

"But I really thought I could trust him, at least I thought Jeremy was a friend. I'm never going to understand how he really set me up to almost go to jail. I feel so betrayed," she told him.

Dr. Andelman put two and two together and came up with his name. Jeremy Collins. Jeremy Collins murdered her. He was still working on how. He knew this.

If the police would not help, he would get him on his own.

CHAPTER 24

This is a beautiful piece—so bright, but so unapologetically dark, she thought as she stared at the portrait.

"Honey, what do you think?" Monica asked Jeremy.

"Umm," Jeremy said distracted. He was busy staring at her two perky breasts through her beige cashmere sweater.

"Eh em," she said blushing. "Eyes up here buddy?"

"This would look good in the breakfast nook," she said.

Jeremy leaned in to read the inscription under the author's name. "*Absence in the palm of my hands.*"

"Isn't that the name of a book?" He asked while shrugging and staring at his radiant wife.

"I'm not sure," Monica said.

"Can we buy it? I hear the artist Milos Argentine is on his way up," she said. Anything his Monica wanted; she could have he thought.

Mrs. Monica Renee Morton-Collins was Jeremy's beautiful six-foot tall wife who had deep chocolate skin and legs which stretched for days.

Monica was the smartest woman he had ever met.

A brilliant mind complimented by the most caring and sweetest personality he had ever encountered in another human.

He was in love.

Jeremy loved watching how women looked at her from head to toe as she walked into a room. Men found it difficult to look away. He guessed they were likely fantasizing about her long legs up in the air wrapped around them, just as he had done the day they had met.

Jeremy usually saw exceptionally tall women who were ashamed of their height and slouched. Not his Monica. She walked like she was regal.

"Sure, let's get it," he remarked, pulling her close to him and giving her a hug.

"Nice, what's this for?" She said rocking slowly in his arms pressing her ass lightly against his groin.

"Nothing, you just feel so good."

Then he whispered, "Let's get this delivered and go home. I have something for you."

She raised her palm and placed it softly on his chin, "I'm ready when you are big daddy."

The year after Father Edwards' death had been a roller coaster ride.

Jeremy spent time trying to find out the mystery surrounding his biological father. Because his name was not on Jeremy's birth certificate, and he could not prove he was truly his next of kin, information shared with him was limited. It frustrated him. The only proof he had was a dead man's tape recording which implicated the people who raised him with murder and kidnapping.

"You're a cutie. What do you need?" An employee at the U.S. Department of Veteran's Affairs who smelled like cigarettes asked as she grinned at him with beige smoker's teeth.

Thanks to her, Jeremy had found out his father's remains were returned to New York from Vietnam in 1972--the same year he had begun the first grade.

Private Alfonso Washington was Hiram Alfonso Washington. That is why Father Edward had likely not found him. That's if he even looked. The man whose sperm created Jeremy was interred at the Long Island National Cemetery.

On Father's Day Jeremy visited his grave. He left a picture of him and Sophia while holding back tears. He would always wonder what life he would have had if both of his parents had lived.

He found out a woman named Pearl Washington, with a Jacksonville address, had received his father's death benefit. Jeremy assumed it was either his mother, wife, or perhaps a sister. It was unlikely it would be a daughter because Pearl was an old-fashioned name. Then again, he could not be sure. At any rate, he was not ready to find his family tree, because the branch he was holding onto himself was broken.

Depression hit Jeremy with a vengeance. At night he took sleeping pills. By day, he was on uppers just to stay awake. He hardly got out of bed or even took a shower.

Such a twisted fate he thought. He felt so alone. The loneliest he had ever been in his life despite what others thought was a great wealthy lifestyle.

Others had cousins, aunts and uncles they could confide in. Now he felt the ones he knew were all pretend. Even calling the women he considered sisters would not help. They had such an angelic view of their mother. If he told them the truth it would likely cause them unnecessary grief. And if he ever found out they knew, and did not tell him, he would be crushed even worse.

Chad had suggested therapy. "At least grief therapy," he said. "Death is hard people and there is no shame in getting help."

Jeremy dismissed it and took to misery on his own terms.

Brooke made sure she checked on him and included them in their family plans. He thought back to the day she had invited him to the funeral for her beloved Maltese, Ginger. Had she not called that day; he likely would have overdosed.

There was something about a dog's funeral of a dog that made him want to stay alive.

Memorial Day weekend was just around the corner. Jeremy had thought he would spend the long weekend high and alone. Or he would jet to Cheetah's in Atlanta where he could easily drop five grand in a night.

Just as he was about to book his flight, Brooke sent a text. He had forgotten about her upcoming birthday party.
Brooke: "REMINDER: Saturday. Party. Our house."
Jeremy: "I'll be there. What should I bring?"
Brooke: "Yourself. I have a surprise for you. REMEMBER: Wear all-white and come alone. Peace."

Jeremy knew he could not miss the celebration of a woman who was like his sister. Her surprise? Likely her trying to hook him up on a blind date.

"Look at you. Damn you falling off? Have you even showered? You smell like you really do want to be alone," Brooke said waving her hand around in his dark apartment, in the middle of the day. She called it a "check-in."

Brooke had walked in on Jeremy, on his couch watching a Quentin Tarantino movie marathon. She had entered using his condo key card Jeremy gave Chad for emergencies.

"Don't walk up in here without calling sis. You almost got shot," Jeremy said looking like he smelled. Fucked up.

"You're looking like 1-800-help a brother dot com," she said shaking her head.

"Do you even know what day it is?" She asked.

"Yeah, it's Wednesday," he said while he looked through the garbage on the coffee table for the remote to turn up the sound.

"It's Friday and when is the last time you cleaned up this place?" She asked walking around doing a dust test on his furniture with her index finger.

"Quiet, this is the part where he kills the doctor in the train station. It's my favorite part. He catches him on the toilet," he said.

"What are you watching?" Brooke asked.

"*Hostel*, it's a classic. This is part one of three. Two more to go. I love Tarantino's mind," he said referencing the notable director and screenwriter who also gave the world *Pulp Fiction* and *Django*.

"My God Jay. I'm going to send Carmen over tomorrow to fumigate this place. Be home and don't fuck her. It's hard finding good help who won't steal your shit or fuck your husband."

"Duly noted," he said staring at the screen.

"And go get a haircut or a shape up or something. You're looking like someone just found you under a bridge."

That was two weeks ago. Tonight, he was standing in his closet contemplating what all-white outfit he would wear. He settled on a pair of white Levi's, a white stretch fitted shirt and a Louis Vuitton belt. Simple he thought.

Although it was an all-white party, he was not about to wear white shoes. A man should never get caught in white shoes unless he was going to play golf, he thought. He pulled out his brown Hermes Palermo loafers and slipped them on. Perfect he thought as he checked himself out on his floor to ceiling mirrored wall in his bedroom.

Sparkling white lights lit up the trees surrounding the long driveway leading up to Chad and Brooke's million-dollar 10,000 square foot mansion overlooking the New Jersey Palisades. At the entrance, there were about forty white doves waiting to be released. Brooke has outdone herself, he thought.

It is a big deal when you're celebrating your 40th year of life. YOLO, he thought as the white tuxedo wearing valet opened his car door and a hostess stood there asking him his name.

"No plus one?" she pried.

"Nope, just me," he said while noticing the sound of crickets. As a city dweller, that was always the first thing he noticed when he was in the suburbs. He liked the sound and could relate. It was the sound of the male cricket attracting the female ones.

"Everyone is out back by the pool. You can ride with those others in the golf cart over there," she directed. "Or I can walk with you?" She said smiling.

"I'm good," he answered.

"Well then, please enjoy yourself," she cooed.

"Thank you," he said. She gave him the verification he needed. He still looked good, even if he felt ugly as hell on the inside.

"You let me know if you need anything. Anything," she repeated. "I will come running."

Someone please dial 9-1-1 he sang in his head.

Before Jeremy could step foot onto the patio by the pool, Brooke, who was obviously a little tipsy, snuck up behind him.

"What took you so long? The party started two hours ago. Black people, I tell you."

"Happy Birthday? Where's my hug?" He asked.

"You clean up nice," she said after checking him out head to toe and hugging him. "Now, come on," she said as she grabbed his hand.

She whizzed him past the beautifully decorated outdoor space. He saw a chef carving a turkey, another was serving some pasta dish. There were a ton of food stations and the smells were delightful. Jeremy realized he had not had a hot meal in weeks.

They whisked by a long table. He salivated as he looked at the inviting hors d'oeuvres.

"Wait," Jeremy said as he stopped and picked up a pastry filled with lobster.

It was within an inch of his lips when Brooke slapped it out of his hand.

"Eat later. Come on, I have someone I want you to meet."

She abruptly halted them in front of an amazon woman. She was almost eye to eye with him. Damn, she is tall, he thought. Maybe an WNBA player?

He admired her sculptured face. Her hair was in a long ponytail past her shoulders. On top she had diamond barrettes. Jeremy thought she looked like a Goddess. Her aura illuminated so strongly, he thought she may have had angels surrounding her.

He immediately perked up.

Maybe she's a model? He thought. She certainly had the slim body and face for it. He looked down and saw three of her French manicured toes arched nicely in some, if he had to guess, Jimmy Choos.

Her heels gave her about two more inches in height. That somehow relaxed him a little. He wanted to know how tall she was barefoot.

Why am I thinking about her feet?

In his eyes she was a chocolate Goddess. Her flowing white silk dress stopped at her mid thighs. She had to be a queen on the Nile in a former life, he thought. He was ready to be her Pharaoh.

Brooke had done well.

"Jeremy, this is Monica Morton," Brooke said as she tried catching her breath. "Jeremy Collins, I mean, this is Monica. Oh hell, Jeremy this is Monica. Monica this is Jeremy. You two enjoy yourselves and please check out the Bellini station—we have flavors—strawberry, lemon, peach."

"Hey DJ, put on 50 Cent," she yelled. "With his fine Cancer ass. Cause we're gonna party, cause it's my birthday."

Jeremy started laughing. "She is something else," as his stomach growled. He hoped Monica had not heard it.

"Miss Monica Morton, how are you this evening?" He asked reaching his hand out to her. He loved the way her name flowed off his tongue. *Monica Morton. M&M.*

"I could complain, but who would listen right?" She said while he noticed she kept her hands at her side.

Okay then, that was a first for him. A woman was always ready to give him her hand. He was stumped.

"I must say you look very nice this evening." He said staring at just enough cleavage, which left something to his imagination. She was classy and sassy. He liked that.

"Flattery will get you nowhere," she said with an impatient look as if he was disturbing her. *You know this man is fine, why are you playing?*

Jeremy smelled her perfume and dreamed of her in his arms, even if it was only one night.

Is this what love at first sight feels like?

"I'm kidding. It's nice to meet you Mr. Collins," she said as she held up her hand. *Damn, she felt bad she had not spent more on Brooke's gift. She had sent her a prize.*

"I like your voice," she said. "Are you on the radio?"

"No, I'm in real estate and the pleasure is all mines," he said as he raised her hand and kissed the back of her palm.

Monica thought she was going to faint.

"Please call me Jeremy," he said adding as much bass to his voice as possible.

"Although I'm sure Brooke would not try and set me up with someone who is married, I need confirmation before we go any further," she said that while thinking he was way too fine to be 100% single.

"Are you married? Separated or living with a woman?"

That was good, Jeremy thought. The first question most women asked was about a man's income, hiding behind the question, "What do you do for a living?" Rarely, did any of them ask, or care, whether he was taken.

"None of the above," He said happy that he wasn't.

"Are you gay?"

"Nope," he said noticing his palms were sweating. "All free and clear Monica Morton."

Thank you, Jesus! She thought, but she would find out on her own. A simple search at check people dot com would help her confirm. A woman had to be careful these days.

"So how do you know Brooke?" She asked easing up a little in her tone.

He explained but he wanted to know more about her.

"Are you enjoying the party? Would you like a drink? Something to eat? A place to live?"

"What?" She giggled.

"I mean would you like to dance?" he asked.

Girl get outta here before the sweat starts forming on the tip of your nose. You do not want this man to see you having your own personal summer courtesy of early menopause.

"I'm sorry I can't," she said. "Will you please excuse me; I see my friend Ericka. It was nice meeting you Jeremy. Enjoy the party."

With that she was gone leaving him stumped again. He wanted to follow her, but he felt like his feet were stuck in cement.

He looked down to see if she had left a glass slipper.

Jeremy and Monica loved telling that story whenever someone asked how they had met.

"I left him standing there with his mouth open," she would say playfully.

"No, tell the truth. You were scared of the big bad Jay," he would reply.

Then they would laugh and warmly touch.

Jeremy believed Monica, who was six years older than him, had saved his life and what was left of his inheritance.

A mature woman was just what he had needed to put him on the right track in life. She had never been married and did not have any kids. No baggage.

"I am a statistic," she told him on their tenth date, which was also about the time he was ready to give up trying to get into her panties. Or maybe he would just join her in celibacy. He laughed at the thought.

"Did you know *Newsweek* reported, a single, college-educated, 40-year-old woman was more likely to die in a terrorist attack than to ever walk down the aisle?" She said as they finished their dinner at the Four Seasons.

"For Black women like me nearing 50, it's probably a nuclear war," she laughed even though she did not look a day over 40. She could give those younger women a run for their money, Jeremy thought. She had aged well.

"Well you don't have to worry about that," he assured her admiring her perfect smile.

"Why is that?" she asked.

"Because you will be my wife one day. One day soon," he said seriously.

This one is not getting away.

"Boy, get outta here. I'm not even sure I like you," she teased.

"You don't like me eh? Then you can pay the check for this $400 meal," he said teasing back.

"Not a problem. And nope I don't like you, I only like the fact that you take me out and feed me. I guess I can return the favor today," she said reaching for her wallet.

He gestured for her hand across the table and she held his.

"You know I'm kidding," he said. "As long as you are with me you will never pick up a check."

That was the exact moment Monica knew she had fallen in love.

After dessert, Jeremy checked them into one of the luxury suites overlooking the fantastic New York skyline.

For the next three days, they did not leave the room and consummated more than a friendship.

One year later, they were planning their wedding.

Monica had no interest in a big ceremony.

When she suggested they wed in the Little Wedding Chapel in Las Vegas, he thought she was joking.

"Well, since my father died when I was young, I never really had a desire for a traditional wedding ceremony," she said sadly. "Fathers are supposed to walk their daughters down the aisle."

Jeremy promised to turn that emptiness into the best day of her life.

"Let's do it," Jeremy said lovingly.

Monica had a few pre-marriage ground rules which she typed up like a shopping list. They reviewed them together as if he were a student in her 8ᵗʰ grade algebra class.

1. No cheating. "I know it's hard for men to be faithful, but I need you to try and not forsake us. It's really important that we are always honest with one another if we may feel the need to stray." *Not on your life. If another man touches you, he a dead man walking, but he agreed and let her continue.*

2. "Don't ever disrespect our home or bed, by bringing another woman to it." Monica would not even let company

into her bedroom. "I lived alone a long time. My home and my bedroom especially, are my sanctuary."

Jeremy agreed. He had learned a valuable lesson about his own mother's deadly choice of visiting another woman's house.

3. "No matter how busy we get, we will always have at least two dates a month." *Check.*

4. "There are two primary reasons for divorce in America. Infidelity, which we've already covered and finances." Jeremy's financial status was bleak. Except for his condo, his net worth was less than $175,000.

Monica pulled out copies of their individual bank statements and credit reports.

"Our FICO scores are decent, let's keep them like that. No purchases over $1,000 dollars without checking with one another. Or should we make it $500 dollars? What do you think?" She asked while Jeremy reviewed his with a perplexed look.

"Do you see an error?" She asked. "Because if you do, we have to get it corrected immediately."

"How would I know if there was an error?" He asked.

"Wait, you have never seen your credit report, have you?"

"No, this is my first time. We had people for this."

"I'll explain it to you after we finish okay?"

"$500 is good. No problem for me," he said.

"What about work?" She asked.

"Can I work at Pet Castle?" He joked. "You could teach me how to be a vet like you."

"You want to work with animals all day?" She asked curiously.

"No, I don't think so," he said. "I just want to be able to see you every day, all day."

"The good news is we don't need extra money right now, but you have to start thinking about our retirement years. No cat food for dinner when we are old and gray. I'm barely keeping my head above water taking care of my mother in that nursing home."

"I've been thinking of something. We are going to be fine, trust me. I just have to figure out how to plug it in."

"Just remember Jeremy. Dreamers don't get nothing but sleep."

"Trust me baby, I'm not dreaming. It's very real."

"That's it then. Let's get married. Sign here and here," she said.

"Wait a minute. Don't I get a turn? I have some rules too," he said.

"Of course, I'm sorry about that."

"Just one," he said grinning. "You promise to give me some of that hot, tight pussy whenever I want it."

"You're always horny," she giggled.

"Yes, to your request but just know this is a no-sex zone during my time of the month and I get cramps like a teenager. Also, don't use up all the Ibuprofen's because I will need them."

"No, I agree that's disgusting," Jeremy said but he knew women and men called blood hounds who did and would even pay for the service.

Jeremy and Monica moved into a fully paid brownstone on West 124th Street. Father Edward had left it to his sister Anna and her children. It was purchased under a shell company, so the IRS had not found it.

"You know my mother used to tell me a woman should never move into a man's home. She always taught me to have my own." Monica said as reviewed the papers for the sale on her Roosevelt Island condo.

"What difference does it make?" He asked. "We're going to live together forever and it's a free house."

"It's a free house in your sister's name, not even yours. A sister I've only met once," she reminded him.

"Listen, you have to trust me," he said. "I know this is a big step for you, but I promise you will not regret it," he said lovingly.

"I truly hope so," she said. "I'm too old to start over."

"I just have one request," Jeremy said.

"What's that?"

"Can we design the master bedroom and bathroom in an Asian theme? Something with white walls, red and black accents. Lately, I've been wanting a room that expresses all that Feng Shui stuff—you know like for our inner peace?"

She nodded affirmatively and said, "I just hope you're right about this house," as she recalled pulling up to her cousin Kevin's house in the middle of the night. He had evicted his son's mother. Monica thought it was the saddest thing to see her in the cold with her belongings in plastic garbage bags crying her eyes out.

S.R. CHASE

CHAPTER 25

Jeremy felt lucky and on top of the world with Monica. He believed he had finally found a woman who was his equal. One who encouraged him and made him believe he could do anything. Living off her was becoming a habit and she was putting on the pressure.

"Have you given any thought to how you are going to earn a living?" she asked again over coffee. "It's been almost nine months and we've had to cash in some stock."

Jeremy knew finding a job had always been an enigma on his life. Collins Realty had been his only employer. The only interviews he had ever been in was someone sitting across from him asking him for a job.

"We'll a job, per say is really out of the question," he said.

"Well maybe you can start a business?" Monica suggested.

"A business like what?" he asked. "I probably can become a masseuse. Don't you think women will pay me for this kind of touch," he said as he got up and started rubbing her shoulders.

"No," she said leaning back and enjoying him loosening her muscles. "This is for me to wake up to each day, nobody else," she said.

Those type of moments with her husband were priceless.

"Why don't you put those political science and psychology degrees to work?"

"Doing what?" As he thought about his framed degrees in a box somewhere packed up.

"Maybe run for public office? The Harlem community loves you and you have name recognition."

Not a bad idea, he thought.

"Plus, the government has excellent benefits, health, vision, and a retirement plan."

Without a doubt he was bitter at what life had pitched to him. Dead parents—all four of them. One murdered, one killed protecting America, the other in a fire and one who went to his grave with secrets. To him, it was a miracle, he was even born and had survived 43 years.

To become an elected official, one had to care about people and be willing to represent their interests. Jeremy had no interest in doing that and would use it to his own advantage. Father Edward left him a clue. At that moment something clicked as he remembered it.

"We were already rich before I was elected, but after I won, well, that is when I became wealthy beyond my dreams."

**

After a year of campaigning and the public resurgence of the Collins name, Jeremy won the senate seat representing Harlem.

Political pundits believed he was victorious because the voters were paying homage to his late father. Running during an off presidential year with low voter out had not hurt either. Jeremy had the cards in his favor.

It was the first time in his life, he was happy to receive compensation that did not have Collins Realty attached to it. He was finally earning his own way.

For the next four years, he would begin a plan that would see him to the golden finish line of life. If all went right, he would walk away with half of a $50 million-dollar payoff.

At every opportunity, he took advantage of his newfound privilege and power. Him and Monica attended A-list parties where they wined and dined among New York's most powerful and elite. He used his senate account for dining out and travel all over the country and the world. He traded in his Maserati for a leased BMW740i and transferred the monthly payments over to his state account.

The senate spending guideline book was like his Bible filled with highlighted text and post its. He made sure he did not miss a perk, such as the fact that elected officials could have a 24-hour security detail if they desired, or the fact he had unlimited parking just about anywhere in the city.

Although it was against the rules and unethical, he accepted cash gifts from lobbyists, business owners and others who bought his votes.

His $79,500 yearly salary was deposited into a joint account with Monica who managed their funds.

When it came to actual work, he passed one-piece of legislation called the *Deceased Veteran's Act* which would allow any public person access to the burial records of any deceased solider, whether they were related or not. After it was made into law, a Texas congressman presented it to Congress and modified it on the federal level.

At the press conference he announced, "I have worked day and night to make this law a reality. It will help so many, including extended family members and adopted children, looking for their relatives. It is utterly important we allow loved ones to pay their final respects at the graves of fallen soldiers."

Jeremy became an overnight hero winning the respect of both his colleagues and the public.

"Babe, you did it. I'm so proud of you," Monica said one Memorial Day as they savored filet mignon at a White House luncheon at the invitation of the President.

From that point, Jeremy practically became untouchable.

His staff worked year-round while the law required state legislators to work part-time only five months a year.

Sure, he would attend an event or two and still visit his district office, give a media interview, here and there; but for the most part, he stayed home filling his days perfecting his con.

Strategically, he had amassed a staff of hard workers who were honored to work as an employee of the New York State Senate. They had sincerely wanted to help the people of Harlem while adding it to their resumes.

Throughout his first four years, their hard work and dedication—often sacrificing their time with their families and personal pursuits with paltry pay, had propelled Senator Collins to one of the most well-liked and revered legislators in the state. If he was re-elected, his staff looked forward to four more years of stable employment.

The summer before the primaries for a potential second term, his staff enjoyed the day at their annual picnic.

Collins interrupted the festivities to announce how much he appreciated them in front of their family and friends.

"Without you, we would not be this far. You all been a blessing to me, and I hope I have been a blessing to you."

The next morning, his true colors emerged and showed his continuous lack of leadership skills unworthy of an elected official. He repaid them all by callously firing them. As icing on the cake, he told the shocked employees, "I hope we can remain friends."

By lunchtime, while staff cleaned out their belongings, Jeremy was on his way to a Connecticut casino.

As a ploy he referred them to a woman in the state's human resources department, who he had been sexing since he first took office.

"If I give them hope for a new job, they would be less likely to sue me," he told her one-night laying in her bed after promising her $10,000 for the gesture.

A lonely single mother, she risked her 15 years of state employment for him.

Her job was to convince them she would help them find another position in the state's government. A position each of them would anxiously seek but would not obtain.

As soon as they walked out of her office, she shredded their applications.

The risk of anyone getting too close or comfortable to Jeremy's deceitful plan was deemed more important than the income his employees likely needed or the fact one of them needed her health insurance because she was fighting breast cancer.

Hurt people hurt other people.

Jeremy had no empathy for anyone. The new crew for his second term would create a new history for him.

CHAPTER 26

Summer 2008

It was an exciting time to be an American. Illinois Senator Barack Hussein Obama announced his candidacy to become the first Black president of the United States.

The pride across the nation was contagious. America was united and coming together to support his candidacy on a progressive, democratic platform.

CNN reported, *"For African-Americans who lived through the civil rights struggles of Selma, Alabama, Rosa Parks and the Rev. Martin Luther King Jr., Obama is a symbol of struggle and success, progress and change."*

Senator Obama's rise to the most powerful position in government signaled the green light for change, not only in the national leadership, but on the local levels as well.

Senator Obama had set a stage for others to walk through the door to potential leadership. Those already in office were almost guaranteed re-election if they were willing to follow his hope and change mantra. Those like Senator Collins who would use Senator Obama's campaign as a blueprint.

His campaign encouraged democrats to vote straight down the democratic line. He also used cryptic marketing messages, such as Senator Obama's signature campaign colors of blue and white with a touch of red, on his campaign literature.

Jeremy had strategically placed a photographer to capture a picture of him with Senator Obama and New York Governor, Judith Harrison, the first woman to hold that position in the state's history.

His marketing team used the photo on his final campaign mailers, and it went viral on social media. Voters were given the impression Jeremy had received an endorsement by them both.

Although expected to win, heading into the 2008 primaries, it was a tight race for him which included two other strong Democrats. He could take nothing for granted. A loss would mean his plan would go down the drain.

"Can you find out when Governor Harrison will be in the five boroughs again?" He asked one of summer interns from NYU.

"Also, I need you to research how to set-up off-shore bank accounts. Look up, the Cayman Islands, Dubai and Singapore."

"Will do sir," Andrew answered.

"Also," he said as he lowered his voice, "Do the research from home, not the computers here in the office?"

"I got you," he answered.

The campaign for Jeremy's re-election was winding down and his office buzzed non-stop with activity. No one questioned where the money from fundraising went that was managed by his elusive treasurer and arrogant campaign manager. No one volunteering had noticed they went from drinking Starbucks and groceries from Whole Foods, to milling over trays of hardened cheese, soggy crackers and instant coffee.

On a busy afternoon, two weeks before the primary, a volunteer grabbed the remote and turned up the volume on the big screen television.

"Listen up everybody," as Senator Collins directed them to watch the broadcast.

"This year's New York Senate race is heating up. The polls are rising steadily. We have reports incumbent Jeremy Collins, is likely to win the Senate seat and once again represent Harlem in the tight-knit race. Collins is the son of the late Edward Collins, a former New York City Councilman and real estate mogul. We will bring you more at the 6'oclock hour. Reporting from Harlem, this is Rod Neptune for FBS-NY. Back to you in the studio Linda."

Volunteers cheered.

"Let's not be so quick to celebrate. This election is far from over," Senator Collins announced.

Although statistics show, it can be difficult to unseat an incumbent, Jeremy had to admit the changing Harlem neighborhood demographics had him a little worried. Harlem's Latino population had grown rapidly over the last several years and was now about 40%.

Hector Torres, Jr., a Harvard educated Rhodes Scholar, who was also heir to the billion-dollar Torres food company, had raised two million dollars. Even though he attended Harvard with his sister Anna, he was giving Collins a real run for his money.

Hector's father, Hector Torres, Sr. had lived a true American dream. Torres, Jr. loved sharing the story in his campaign commercials.

"My father came to America in the late 1960s with no money and unable to speak English. In fifteen short years, he built the largest Latino food brand in America and donated millions of dollars to various charities, programs and political leaders right here in Harlem..."

Jeremy knew Torres was a longshot because their company headquarters was in Washington Heights, a predominately Latino enclave next door to Harlem. Voters kept asking when he planned to move his operations to an official Harlem address.

The other candidate, Lasailla Adams was also hard at work. She announced it was time for Harlem, "To elect a person who represents the LGBTQ community, who happens to be a Black woman." She also made sure to point out, "the majority of voters are women."

The 52-year-old Harlem native was also the award-winning founder of the Harlem Rescue Mission.

Jeremy and Monica had donated thousands to the nonprofit which helped LGBTQ homeless New Yorkers. They had hoped she would join Team Collins instead of challenging him. Jeremy had wasted their time and money.

Jeremy had to give her credit because her leadership in the grassroots sector was revered by everyone from the mayor to the bodega owner.

Adams also had a lot of media savvy. Jeremy thought the way she postured herself in front of the camera speaking against her perceived injustices such as police brutality, inequities in the school's system and gentrification, reeked of desperation.

Just like Jeremy, she had a hidden agenda.

A win for Adams would propel her to the national spotlight.

Jeremy knew he had no time to waste. His win would mean the next four years would set the stage for the rest of his life. He was not going to lose. His new team were good, and it was just the type of motivation he needed.

The stragglers, the opportunists and the lazy had been weeded out.

What remained were four core people who represented the best minds Jeremy could find. True A-type personalities that would need little supervision and more importantly, would have their own agendas as well. While they thought they were using him, he would be using them.

At the request of a consultant, Collins summoned key members of his strategic team one summer night to report on the feelings of voters as they entered the campaign's homestretch.

Senator Collins was happy to see Jack Rollins, an elderly, but very youthful, 70-year-old political consultant, which is how everyone referred to him in public. Behind closed doors, he was feared like a mob boss.

Rollins had helped launch the careers of several local and state leaders, including two New York governors. Careers he could also end if he truly wanted.

The only time political party leaders got together and played nice was during Rollins's annual golf tournament. Even the most powerful politicos would reschedule family vacations, medical appointments and probably their own funerals, to attend.

Rollins had an uncanny ability to correctly predict election outcomes as far back as the 1960s.

Today, he was on Team Collins and now, for the most part, Jeremy was just playing the waiting game.

"Your father was one of my best friends," he told Jeremy before the meeting began. He looked like the sophisticated gentlemen of the old days with a tailored business suit, perfectly folded handkerchief in the pocket and a Stetson hat, which he had on the table in front of him. Considered a true OG, he also had rings on three of his five fingers and his ear was pierced. A big brawly man, dressed in all black, who served as his bodyguard stood standing a few feet away watching everyone's movements.

"You know we went to Shaw and pledged together."

"Yes, I know that sir," Jeremy said.

"Ed Collins and I did a lot together to help Harlem," he said smiling displaying a perfect set of dentures. "He was really a good man."

"Like what?" Jeremy asked.

"Shit, what didn't we do. But if I told you, I would have to kill you," he laughed.

"Please everyone, let's get started," Trent Murphy, a chubby 28-year old graduate student from City College announced over the glaring sounds of sirens and car horns coming through the window from outside on the busy 125th Street thoroughfare.

Trent was from Minnesota and was now calling Harlem home. He wore a snug white T-shirt with the words, "Damn Gina!" scrawled across in bright pink lettering.

"What's up with your shirt Trent?" Jeremy asked the hipster from Columbus, Ohio.

"Mart-innn," he shouted like the show's song. You know that was the show of the 90s."

"How old were you in the 90s?" Mr. Rollins asked, looking at Trent's ponytail and wondering whether he was transgendered. His grandson had recently transitioned, and he was trying to keep up with a new world.

"Those were my teen years. My parents never let me out of the house. All I had was books and TV shows," he said.

A nice icebreaker, Jeremy thought.

Trent noticed him staring at his chest, which made his nipples hard. Jeremy carefully looked around at the others, before winking at Trent causing him to blush.

Jeremy noticed his backside was a little pudgy and a little higher than usual for a man, but he liked the way it looked in his tight khaki pants. Each time Trent turned his back, Jeremy would take a quick glance.

"According to the data and research, Senator Collins has all of the tools to complete this successful electoral run. We should try and get him into something more beastlike in the next two weeks. For example, his social media is way corny," Trent presented. "People respond to him, but it does not translate into donations or votes," Trent said.

"Also, I'm not a big fan of social media, but I can tell you this, the number of friends and likes does not mean people really like you. That's the mindset of a narcissist. What matters is how does that transition into real life? Who is giving you financial support? Votes?" Jackie Potter, his campaign manager added.

"Agreed," Trent said. "Most people who seek validation from social media are the loneliest among us all."

Jeremy was not paying them any attention. He was focused on Trent. He thought Trent had swag. His voice was a mixture between, urban and suburban. Like I go to college during the week, but I smoke blunts with my Jamaican homeboys in the projects on the weekends.

"He is straight savage on the new residents moving into Harlem—they love him," Trent said continuing the presentation. "His views on a new Harlem are right on point. He is woke."

Trent was dramatic and thematic about the Harlem community. Jeremy envisioned the two of them getting to know one another more intimately as he stared at his semi-full lips. Maybe his mother or father is Black, Jeremy thought.

Trent represented an interesting demographic himself. Harlem was becoming more diversified and that meant he would need more than just the Black vote to win. The millennial vote was also important.

"Does anyone have any questions?" Trent asked.

"Yes," Mr. Rollins said. "What does woke mean?"

"My bad," Trent said. "That means he is knowledgeable about Harlem. He understands the changes, the diversity, the different perspectives and embraces it well."

"Wow all of that in one word?" Rollins responded. "Then I guess I have been woke a long time."

Everyone laughed.

"May I continue?" Trent asked. "I'll try to speak without all the slang."

With a press of a button another slide appeared with volunteers on telephones.

"We have learned through our phone polls in the largest primary zip codes of 10030, 10037 and 10039 that Collins is leading among male voters 30-55 years old and women 18-35 years old."

Trent clicked to the next slide.

"Women over 35 appear to be more aligned with Lasailla Adams."

No shocker there, Jeremy thought.

"We should try and get Monica out more on the campaign trail," Trent suggested. Collins nodded affirmatively thinking it would be nice to have his radiant wife by his side.

"The Collins name was recognized among 93% of the callers and 47% said they would like to see him out more in the streets." *Not gonna happen, Jeremy thought.*

"The rest of the zip codes, which include 10026, 10027, 10029, 10031 and 10035 will be polled this week and reported to you via email," Trent concluded.

"Were there any concerns?" Mr. Rollins asked.

"Yes," Trent answered. "But they were more like suggestions. The most common was people felt Senator Collins lacks a clear connection with Harlem's young people."

Most young people don't vote, and they sure don't give money to campaigns, Jeremy thought. We won't be fixing that.

Trent clicked off the projector and said, "I would just like to add. As you are aware, there are no Republican candidates. All we have to do is get through the primaries."

"Remember, winning an elective office is not hard," Mr. Rollins added. "It's staying in office that's the hard part. People will want to see you fail as much as succeed." He paused to catch his thoughts during what he called a "senior moment."

"I already see you at the finish line Collins or I would not be here."

Yes! That is exactly what they all were waiting to hear, Jeremy thought.

"There are only three things a candidate needs to win," Rollins continued.

"One is money. Two is knowledge of the community you want to represent. Get to know as many people as you can, by name, from the bodega owner to the latest real estate developer; and three, keep your friends close and your enemies even closer, including your opponents. You will need them all."

"No disrespect Mr. Rollins, but I was taught to keep my enemies far, far away. Like go that way," Jeremy said while pointing to an imaginary place. Another round of laughter by everyone.

I've got them right where they need to be.

Rollins thought Collins was foolish. He was sent there to watch him. It was true Ed was one of his good friends, but he was dead now. He owed him nothing. His son was a sloppy politician and a womanizer. Harlem's legacy, which will be around long after he was done pretending to represent the people, had to be maintained.

Rollins also did not like him, as he looked over at his manicured nails. The boy probably never even picked up a hammer a day in his life, he thought. He was looking forward to when he would just be a footnote in Harlem's chapter.

"Yes, children, once upon a time, there was a Senator named Jeremy Collins."

"Who?" They would ask.

"Never mind. Please turn your pages to..." Rollins smiled at the thought. History never remembers the fake ones no matter how much they believe they have accomplished.

Jeremy talked a good game, but real hardcore Harlem people considered him soft. This Rollins knew.

Unbeknownst to Jeremy, his protection on the streets was due solely out of the respect most had for his late father. A lot of people believed Ed Collins helped launder money from some of Harlem's most notorious drug dealers and gamblers. They all felt they owed him and his family.

It was rumored, when the feds came to get one of Harlem's crime bosses, who had been caught red-handed with a trunk full of cocaine, Ed Collins had paid off a judge for him to walk. He then quit the game and quietly moved his family to California where his son is now one of Hollywood's top black television producers.

Were it not for his father, Jeremy would have been hit a long time ago by men who preyed upon weaker men and especially on those who hit women. Elected official or not, in the least, he would have been carjacked.

"Man, that fool is so lucky he is one of my best customers. I hear he likes to beat on women and shit," Kev said to his friend after Jeremy walked away from copping a $1,000 worth of marijuana and pills.

Game recognized game.

"Can I see you for a moment in my office?"

"Sure, let me just wrap up," Trent said.

I mean, "Let me just wrap up this stuff up," he corrected.

Yeah, he knows what time it is.

CHAPTER 27

On a brisk fall night in late October, nearly 500 people and representatives from every major media outlet patiently waited for the final senatorial debate hosted by the Upper Manhattan NAACP.

The Marvin Gaye classic *What's Happening Brother* played as Jeremy and Monica entered St. Aquinas' Episcopal Church on Fifth Avenue.

His mood was good and upbeat. If had to choose another word, he would pick fearless. He knew he was among friends who were seated in the church's basement.

"Ms. Judy, how's your sister Peg doing?" Jeremy stopped to ask.

"She is just fine Senator. Thank you for those lovely lilacs you sent her in the hospital," she said with a big smile feeling special.

Those two guaranteed votes cost him $29.99.

Jeremy was among the usual suspects elected officials had to cultivate for votes and financial support: tenant association presidents; union representatives; pastors; and the largest voters, women.

Ladies who would likely love to meet with him privately concerning some fake issue of an urgent nature. There was always someone in line for the attention of an elected official.

Jeremy noticed most of the audience were seniors. He pulled out some index cards and wrote down talking points. Senior housing, check. Social security, check. Elder care, check.

He waved over Jackie to join him.

"Do me a quick favor. Get me the number of newly constructed senior housing in our district within the last two years."

"That is 512." Jackie answered quickly.

"The Hopewell Residence on 140th and Lenox-70 units; Adam Clayton Powell Senior Housing on 152nd and 8th Avenue-300 units; and the building at 400 St. Nicholas Avenue-142 units."

"High five to you lady," he said impressed.

"No biggie, your old chief kept excellent records."

At only 56 years old, Jackie looked much older than her years—almost like a senior citizen herself. Bitterness, blended with a head full of gray hair, had seemingly stolen her grace like a thief in the night.

Collins had met Jackie at campaign function for the borough president. Her business card had the title of special assistant, but Collins found out she was a lowly aide in charge of coffee and copier paper.

Her face always had a frown. Collins found himself regularly telling her to smile. She was one of the few women he could not find any physical beauty. Yet, there was something about her satanic aura that attracted him.

Her demeanor reminded him a lot of that child molester pedophile who had pretended to be his mother, Mama Ernestine.

She had grown up in the projects where she said, "The scent of urine from the elevator attached to your clothes." He could only imagine.

Collins had suspected she had leeched on to people like him to make a name for herself. An opportunist who had never done anything except off the name, and plight, of others.

Most of the time she walked around like Jeremy's personal bodyguard. If he abruptly turned around, she was there standing on his heels. The only time she gave him space was around his wife. Then she would almost remain hidden.

Jeremy liked the protection and knew she had a crush on him. Maybe one day he would oblige her, but he would have to be highly intoxicated.

Jackie was a borderline anorexic and was always eating. Campaign volunteers had suspected she was going in the bathroom after she ate to throw up her food.

Jackie had hinted at becoming his Chief of Staff, but he still wasn't sure the title would not give her an air of superiority. Jeremy noticed when she spoke to people in the community, mainly Blacks and Latinos, she was arrogant—as if she was doing them a favor.

Back in the 1970s, she would have likely been called a "poverty pimp." For people like her, it was to their advantage that someone was always less fortunate. They would grab a bullhorn, and advocate on their behalf as long as they received a check.

For all her attitude, Jackie stumbled around educated intelligent women. She was jealous of the Black ones, and nervous around the White ones. Jeremy thought she would be good to represent him in the district office, but he knew she would be out of place in the hallways of the state capitol, even with her good fashion style. At the end of the day, she was an old, well-dressed hood girl.

"She seems to be the type who has forgotten where she came from," a good friend told Collins when she saw them together at a community rally.

Jackie had climbed the hood ladder likely cutting anyone in her way. He could feel it. At her age, there were not too many opportunities left for her. Maybe he would throw her a bone? Maybe she would be the perfect type to lead his office after all, he thought as NAACP representatives made introductions and led him to the staging area.

Jackie had followed and stood patiently for his next request. He could not remember what he wanted to say. When he was a child, Mama Ernestine used to tell him, "You can't remember because it was probably a lie."

"Anything else Senator Collins?" Jackie asked.

"Would you like some water or something? They also have a tray of donuts over there."

"No, I'm good, thanks." Just then, he heard the moderator began addressing the crowd.

It was showtime.

The other two candidates walked over near Collins. They exchanged phony pleasantries and fake smiles before walking to the three podiums.

The moderator read their bios and announced to the crowd, "Each candidate will have three minutes to make an opening introduction. We ask that you save your applause for afterwards. Ms. Adams, ladies first. So, we will begin with you."

Adams stood looking rather unappealing in her gray pantsuit and black buttoned-down shirt with some fake pearls. Her orthopedic black shoes did not help her look, but she stood with confidence.

"Good evening. My name is Lasailla Adams and *I* am running to be your next senator—your first female senator from Harlem.

In your chair, you should have found marketing materials telling you about my background, along with information to volunteer. This run is important for me. Important for Harlem. We do not have time to waste."

The crowd sat attentive, but she was not connecting much with them, Jeremy noticed.

"I am having a hard time understanding how we can continue to entrust our community's finances to an incumbent who has filed for bankruptcy."

The room went so quiet, you could hear a pin drop.

Jeremy faked a smile.

What a true bitch.

"He wears $2,000 suits, drives a $75,000 car, and was born into wealth. How is broke is he really?" She asked.

She has no idea what I was born into. Shit, I don't even know what I was born into. Was it a hospital? A house? For all I know I could have been born in a shack somewhere.

Amidst the audience's whispers, she continued: "Gentrification has hit Harlem hard. His father started this trend."

Some people in the audience booed. She should have known better than to bring up his father. He was Harlem royalty.

"You can boo me, but those are the facts. His son has bombarded us with literature highlighting family values and the relevance of marriage with a women's right to choose," she said while holding up one of Collins' red, white and blue brochures.

"Yet, he is on his second wife. When he was with his first wife, Rev. Tyler's daughter Dana, he got a side chick pregnant."

Someone yelled, "Man, he's ratchet."

We need to elect a leader without, dare I say, ghetto baggage. One who actually respects women."

She paused to get the reaction of the audience who were nodding their heads affirmatively.

"Although he is quick to discuss a better public-school system and attack our chancellor, he had a private school education and neither one of his children have ever attended public schools in New York, let alone Harlem," she continued.

The audience gasped.

"Thank you for your time and I look forward to the rest of tonight's forum," Adams said beaming and giving Jeremy a 'take that' kind of expression.

A deafening silence filled the room while they gave her a lukewarm applause.

"Well that was quite an introduction, Ms. Adams. In all fairness to Senator Collins we will allow him five minutes instead of three, so he can provide a rebuttal if that is okay with the candidates?" The moderator asked.

"That is fine with me," Torres said surprised at Adams, but thankful she had not mentioned him.

"By all means, take as much time as you need," Adams said.

Jeremy was used to the attacks—it came with the job. He looked at Monica who gave him thumbs up.

Monica thought he looked exceptional in the black pin striped suit with the crisp white shirt and the American power symbolic red tie. She knew he was ready.

"Good evening Harlem!" Collins yelled.

"Good evening," some mumbled back.

"No, you all can't hear me. I said, "Good evening Harlem!" He repeated.

"Good evening," they yelled back. Better he thought.

"Lasailla, I want to thank you for so graciously sharing that information on me which is also available through a simple Google search."

Some in the audience laughed.

"I would have hoped you would have taken your three minutes to discuss the Adams' agenda. The platform for your own campaign." So, let me clear up some things.

Let me start with my suits. They don't cost anywhere near $2,000. Ms. Emma from 140th street has been making my clothes since I was this high," he said has he put his hand near his knee.

"She is here somewhere tonight, I saw her," he said as Ms. Emma stood up and everyone clapped for the elderly woman with beautiful silver hair that flowed down her back.

Collins continued, "My suits may look like thousands, but that's because Ms. Emma has talented hands. I hope she never charges me $2,000. If she does, I will find a way to pay her because I support businesses in our community. I hope some of you will do the same." He looked out at the crowd and saw many were smiling.

"As for privilege. I was in a family that worked hard. My mother and father immigrated from good old South Carolina. I say immigrated because we live in the country of Harlem, as you can see from all the immigrants who are living here now from the country of the Midwest," he said laughing. Some joined in the joke with him, including some of the White people likely from the Midwest who were in attendance like Trent.

"My parents came up to Harlem after my dad graduated from Shaw University. Where are my HBCU folks tonight?" he asked.

"Heyyyy." Some yelled. *Those so-called parents came up here and became murderers.*

Jeremy paused to reroute back to his current thoughts and shake the vision of his old backyard. The nightmares still haunted him.

"You know years ago, there was a law—a hidden code if you will, that dictates in a battle, no women, no kids. They were valued, they were protected. Do any of you remember those days?"

"Sure do," some people yelled.

"Take us back to the old school," another yelled.

"Well, it's a lot like that in politics. Instead of discussing my record, or even my plans for our great community, Ms. Adams personally attacks me and my loved ones. I'm afraid that's not leadership. That's not even good manners Ms. Adams," he pointed out while looking over at her.

"She should be ashamed of herself," someone yelled out. Even Torres frowned.

"I have two children. Yes, I do. Jeremy, Jr who lives in California and my daughter Christina who was born with Down's Syndrome lives in Georgia."

Preying on their sympathy was his goal and if he had to use his children to do, so be it.

"Many of you do not know Christina was a twin. The other baby did not make it."

There were sad looks in the audience and parents clutched their children tight.

"Her mother's sacrifice has allowed me to stay in New York to continue to help the community that I have grown up in and love."

Adams looked uncomfortable. She was expecting an attack from Jeremy. Perhaps a slip of his tongue or some negative connotation about her sexual identity. Then she could label him homophobic.

Yet, his cunning ass had done the opposite, she thought as he shifted her feet.

"Yes, I have filed for bankruptcy. That is a fact."

Collins blamed the fiduciary mismanagement on his father's accountant, another senior in Jeremy's arsenal.

"I'm apologizing for Mr. James, many of you know as Pop James. He was our bookkeeper at Collins Realty, which provided housing to many families, including some of you who are here tonight."

Many in the audience nodded in agreement.

"Mr. James worked with my father a long time, but he told me he should have retired long ago, especially due to his health. You see because of his diabetes he had a hard time adjusting the financial records. I told him it was alright and for him to do his best," he said reeling them in with another lie.

"People have wondered why I sold our house and the business. Well it's because when the IRS says when you have to pay, well you pay." The audience laughed.

"I miss my father so much." He paused and put his head down as if he was sad to speak about his father. *Yeah, do you see this. Thanks for the clue. Is this how you did it?*

"Take your time, take your time," someone in the crowd yelled.

"We must support our own. We must keep our legacies alive. If Pop was good enough for my father, then he was good enough for me. Sometimes we all go through a rough patch financially and otherwise."

"I know that's right," someone yelled out.

"I've committed no crime, do not owe the government any taxes. My bankruptcy is a personal matter. During my first term we have managed the state's budget so well, this year our state has a surplus for the first time in a decade. In the past three years we have made some great strides in our district. Did you know we were able to get over 500 new units of senior housing built?"

"I got me one. Thank you, Jesus," an older woman shouted.

Adams looked like she wanted to disappear.

Collins took his introduction home like a veteran politician.

"Let us continue to work together toward four more years. And just like Senator Obama says, 'Be the change you want to see.' Let us put Harlem first. *I am* Senator Collins *always* at your service."

The crowd began chanting, "Collins, Collins, Collins."

They were so loud, the moderator had to wait a few minutes before he could introduce Hector Torres.

I'm not new to this, I'm true to this. Rollins left out one point. To win an election, you must also know the art of bullshitting people. Jeremy knew he excelled at it.

The next morning Collins' social media was ablaze with positive comments. Even the *New York Sun*, sometimes known for their divisiveness, referred to him as, *"A political veteran who had swept the floor in the last night's political debate."*

Jeremy won the primary with 51% of the vote and without a Republican opponent, it meant a guaranteed re-election. It was celebration time.

After the November election, his office issued a press statement. If he had his way, it would be his last as a Senator.

"I am honored to continue serving as a strong voice for Harlem. A community I support and believe in. I look forward to working another term on your behalf in the state legislature."

Jackie was appointed as his Chief of Staff and Trent officially became the Director of Constituent Services. His new assistant Katie Romano would arrive any day.

Just four more years to go.

CHAPTER 28

Twenty-seven-year-old Katie Romano sashayed her way down West 35th Street. In less than 10 minutes she would meet her real-life prince charming at the most romantic of all places—the Port Authority Bus Terminal.

When she had asked the prince to pay for a bus ticket for her, he seemed offended. She had underestimated his charm, and obviously his class.

"No girl of mines takes Greyhound," he said while insisting she allow him to send a private car to her New Jersey home.

"No, please do not spend that type of money on me. I'm right next door and the bus ride is only 90 minutes. She had lied and let him buy the ticket. That bus ticket went unused. Katie had just finished parking her Mercedes Benz in a midtown garage and was walking to beat him to the terminal.

At 5'10" her legs moved like a panther with her four-inch boots that not only boosted her height, but made her hips move like she was on fire. Katie ignored the cat calls from the men. Had it been summer instead of November, she would have worn a mini dress. Instead she settled for a long jean skirt and a top with a plunging neckline that followed the contours of her large boobs.

Her mother had warned her about indoor tanning.

"It's going to wrinkle you early and give you skin cancer," she said. Katie felt the risk was worth it as her bronzed skin gave the impression she had just returned from a place with a lot of sun. It matched her golden blonde hair that included a track of no. 18 Remy human hair she purposely flung side to side.

Yes, White girls wore hair extensions too, she would tell anyone without shame.

A UPS truck driver tried to say hello. Katie waved and smiled letting him see a set of pearly white teeth.

Her father always told her, "It doesn't cost a thing to smile. Be nice, it just may make someone's day." That smile had gotten her far.

There was only one thing on Katie's mind and that was to become the real-life girlfriend of her internet fling known as screenname: winkforyou740. When she learned he was Senator Jeremy Collins, she saw another way to live life on her own by letting a powerful man take care of her. So much for finishing college as her entire family had wanted her to do.

It had taken an entire year of her pretending to be interested in his life. A year of sucking him in through calculated live sex shows, mainly when he was alone and drunk in a hotel room or in his office.

When he had finally suggested she come to New York and join his staff, the sounds of casino slot machines began ringing in her head. Jackpot!

They say pimps work through mind control to program a woman to sell her body. Katie had used that cult-like strategy to her advantage mainly with married men like Collins.

With the internet, a woman could get into a man's mind before she ever physically met him. It created a physical desire for a woman that sometimes worked well. Katie had men paying her bills, and sending gifts, who she had never met offline. Collins had not sent any money, but he was big on sending her flowers and gifts for her online services.

He thought her screenname: vanillatrail meant she was from a trailer park and she had not corrected his assumption. "We have to get you out of that Jersey trailer park," he joked one day.

"What makes you think?" She stopped and caught herself. Sometimes men were so dumb. Even though he was some big Ivy league educated senator, Katie thought he was naïve as hell. Since he wanted to be her hero, she was ready to be rescued. Let him think she lived in a trailer park. That kept her in groceries for months.

Truthfully, she did not even know whether New Jersey had trailer parks and she certainly had never been to one.

The reality was she lived with her widowed mother, and her 21-year old brother in a 4,000-square foot home near the Jersey Shore in Colts Neck--home to such celebrities as Bruce Springsteen, Queen Latifah and football hall of famer Joe Klecko. Another brother lived in a house in the Bay Ridge section of Brooklyn.

It was time for her to level up to the life her parents had built for themselves. She could care less if he had three wives, she thought as she walked into the terminal.

Bill Wither's song *Lovely Day* played over the speakers. Jeremy tapped his fingers on the steering wheel. Yes, a lovely day indeed, he thought.

With his victorious win last week, the final peg was on a Greyhound bus. Finding the right woman for his plan had been easier than he had thought. The values of some women had plummeted faster than Blockbuster stock he thought as he drove to pick up Katie.

Men across the country should hold a conference on how easy it was to get a woman to do their bidding, especially a mistress, aka side chicks, he thought. Most were lucky these days if they got a Netflix and chill night.

Choosing Katie, a young hot and very eager 27-year-old from his online crew of women was genius, he thought. She was from another state and not a part of any of his circles. The fact that she was Caucasian would make the story she would need to tell of him sexually harassing her almost infallible.

The insurance company would pay, and everyone would keep it moving. Yes, he knew had a lot to lose, but the chance of obtaining $50 million dollars was worth it. He would act embarrassed, even humiliated, but that shame would quickly diminish as he sat on his yacht docked at some island cove sipping a fruity drink under the warm sun for the rest of his days.

The phone rang in his car. It was his son Junior. He was already 12 years old. Time had gone by fast.

"Hi dad," Jeremy noticed his son's voice was getting deeper.

"What say you? How's sunny California?"

"It's raining."

"It never rains in southern California someone once said in a song."

"Really? It must be old, because I've never heard of it."

"It's from the 90s?" Jeremy said. "Tony, Toni, Tone, the group."

"The 90s?" Junior answered. "Dad that was a really long time ago, but I'll look it up on YouTube, if they still have it."

Jeremy knew he was getting old, but these kids today thinking the 1990s was ancient was too much for him.

"Anyway dad, I gotta be quick. I'm calling to see if I can come to New York over the Thanksgiving break? Mom and Bob want to go on some camping trip, but I would rather be with you and super stepmom Monica. Can I come?" He asked speaking faster.

Junior was already 6 feet tall in the 7th grade. He was a formidable basketball player and Jeremy watched his videos with excitement. Maybe someday he would go pro.

"Don't you have any games over Thanksgiving?"

"Nope, the season doesn't start until December."

"Well, you know my answer is always yes, whenever you want to come east. It's up to your mother."

"She said to ask you."

"Then it's settled. I'll see you for Thanksgiving."

"Thanks dad, I have to get back to class. I'm sneaking."

Jeremy missed his son. Dana had remarried some writer named Bob and they were raising Junior in a gated community in Hidden Hills, a luxury suburb outside of Los Angeles.

Jeremy and Junior's father and son relationship was primarily taking place through social media, emails, phone calls and ten-hour round-trip flights. Jeremy felt he was watching his son grow up through pictures and characters of 140 or less.

Jeremy had not gotten around to telling Junior about his real heritage. He really did not know how.

"Junior! You know better than that. Get back to class. But I'm glad you called. I love you son."

"Love you too Dad. Bye."

That call prompted him to call and see how Christina was doing.

As usual, Sha did not answer. He was not even sure he had the correct number anymore.

The last time they had spoken, it was on a three-way call with Dana. He was trying to coordinate taking the kids to Disney World together.

"Listen they may have the same father, but they are not siblings," Dana said coldly.

"Fuck you bitch," Sha yelled and hung up.

So much for his kumbaya Lion King moment.

Jeremy pulled up and texted Katie.

As she walked out of the terminal, he was pleasantly surprised to see her dressed well. A woman's clothing usually dictated where he would take them out. Katie's outfit let him know it was okay to take her someplace classy.

He got out of the car and opened the door for her.

"Well, well, well," Katie said settling in the passenger's seat.

"Hello my gorgeous Jerzee girl," he said.

"Good to finally meet you sir."

"Sir? That makes me sound so old," he said smiling.

"Well, what should I call you?"

"Call me daddy," he said chuckling. "We know each other well enough. Well I feel like I know you. I've just never had the chance to touch you," he said as he rested his hand on her thigh.

"Daddy, it is," she said as she slouched trying to get his hand to the middle of her crotch.

He seductively smiled giving her the hope of sex. He had no plans to cheat on Monica with her. Their relationship would be strictly business.

"So where are we off to?" she asked watching the pedestrians walking fast. New Yorkers were always rushing somewhere she thought.

"Are you hungry?" he asked.

"Sure, let's get something to eat." *Spending money already, I like that.*

"How about Italian?" he asked.

"Hey, I'm Italian," she said smiling.

A few minutes later he pulled over and a valet opened her door and helped her out of the car.

"Welcome to Cipriani's," he said giving her a once over.

Expensive. He just got himself a blow job when we get back on the road.

"We'll start with a bottle of Antinori Guado al Tasso Superiore, two entrees of Rigatoni all Bolognese, and for dessert we'll have the crepes de la creme please," he said to the waiter handing him back both of their menus.

"Also, please bring me a glass of cherries."

"Excellent," he replied while he stared at Katie.

"Come here often?" Katie asked impressed.

"Only on special occasions like this," he said as he reached out for her hand on top of the table and she got lost in his eyes.

"Why the cherries?" she asked curiously.

"It makes any drink taste like magic," he answered. "Do you like magic?"

Before she could answer, they were interrupted by his phone buzzing. Collins then began a series of texts to someone.

During their meal, he stayed on the phone the whole time. His conversations bored her. When their food arrived, he disappeared for a few minutes. Katie thought about taking a Xanax she had in her pocketbook to relax her.

While she waited alone, she took advantage of the tables which were so close together she could hear the conversation of the middle-aged couple next to her. They were clearly tourists and were complaining about the menu prices.

"Thirteen dollars for an asparagus appetizer? I bet there are only four on the plate," the man dressed in a wrinkled shirt said.

"Why didn't you look this place up online first?" a woman who appeared to be his wife shot back.

The perils of married life, Katie thought. She was not anywhere ready for that. No, she thought she was a much better mistress than a wife.

When Collins returned, he ate his food quietly.

"Maybe I should text instead of us talking?" Katie asked sarcastically.

"What's the matter? You didn't enjoy your food," he asked looking at her half-eaten plate.

"No, it was fine," she replied as she played with her fork in her pasta.

"I'm not used to really talking while I eat. It's just the way I was raised," he paused as he remembered eating with his family. The children could only listen around the table, not talk. Sometimes he forgot you could have a conversation over a meal.

The Collins' had jacked him up.

"Plus, for some strange reason, I got busy," he said.

"You do know I'm a Senator, right? It is the middle of the workday. Don't take it personally," he smiled.

His smile got to Katie. She loved it and she loved the way he chewed. *The man is sexy I must give it to him. His wife is a lucky woman.*

"Well, that will be good to know as your new assistant. I want to thank you for hiring me. I really need the job," Katie remarked.

"Also, and I know this is a lot to ask, but my brother does all this law enforcement stuff. Right now, he's a correction officer at Riker's. Kevin Morrellio, have you heard of him?" She may has well try and get all she can get, she thought.

"No, can't say that I have."

"Well, he's been trying to get on the state police forever. When he found out I was going to be working for a big politician, I promised I would ask."

"Remind me later. And it's my pleasure to give you this job. But you know it's more than a job, right? I have a plan for us to become millionaires—that is if you are willing?"

"Millionaires? I'm all ears," she said grinning.

The waiter appeared with their dessert which had fire on top of a beautiful pudding.

"Wow!" Katie said. "I am going to enjoy this ride."

CHAPTER 29

Jeremy and Monica strolled down East Bay Street in Nassau enjoying a picture perfect sunny day in the Bahamas.

When Chad and Brooke invited them to spend a few weeks with them at their villa, it was right on time.

It was the perfect excuse for him to conveniently skip all the year-end holiday invitations.

Jeremy suddenly stopped.

"Come on, I need to go inside for a minute," he said. Monica looked up and saw they were standing in the front of the First National Bank of the Bahamas.

"Give me a minute," she said, as she held up her halfway finished Pina Colada.

"I'll be right back," he said.

Although they had been inseparable for most of the trip, she was sure he could use the ATM machine alone.

Monica glanced at the quaint street with buildings painted with bright tropical colors. Everyone seemed to have holiday cheer and were peaceful. Children in nice school uniforms were walking home. Older women were shopping with baskets instead of plastic bags. Men were sitting on makeshift tables playing dominos. The wonderful smell of conch, their native dish, stirred her appetite.

The drink was making her feel tipsy and the warm sunshine felt good on her skin. She stared at the view across the turquoise water to Casuarina Beach. It was spectacular.

I could get used to this life, she thought.

Jeremy returned and said, "All done."

"Come here you fine husband of mines," she said as they smiled for a selfie.

"Come on, I have something to tell you," Jeremy said excited as they walked hand in hand to the beach. He hoped she would agree to what he had to say.

"That is so sinister to the other woman," she said after hearing the details of his plan to fake a sexual discrimination scandal.

"Another woman who wants to sleep with your husband," he replied while putting down a blanket for them.

He had a point there, why should she care about some other's woman's feelings? She certainly was not thinking about hers from what she had heard. Nevertheless, Monica just felt some things women had to stick together on, especially a con by a man.

"Baby, this is not an innocent woman. She is plotting against not only you, but me as well."

"I understand but I just think," she managed to say before he interrupted.

"Do you think these sides chicks are in it for love?" He asked.

"I had no idea Jeremy; I've never messed with anyone's else's man. I always could get my own, so I don't know how they think."

"Some are in it for the sex. But most of them are opportunists. Vile women who want to break up marriages and hurt families," he bitterly said.

"Look at what Dana and Sha did to me."

"You weren't exactly innocent. It takes two to Tango," she responded.

Just then he grabbed her hands and started moving her to an imaginary Tango beat.

"Stop it silly," she said playfully as people walking by began encouraging the happy couple.

"All I'm saying is now it's my turn. Our turn to flip the script and use them," he said as they sat back down on the soft white sand.

"Let me get this straight. Did I walk door to door for months handing out flyers, making calls to voters and smiling at fundraisers so you can get in office just to pull off a con?" She said leaning into him.

He shook his head affirmatively.

"A con that you want me to agree to scam the government and possibly commit perjury?" She asked while staring out into the ocean. "Then on top of that give my approval for you to have sex with another woman, who by the way, will be taping the whole thing?" She said shaking her head.

"All of that so she can sue you for sexual harassment?"

"You got it," he said while applying some suntan lotion on his legs.

"Did I get it all right?"

"Pretty much," he said offering her the bottle of lotion.

"You know what, we are going to have to get the ION and ID channel dropped off our cable package. You're going bonkers."

He looked at her with the most serious face she had ever seen on him.

"I'm not joking. This is a real plan that I have been working on since you suggested I run for office," he said as he lifted his sunglasses and gave her a stern look.

"Life has fucked me over more than you even know. It's time to fuck back."

"You know you're taking an enormous risk here? You took an oath on the Bible. I remember it, because I was there right by your side," Monica said hoping he would change his mind. She had never intentionally broken the law in her life.

"Yes, I know all of that," he said growing impatient.

"Who is the woman?"

"Katie Romano," he answered.

"Katie, who you just hired as your assistant?" She asked.

"Yes."

"How old is she? She looks like a kid who just got out of college."

"Far from it, she's 27 and seasoned."

"Seasoned? Like when you are preparing chicken for dinner?" She said to lighten the mood.

"No. Like very mature for her age, seasoned."

"Have you been sleeping with her?"

"No. It's all fake," he said giving her a surprised look.

"Fake sex like in the movies. A couple of scenes, some dick texts and promises of a promotion in exchange for a blow job. Shit like that," he said.

"I can hear see you now on News 28 sounding like President Clinton, 'I did not have sex with that woman,' she said while still wondering if she really believed him.

"You're focused on the wrong things," he said.

"I'm talking about $50 million dollars. That's a lot of zeros. We can get out of New York. Maybe live in a place like this," he said moving his hands to emphasis the beauty of the island.

"What about Pet Castle? You know my business?"

"Baby, with that type of money, you can open up Pet Castles across the planet!"

"You know Jeremy the Bible states, 'Though one may be overpowered, two can defend themselves, but a cord of three strands is not quickly broken.' Be careful."

He ignored her Bible reference.

"Let's go take a swim. I need to cool off a little," she said while removing her coverup revealing her voluptuous body in a royal colored bathing suit.

With or without her, Jeremy knew he was moving forward he thought as he picked her up and carried her to the water.

CHAPTER 30

Jeremy placed his new monogrammed desk plate Monica had bought him on his desk and glanced around the office he had spent the last four years in. This time he had to make sure it always reflected what a busy person's office would look like.

Stacks of paper piled up on the desk, an empty cup, some pen, file folders with empty papers. His television always tuned to C-Span or the state's public access government channel.

Each morning Jackie would log on to his senate email to give the impression he was in his office while he was out doing whatever he wanted. He instructed her to be especially careful when responding to emails.

"Dance like no one is watching, email like it may one day be read aloud in a deposition," he read once online.

Katie would need to keep his schedule on track, especially from January through mid-June, when lawmakers had to spend most of their weekdays in Albany. He briefed her on a list of other important rules.

"The only calls I will answer, or immediately return, are from other elected officials. All press calls, office administration and personnel matters should go to Jackie, constituent matters to Trent, everything else you handle. Make my life around here easy," he said.

"I got it daddy," she said.

"Another thing don't call me daddy in the office or anytime we are working. Always remain professional and follow my lead. Speak when spoken to in public and watch my back."

He continued. "Make sure when we are out at events pictures are taken and they are immediately posted to my social media. Also, never respond to any posts."

Staff meetings were a necessary evil. Jeremy planned to conduct them twice a month alternating between his Harlem and Albany office.

Today was the first one of his new term.

Katie entered first bringing with her the scent of a floral fragrance. She looked professional and he liked her hair out. She wore a black suit with a light green collared turtleneck and high heel leather boots. It was an expensive suit, and it made him curious as to how she had such a great wardrobe. He had thought she was financially challenged.

"Good morning sir," Katie stood over his desk and gave him a salute. "Executive Assistant Katie Romano reporting for duty."

"Good morning Katie, have a seat over there." He said pointing to the conference table in his office. "We are waiting for the others."

Jackie Potter marched in in carrying four cups of coffee on a tray and a bag of sausage biscuits.

"Good morning all," she said dryly.

"All of the coffees are regular, but everyone can tell me what flavors they like. I'm a caffeine addict which reminds me, can we get a Kronos machine?"

"Whatever you need. Also, can you get a water dispenser while you're at it?" Jeremy asked before making introductions and watching her dig into her smelly swine sandwich.

"Jackie Potter, our new Chief of Staff, meet Katie Romano, my new executive assistant." Katie reached out and shook her hand and told her thanks for the coffee.

Jackie pretended to be pleasant when she said, "Nice to meet you too."

The coffee had been a rouse. Jackie was not happy his assistant was some college dropout from New Jersey. The position should have gone to a Harlem native, or at least a New Yorker. Someone like Imani, the journalism major from City College who had worked her ass off all summer setting up campaign stops and his appointments.

Trent entered breathing hard. He plopped down loudly in a chair. Jeremy looked at his watch and then at Trent.

"Good morning everyone, apologizes for my tardiness." Trent announced.

"Trent Liu is the head of constituent services. Trent, this is Jackie, the chief of staff and Katie, my executive assistant. Mr. Rollins who you all met at our last strategy meeting is onboard as a consultant. I'm also recruiting for a fundraising person soon."

"Welcome to Team Collins 2.0," he said grabbing a cup of coffee and taking a seat at the head of the table.

"You, along with all other staff, will report to Jackie who will report directly to me," he said before handing Jackie a file.

"Inside are resumes of the people I need you to hire for the Albany office. I have already interviewed and approved them, but their paperwork will need to be processed with human resources."

Jackie took the folder but was surprised the staff was already selected.

"Do I have the final say on their hires?" Jackie asked.

"They are already hired. I need you to meet and process them. I will do all the hires myself."

Jackie nodded to let him know she understood.

"Make sure you all share information with others on a need to know basis," he told them before going over their short agenda.

CHAPTER 31

Jeremy stared at himself in the mirror admiring the way his tailored tuxedo fit. His gaze was interrupted by the phone ringing over the surround sound speakers installed throughout the house. Answering the phone via Bluetooth from any room was still weird to him.

"Hello darling," Monica said. Hearing his wife's voice instantly put him in a good mood.

"Hello Mrs. Collins. Did you get your delivery today?" he asked while looking for a set of monogrammed cufflinks.

"Yes, the lilacs are beautiful. I'm looking at them now."

"Beautiful just like you," he said. "How are you feeling?"

"I'm a little tired. I've been to a ton of workshops today and it's hot as hell in Phoenix," she replied.

"It's 104 degrees," she said looking out the window at the scenic mountain terrain.

"Get some rest then," he replied.

"Hey, are you aware, there is no mention of a cat anywhere in the Bible? Or that hippos create their own sunscreen through the secretion of sweat glands located under their skins?"

"No, I did not," he said intrigued. He still had not gotten used to speaking hands free. It felt like he was talking to the ceiling.

"My wife the animal kingdom Wikipedia.

"Is the conference productive?"

"Yes, it really is. Every animal caretaker in the world is here, even those who run shelters," she said.

"I think I was an animal in my former life."

"Yeah, probably a cat, because I like the way you purr."

"Stop it. I am too far away for you to be getting all hot and bothered. I've already taken three showers today," she laughed.

"Hey baby, what could a man say to you that would make you believe he was going to leave his wife?"

"Are you trying to be funny?" She asked a little peeved he took away her fantasy thoughts.

"No," he said. "It's for the plan."

"Well, there is nothing better than I'm divorced or I've moved out."

"Well I can't say either of those."

"Should we even be having this conversation over the phone?" Monica asked.

"It's fine for us to talk. I'm asking for a friend. You remember Anthony? We met him at that thing in the Bronx?"

"Are you getting ready for tonight?" She said changing the subject.

"As a matter of fact, I am. I had just finished getting dressed when you called. You want me to Facetime you, so you can see how fine I look in this tux?"

"Dressed already? Wait, what time is it there?"

"It's after 6," he answered.

"I totally forgot about the time difference. And I would rather see you without the tuxedo on. How about later tonight when you get back?"

"Yes, we can play naked Facetime," he said.

"Later, I can't wait to see my sexy chocolate ice cream cake licorice wifey."

"And she can't wait to see you. All of you," she said seductively.

"No trouble tonight," she warned.

Monica was joking. She trusted Jeremy without reservation. They had an awesome sex life. She knew they left one another fully satisfied.

"Scouts honor, I promise. I miss you," he said. "I'll call you later."

"I will be waiting with bated breath sire," she said with an English accent.

"I love you," he said.

"I love you too," she responded.

Their fourth anniversary was just around the corner. She always talking about knocking England off her bucket list. Maybe he would surprise her with a trip to London.

**

Seventh months had passed since Jeremy had told Monica about the con. The less she knew the better she thought as she smelled an unfamiliar scent on one of his shirts.

Monica admitted the prospect of spending millions of dollars with Jeremy was intriguing. In lieu of children, they would travel the world without worrying about a bill for the rest of their lives.

The downside was she was growing impatient with the excessive number of pictures Jeremy took with Katie that were on his social media. None of his other staff appeared by his side as much. Were their alleged sex tapes fake or were they really having sex? When were they going to go public?

Whenever she asked him about it, he told her by the end of the year.

"After everyone returns from the holidays," he said. "It will be a slow time for the press, of course unless there is some breaking news. I've already prepared a statement. Trust me, I'm ready. Be patient."

CHAPTER 32

The Parksdale Annual Summer Benefit was the most sought after ticket in Westchester County. Each year, it raised millions of dollars for charity. Attendees were some of New York's most prominent friends of law enforcement in New York's most expensive zip codes outside of the city and Long Island.

Jeremy had attended each year since him and Dana lived in Parksdale.

Jeremy stepped out of the limousine at the entrance to the event cool, calm and collected. He glided up the steps leading inside the venue with an air of authority. People were mingling and staring at him. They knew he was someone important and he liked it.

Jeremy entered the main hall decorated in a Moroccan theme with vibrant colors. It reminded him that Morocco did not have an extradition treaty with America. That may come in handy soon, he thought.

He glanced around the room and estimated there were about 200 people in attendance. Some sitting around tables, a few dancing and others staring at belly dancers who were winding their hips much to everyone's delight. He turned around and saw a familiar face. This time he remembered her name.

"Hello Esquire," Jeremy whispered in her ear.

"Hey, you," she said pleasantly surprised.

"Elena Harris, Attorney," he said smiling.

"Actually, it's Harris-Davis now." She said as she showed off a big diamond wedding ring.

"It's been a long time," he said.

"Yes. What eight, nine years?" She asked.

"Well, what brings you here?"

"My husband works for the Parksdale Police. We're newlyweds. Tonight, is our two-month anniversary. I couldn't be happier," she said.

"Congratulations," he said.

"You know I've always imagined what would have happened if you called me," she giggled as usual. He looked at her and could not believe she still had a crush on him after all these years. Should I go for it? Her flirt game is live and direct, but he decided to be cool.

"I probably would not have found my wife," he said.

"Is she here?" She asked while looking around.

"No. She is away on business," he answered.

"She must be a real secure woman. There is no way I would let you out looking like that without me," she said as she looked at him from head to toe.

Jeremy smiled and wondered why she had been one of the few women he had wanted head from. Then it clicked. She had lips just like Carl, the ice cream licker.

"I'm sorry to hear about the loss of your father. He was a good man." *Great idea change the subject before I take your hot ass to some empty room.*

"Thank you, I really miss him," he said lying.

An Arab looking server approached them offering a drink from a silver tray.

"These look refreshing, what are they?" She questioned.

"Cold mint tea," the server answered giving Jeremy the eye probably thinking he was Middle Eastern.

"Mint tea is a tradition in Morocco, what a nice touch," she said.

"Yeah, this might work," Jeremy said as he took a glass off the tray and winked at the waiter. He frowned and said something in Arabic.

"Thank you," Elena said.

Jeremy looked at the floating mint in the glass and said I need something a lot stronger than this.

"This is America, we take the real hard stuff."

The server lost his balance and almost dropped the tray before walking off upset.

"Careful now," Jeremy said laughing not aware how close he was to getting knocked out for flirting with a Muslim man.

"Are you still practicing law?" Jeremy asked.

"Yes, I sure am," she said while glancing around the room.

"I miss the money in real estate, but I thought it was more important to focus on criminal matters. You know to help and thwart the pipeline to prison happening with our Black boys," she said as she waved over to a man dressed in full uniform standing across the room who joined them.

"Honey, I would like you to meet Senator Collins of Harlem. Senator this is my husband, Captain Timothy Davis."

"Nice to meet you Senator, just call me Tim," he said as he gave Jeremy a surprised look.

"Senator Collins of Harlem?" He repeated. "How interesting," He said as they shook hands.

Tim knew him as screenname Ithacamaverick. They were followers in the online sex group Men for Men. Tim had shared many long chats with the Senator.

Jeremy recognized him as well but played it off. *A cop? No wonder why he had a fetish about handcuffs and tying men up.*

"Nice to meet you as well," Jeremy said giving him a look of discretion.

"Harlem?" he repeated. "What do you think of the gentrification taking place there? I mean the displacement is such a huge issue, you must get calls all the time." He said thinking he was much taller than he imagined.

"Yes, we do get a lot of calls," Jeremy said not having a clue. "I think we, as Black people, have had ample time to take advantage of the real estate there. Some have made a pretty penny."

"Yes, but you must admit some are being displaced," he said while smiling at Elena.

"It's a heated issue and one thing is for sure it's not stopping anytime soon," he said feeling uncomfortable. He had never bumped into one of his male online friends before.

"That's true," Tim responded while Elena stood there holding onto his arm and sipping her drink. Jeremy did not know which one wanted him more, maybe both. Together.

"Elena and I are having a get together on the 28th at our house here in Parksdale. If would be great if you could come," Tim suggested while squeezing Jeremy's shoulder.

Elena stirred her drink with her finger and sucked off the liquid. She was likely imagining the three of them engaged in some sexual encounter as well.

"That sounds inviting, I'll give Elena a call," Jeremy said slightly licking his lips as he felt his little man rise a bit in his pants.

"If you will excuse me, I need to say hello to your chief before I miss the chance," he said. "Good meeting you Tim."

"Yes, let us let you go, we'll chat soon enough," he said confident he would take them up on their offer.

Jeremy went to find a restroom.

When he came out, he caught the eye of a woman wearing a bright red dress staring at him from the dance floor. His first thought? She was a mediocre call girl. They worked premier events all the time.

Her hideous blue eyeshadow which reached her eyebrows and fire red lipstick gave him the impression she was on the hunt for male company. Her mocha skin was too dark for such colors.

The inappropriate dress she wore screamed vixen, although Jeremy had to admit it blended in nicely with the event's

Moroccan theme. Most of the women had worn black dresses seeking to hide an extra pound or two.

One thing was for sure she had the attention of the men who were staring at her like a piece of raw meat they wanted to devour. She was brown skinned, average height but had a body like a porn star. Jeremy wasn't yet sure if it was her natural body or bought. Like the Commodores sang, "She was mighty, mighty and letting it all hang out." If she wasn't a hooker, she probably could make a good living in the sex industry, he thought as he walked to the bar, never taking his eyes off her.

Her hips swayed unapologetically to the music and her long black curly hair shined under the dim lights from the dance floor. Jeremy was engaged with her as if he was a horny teen watching a porno movie for the first time. He pictured her crawling for him.

Jeremy wasn't sure if whether she knew there were hordes of men watching. She certainly was enjoying herself and so was her dance partner who was happily partaking in his own version of dirty dancing.

Her demeanor was unbothered. Or perhaps she was just being coy, Jeremy thought. Pretend we are not all looking at your ass shake.

"Senator, I see you made it. Good to see you," declared Chief Polowski, as he greeted Jeremy at the bar.

"You know I still think about that fabulous lasagna Monica made the last time we were over for dinner," he said as he rubbed his pot belly.

"Yes, I know she puts love in every meal. And Claire?" Jeremy asked.

"Still the same ole Claire. Married for 27 years and she still can't boil water. But I didn't marry her for her kitchen skills, if you know what I mean?" He laughed.

A photographer came over and they posed for a few official photos.

"Listen," the chief leaned in and whispered after the photographer finished.

"I've been asking the state police Chief O'Ryan if Parksdale could get a few extra state police cars that are out for pasture. Our budget is short this year, so we can't get any cars without a little help," he said while sticking an olive in his mouth from the martini he was holding.

"He's been a real prick about it. I was hoping you could have a conversation with him, nudge him a little," he said as he handed Jeremy a thick envelope. Jeremy knew there was cash inside and quickly put it his jacket pocket.

"Sure, thing Chief. That's easy," Jeremy said. "How many cars do you need?"

"Three, four, if we can get them," Polowski answered.

"I'll set something up. I'll have my assistant call your office next week."

"Much obliged Senator," he said pretending to have a southern accent.

"Enjoy your night. Give my regards to Monica."

With the mention of Monica's name, Jeremy felt it was the perfect time to send a random text to his wife.

"I love you," he typed. In less than a minute, she texted back, "I love you more ♥."

Jeremy smiled and looked around at all the couples. He missed Monica and was getting bored. He looked for the red dress woman, but she was gone. Probably off somewhere with her husband after their dance he thought.

He decided to go and check out the veranda which overlooked the Hudson River. He had missed living in Westchester, it much more peaceful than the loud city.

To his pleasant surprise, Miss red dress came out shortly afterwards. He smelled her scent even before she walked up next to him. She smelled like honey.

"Are you making a wish?" She asked.

"I don't believe in wishes," he said.

"Is that right?" She said glancing at his wedding band.

"Are you here with someone?" she asked while holding out her hand. "I'm Amber Williams."

"Nice to meet you Amber. I'm Jeremy and I'm solo tonight." He could have a conversation with a woman without anything happening, or so he thought.

"I see you have one too," she said as she pointed to her wedding ring.

"Yeah, I'm on lockdown," he said. "Most days," he added which made her smile.

Jeremy turned to look over the terrace instead of facing her because she was overly displaying a set of huge breasts. He really did not like women who advertised so freely in his face. He thought they were trying too hard.

"What brings you here tonight?" Amber asked.

"Just a night out on the town. It's always a great event. I've been supporting them for years," he said wondering where her husband was.

"I'm here with my cousin, Officer Smith. The one over there." She pointed to a guy sitting on a chair stuffing his face with some cocktail shrimp.

What a pig, Jeremy thought. Can't take some folks nowhere.

"I must say you look very nice in that tux."

"Are you flirting with me?" He asked. "Where did your husband go?"

"That wasn't my husband. He was just some man who wanted to get his dance on," she said.

"Thanks. You don't look too bad yourself," he said nonchalantly. Although, I'm curious why you chose to wear red?" He asked thinking about how loose she danced with a stranger.

"Thanks," she said looking down at her dress which still had the store tag inside.

"Red? Because I'm the devil."

"I'm definitely not a stranger to the devil, but I could have sworn he was a man," he said laughing.

"You're not a man, are you?" He asked although it would not have made a difference to him.

"All woman," she said smiling and poking out her two cantaloupe sized breasts even more for effect.

"What does the devil do as a profession, besides try and rule the world?" He asked.

"She is a social worker."

"That's interesting," he said. "For who if I may ask?"

"Well, I was just laid off from the state university."

"That sucks. Sorry to hear that," He said.

"Yes, just shy of 20 years. Eleven more months and I could have retired still young enough to start a second career. Then budget cuts from our great elected officials in Albany, and boom, I may lose a large portion of my retirement. Got me worried about whether I'll have enough money for my son to attend college soon.

"What are you doing now?"

"Just taking some me time, meeting with attorneys about the job situation and figuring out next steps for my life. I'll be 40 soon," she said.

"And you, what do you do handsome?" Wait let me guess, you're a cop?" She asked looking down at her empty glass as if she was wondering how that happened.

"Not a cop. I'm one of those great elected officials in Albany. Senator Jeremy Collins at your service," he said smiling.

I know exactly who you are. My new meal ticket.

"I know the name. Were you one of the ones who voted on the cuts?" Amber said while thinking about Laz Alonzo from CSI Miami, the actor who he favored.

"I can't say I remember that vote, but I promise to see if I can be of assistance." *Now my little head is talking. She did not ask for your help.*

Yeah, you can offer me some assistance right here and right now, she thought.

"Would you like to dance?" she asked him. "But let's get another drink first."

Jeremy was surprised. Not even his wife had ever asked him to dance. These 30-something women were different. They were bolder. Madam Ernestine would have said she was being whorish.

"Sure, why not," he said as they walked to the bar and he ordered their drinks which they sipped and had the usual, "I just met you," preliminary conversation.

"Let's dance," she requested.

As soon as they hit the dance floor, the music suddenly changed to the waltz. *Of all things he thought.*

He pulled her close and smelled her weave glue mixed with perspiration and alcohol. An odd smell he thought.

They both chuckled as she stumbled a little in her red four-inch heels.

"I'm sorry this is my first waltz," she said looking at other couples moving in perfect coordination.

"It's okay just follow along with me. It's a really an easy dance. Just count 1-2-3, 1-2-3. Just move like you're making a square with your feet 1-2-3," he said before the music changed to the instrumental of Stevie Wonder's *Sir Duke*.

"Now this is more like it," she said.

"I see you girl," he said as he eyed her large ass, she kept backing up on him. He copped a feel. *Damn it's soft...and real.*

When the song ended, Jeremy whispered into her ear, making sure his lips barely touched her earlobe. She felt his saliva drop on her neck and it sent a tingle throughout her body.

"Would you like another drink?" he asked thinking they had a strange chemistry.

"Now that I can do," she said thankful she had a pantyliner on or her panties would have been soaked.

Jeremy summoned the bartender, "Whatever the lady wants."

"A honey Jack Daniels on the rocks." From what he gathered this was at least her third one.

"Such a strong drink for a lady," Jeremy remarked as he asked for a scotch on the rocks.

"It's the drink you need when two people who are married to others, who aren't here, get a drink a together," she said smiling.

"Touché," he said, while thinking it was time for him to circle the room because of the stares. He did not want anyone to think she was his date. You never knew who knew who.

"Well enjoy your drink, I'm going to go walk around and check out the silent auction. See if I can pay $1,000 for a saved peppermint from Michael Jackson or something."

"That's funny. Maybe another dance later?"

"Sure," he said as he walked away.

Amber watched him the whole night. He could see her out the corner of his eye. Sometimes they would smile at each other. Others, he would just send a wink.

They became familiar strangers.

At about 10 pm, Jeremy walked over to her with the intent of saying good night and giving her his card. He wanted to help her. Or at least that's what he told himself.

"Leaving so soon? I was saving the last dance for you," she said holding out her hand where Jeremy noticed her large biceps which were like a bodybuilder. There was something real masculine about her physical physique he thought.

"A politician should never be the last person to leave an event," he told her.

"Why is that?"

"Someone may want to come home with me."

"Is that so," she said eyeing him curiously.

"I'm kidding," he said. "I'm leaving because I'm a little tired." The truth of the matter was he had to get home for his nightly chat with Monica.

"Can I have your number?" She asked. "I want to follow up about my employment situation."

He handed her a card.

She sucked her teeth.

"Really? A card? Hand me your phone."

He briefly hesitated before handing it over. He looked down and saw she put her number under the name Alvin.

"Another man's name?" he said while checking for an Adam's apple on her neck.

"No, I just don't want to get any calls from wifey."

"That's a bit presumptuous," he said. "Besides my wife would never do such a thing," he responded confidently. Neither him nor Monica ever went through each other's things.

"That's what they all say. From now on I'm Alvin," she said boldly.

Her body, along with that challenging attitude, made him think about taking her back to his waiting limo. *No, be a good boy, you promised Monica.*

"Alright Alvin don't stay out too late," he said before walking away.

"I won't. I look forward to hearing from you Senator."

In his limo, he counted out $10,000 in tax-free money. It was like taking candy from a baby.

An hour after arriving home, Jeremy spoke to Monica. Their conversation was so steamy he had to take a cold shower. He was now sitting in the middle of their bed with a towel wrapped around him staring at Amber's number.

Reviewing the night's events made him smile.

He went into the guest bedroom, so he could keep one of his wedding rules to Monica—*never have another woman in our bedroom*. He figured that meant on the phone as well, he thought as he hit the call button.

"Home safe?" he asked Ms. Alvin when she answered.

"Yes, I am," she said surprised.

"Unfortunately, I can't really talk now because I am home. If you know what I mean."

"What do you have on?" He asked ignoring her.

"I wish I could tell you that right now," she said as she heard her husband Richard turning off the house alarm.

"I was hoping you would tell me some of your fantasies?" He said disappointed.

"Can I have a raincheck?" She asked speaking faster.

"Yes, you may," he said. It was kind of funny that she was getting nervous, but she had not hung up yet.

"How about dinner tomorrow?" Jeremy asked.

"Text me an address and I'll send a car."

"Yes, okay. I really have to go," she said.

"Good night," Jeremy said.

Although she knew she had him at hello, Amber had not expected him to call so soon. She liked him already. He was tall, smart and she pictured him spending his free time in a cabin somewhere reading Shakespeare.

She did a quick google search and stared at his wife's picture.

A doctor. Well a doctor for animals. Does that really count? She asked herself. He was probably only with her for her money.

She was decent looking, but older. She looked about 50 or so. Jeremy must be tired of her old ass, Amber thought.

Poor woman. She doesn't even know what's about to hit her, she thought as she heard her husband say, "Amber are you here? I'm home."

CHAPTER 33

Thursday night NFL games on television proved to be a genius move for men across America. Men who needed something else to do while their wives were busy.

How did they spell relief? A-B-C, as in the network their women were tuned to waiting to find out what America's #1 side chick was up to next on *Scandal*. Some men wanted to personally thank the show's creator, Shonda Rimes, for giving mistresses hope.

When Congressman Milton had convinced the Rockville Country Club to open a clubhouse on Thursdays, almost every elected official from Staten Island to Throgs Neck did not hesitate to pay the extra dues. Now there was a waiting list.

Women ready to please, showed off their sexiest outfits with perfectly manicured hands and feet. They would brag to all their friends how they were going on a date to one of the most elite places in the metro area for cocktails and dining. They would conveniently leave out the part it was with someone's else's man.

"We never bring our wives here. This our own private place." The legislators would lie to the women, some of whom they called bimbos.

Queens Assemblyman Ben Haslip was in a jacuzzi with a woman with a skimpy bathing suit and a big smile.

"Ain't life grand? What's the point in having power if you can't reap the benefits?" He asked Jeremy who gave him a thumb up confirmation.

Jeremy decided it would be the perfect place to bring Amber.

"My wife was a damn good girlfriend, but she makes a lousy wife," Jeremy said lying as they casually strolled around the club's beautifully manicured grounds on their way to the clubhouse.

"I didn't mean to pry, it's just that I was wondering why you are out here with another woman?" She asked while thinking she should have worn something dressier rather than the simple white skirt and sandals she had on. All the women were dressed up. Even Jeremy had on a suit. She would not make the same mistake twice.

"Don't misread this. We're just having dinner which I do with women all the time," he said.

"Excuse me, but you know you're lying," she chuckled.

"This looks like a date to me. You know we had chemistry last night. I bet you thought about me all night," she said as she started skipping.

"Well, let me ask you something," he said. "What make a woman cheat on her husband?"

"Ha! Who is cheating? I'm just going to dinner?"

"Sure, you're right," he retorted.

"Well I can't speak for all women. I've been married for twelve years. My husband bores me, and he sucks in bed. We haven't had sex since New Year's Eve. I'm sure he is doing his thing somewhere," she said. "They say a man can't go without sex for more than five days," she laughed.

Damn, she was cold. No loyalty either. He knew she was likely telling the truth because unlike men who can fake an entire relationship, rarely do you meet a woman who can fake her heart. By the time she was ready for another man, it was likely over. Or maybe she wanted a side man--a concept it seemed younger men were caught up in.

Let's see how far she wants to go, he thought.

"So, what kind of man do you like in bed?"

She giggled and acted bashful. Then stepped into him, tiptoed and put her hot lips and tongue in his mouth. She then put her hand between Jeremy's crotch and whispered, "This kind."

He was surprised to smell and taste alcohol from her mouth, but she tasted good nevertheless. *She likes to drink. Maybe too much?*

He pulled her closer, put his arm around her and kissed her passionately.

"Let's get out of here," he said.

"But we haven't even had dinner," she said.

"We'll order room service. Or am I moving too fast?"

"No, you're fine, I'm ready. Told you it was a date."

By the time they walked into the room at the Rockville Marriott they acted like hungry dogs in heat.

They had aggressive sex with an unbridled passion. It was rough. It was vigorous. They fucked hard as if they both had just been released from a long prison sentence.

Amber felt it was the best sex she had ever had.

Jeremy was delighted she had not only let him fuck her in her ass, but she let him choke her into an orgasm.

She was a keeper for sure, he thought as he stared at her walking naked to the bathroom.

"Can you get us something to eat and a bottle of honey Jack?" She asked sweetly.

Her and this drinking. It was her liver, he thought as he picked up the phone to call room service.

CHAPTER 34

Amber was excited. It was time to introduce Jeremy to her friend and mentor Lauren Harrison. She called her to spill the tea.

"Good morning. Time to rise and shine," she loudly said over the phone.

"Good morning," Lauren said half asleep looking at the clock to see it was only 7:30 am.

"What are you doing tonight?" Amber asked.

"I was planning to go to see the new movie with the actress A'Shey. I'm trying to figure out what lucky man will have the honor," Lauren said sitting up trying to remember whether she had programmed the coffee maker last night.

"I saw it last week, it was good. I won't give it away, but she rocked it. I hear she may be up for an award already. I thought it was cool they featured Kid Cudi as her boyfriend. He was good. An actor and a singer, double jeopardy.

Good ole Amber. If Lauren had on a new sweater, Amber had the same one at home she would say. If Lauren wanted to go see a movie, of course she had already seen it. Lauren wondered, "If I jump off a bridge are you coming too?" It was annoying, but Lauren knew everyone had a pet peeve. True friends ignored them.

"Must be nice to sleep all day. I had to clock into a plantation for twenty years. I get up at the crack of dawn," she said.

"Yes, but remember when you are asleep by 11, I'm up working. I just went to sleep about five a.m. Anyway, what's up?"

"This guy I've been seeing is taking us out tonight for drinks at Rico's. I want you to come. How's 8 pm?"

"This guy?" Lauren asked.

"Just come I want you to meet him. I've been seeing him for about nine months," she requested before sharing details about his life and their relationship.

"I think he is the one, and you know your opinion matters."

"He's the one for what?"

"To be my next husband, my next baby daddy. The forever man," she said with laughter.

Another one, Lauren thought. She was the ficklest person she had ever met. Now this new one was a politician. Last week they had just been out with two other guys they had met at a bar. Less than a week later, she was spending the night with him in the same house, the same bed he shared with his wife. Yet, she had a new guy?

Lauren could not understand it. Amber had come to her crying when she found out her own husband may have been cheating on her. A husband who was seemingly a good man who owned several Caribbean style restaurants in Brooklyn and Manhattan.

A single father, he had allowed her and her son to move in with him and his own son. It helped get her out of the subsidized small apartment she shared with her two sisters and their children in the Bronx. Lauren had given the man credit for doing that type of thing.

The reason Amber had men on the side was beyond her comprehension, but judge not, lest ye be judged was her motto.

"Alright, text me the location," Lauren said.

"Okay, I'll see you later."

Lauren hung up and went back to sleep.

**

Rico's was a dump on the Lower East Side. It was in a neighborhood where some streets were modern, others ghetto.

Rico's happened to be on the side with cheap real estate. Lauren turned up her nose and her attitude that some guy brought her friend here for anything as she watched a rat eating garbage at the curb.

Lauren regretted going inside as soon as she walked through the door. She had a funny feeling in her gut. She quickly scanned the narrow establishment taking note of where the emergency exit was.

Lauren figured out looking at the couples off in dark corners, Rico's was the place people came to hide. The chairs at the bar were filled with a mixture of bikers and women with tattoos wearing black lipstick and nose rings. The bartender served beer from the tap and nachos with artificial cheese. Lauren felt out of place.

Lauren joined Amber and her friend, who were sitting at a table too far away from the door as far as she was concerned. Her first thought, although he was handsome, was that he was too old for her. He was already going gray. Her second thought, as she stared at an old version of a Yankee baseball cap down low on his head, was that he was trying to disguise himself.

"Greetings and salutations," Lauren said while pulling out a chair to sit. Amber's friend had not even bothered to stand. What a gentleman, Lauren thought.

Amber was all smiles as she introduced them.

"Jeremy, I would like you to meet my good friend and mentor Lauren."

"How are you doing?" He said dryly as if it hurt him to speak. Was he high? Or maybe tipsy? Lauren questioned.

"Lauren meet Jeremy. I mean Senator Collins," Amber said smiling.

"I know your work for veterans. It's nice to meet you." May as well be cordial, she guessed.

"What are you drinking?" Amber asked as she put her hand up to get the attention of a waitress.

"You know me the usual. Margarita please, no salt," Lauren said to the waitress debating whether she would bring any glass to her mouth from that place.

"Make hers a double with Patron," Amber said while looking at Lauren for confirmation. Lauren nodded.

Lauren noticed Collin's wedding band. *Wait, two married people out on a date? This was different.*

"I like your hair chicka and your bangs look great," Lauren said. Amber always wore weaves. Long curly weaves. Lauren called them "hair hats." Amber's $900 monthly investment on her hair was excessive to Lauren.

"Not all of us have good hair like you," she told Lauren one day referencing her mixture of Caribbean, African and southern hair roots.

"Almost a $1,000 a month?" Lauren said. "You don't need all that to look pretty."

"Yeah, it's a G, but errbody know it ain't trickin' if ya got it," she said sounding like her favorite Hip-Hop artist T.I., while swirling her head side to side showing off all 24 inches.

They laughed together but Lauren knew all that hair was a part of a low self-esteem issue.

At Rico's the three of them talked about the weather, politics and Harlem where Lauren grew up.

"Come with me to the ladies' room," Amber requested.

"Why do women always have to go to the bathroom in twos?" Collins joked.

"Because we go to talk about men," Amber said laughing. "Come on girl."

"What are you doing?" Lauren asked as soon as they got through the door and the smell of stale urine hit her face.

"Look at this place, it's disgusting."

Amber looked under the stalls before she spoke.

"It's not so bad," she said.

"Make sure you don't touch anything in there," Lauren said while looking at the smudge filled mirrors.

"Do you like him?" Amber asked as the toilet flushed.

"He's alright. A little cocky, but he is cute," Lauren said while Amber washed her hands.

"I'm in love," Amber said.

"I can see that," Lauren said. "He is married and let me remind you, you're very much married too?" Lauren said as she decided to wash her hands for the hell of it.

"I'm tired of Richard. He doesn't do anything for me anymore," she said while checking herself out in the mirror.

"Beside we won't be married to those others for long. I'm going to be a Senator's wife," she said smiling as if she had already picked out the color of her bridesmaid's dresses.

"Why don't you try and work on your marriage?" Lauren said knowing her and Richard had been having problems. What marriage didn't. Surely another man was not the answer.

"Well, Richard wants to go to marriage counseling. Meanwhile, I'm living my life," she said while freshening up her makeup.

"I'm hashtag #TeamRichard for life," Lauren said as she shrugged. "And don't talk to that man about your husband."

"Too late! Besides, he tells me about his wife all the time. I'm also getting ready to start working for him as his assistant. I've also convinced him to hire you as a consultant to help with his fundraising," she said as if Lauren was hired on the spot.

"Really?" Lauren said surprised.

"I know you need the money, so act like you don't," she said. "Tonight, is kind of like your informal interview. We're talking serious money."

"How much? I don't know how much do you want? Anyway, you two can talk about that later. Be nice to him please," she said with glee. "It will give us a chance to work together again."

Years earlier, Lauren had given Amber her first job out of college. Amber at the time was a struggling single mother, on welfare and living in an overcrowded house with little privacy. A job which propelled her career. She urged her to continue her education and become a social worker. She considered her more of a little sister than a friend or mentor.

This job offer was her way of saying thanks, Lauren believed. It was a nice gesture, but Lauren really did not need the position. Amber had no idea Lauren's family had wealth. They had Black privilege since slavery although Lauren was not exactly proud of how they got and kept it. She guessed it would not hurt to take an offer to make a few extra bucks working for a politician.

When they arrived back to their table, a pitcher of margaritas awaited them. Lauren saw Amber wink at Collins who nodded his head.

"Lauren what do you do?" Collins asked. She explained she was a fundraiser and had worked on several campaigns raising money.

"Well, Amber has spoken very highly of you," he said putting his arm around her and pulling her closer to him. I'm looking for someone like you to join my team. Trust me, if you're good, I'll have every elected official in New York beating down your door."

Politician talk 101, Lauren thought.

"We can talk more about it during business hours. That's if you're interested," he said as he looked up at the television screen.

Lauren looked at Amber. She nudged her on.

"Let me know what you need," Lauren said.

"Send me a written fundraising plan and your resume. Here's my card with my email. Send it and we will go from there. Let's say next week?"

"Sounds like a plan," Lauren said not trusting a word he said.

Amber thought that worked out perfectly. No one turns down money. Lauren was her friend, but she would need a spy to give her intel when she was not able to be in the office. She needed to know everything she could about Jeremy. Lauren would also serve as a decoy so when the three of them were out together, like tonight, no one would suspect he was on a date with her.

Jeremy knew he was giving Amber a gift--a favor. He was looking forward to repayment later while she was naked.

That night, Lauren called Amber.

"What have you gotten me into?" She asked. "I'm not sure I like your boy toy. There is something about his spirit. Also, he has shifty eyes."

"Look let's get the paper from him. He got it, so let's get it," Amber said. "He's my three F man.

"What are the three Fs?"

"Food, fucking, and financial. In that order," she said. "But I promise you, the fucking part, leaves much to be desired. He's not all that," she laughed. "He is old."

Lauren had known Amber for a long time. She knew she was always trying to level up. It probably was the only reason she hung out with Lauren in the first place. In life, there was always an opportunist lurking that you had to feed them with a long-handed spoon.

Amber grew up poor in the South Bronx. Her extended family were from some town in West Virginia.

Her mother was raising three children by three different men by the time she was 30.

When she moved to New York, she found a man with a job as a city bus driver. At the time she was on public assistance and struggling to make ends meet. When he asked to marry her, she was happy to say goodbye to public support.

That man was willing to be a husband and a father to the child they had shortly afterwards, but he let know he was not signing on to be a stepfather.

"I'm not taking care of children by other men. If you don't want to be with me that's fine." He had made clear from the start and her mother chose him over her children.

"Listen this job is my way of saying thank you for helping me," Amber said. "I never told you this before, but my mother and my stepfather abused us. I mean while they ate good, me and my two brothers had to eat things like eggs with rice for dinner, if we even got to eat," Amber said sadly.

"I never want to know what it feels like to ever be hungry again," Amber said. "My mother hated us. When I turned 18, she put me out," she continued.

"Where was your father?" Lauren asked.

"Somewhere else with his wife and their children."

Were it not for a guidance counselor at school who got me into college and campus housing, I probably would have been homeless," she said. "That's why after college, I will always be grateful to you for giving me a job. With it, I finished graduate school and never looked back."

"That's must have been hard on you, but you know what?" Lauren said.

"What?"

"You survived," Lauren said. "Besides, for some, the best thing about a bad childhood when you grow up is that it's over."

"That's good. I like it," Amber replied.

"The 3 Fs homie," remember that."

CHAPTER 35

Senator Collins gave Lauren a $50,000 six-month contract. Cheap, considering he wanted her to raise a million dollars.

After two months on board, Amber had still not started working in the office.

Each day, she would check with Lauren to get her daily dose of information as if she had the questions already pre-planned.

Lauren fell for it and innocently answered any questions Amber asked. Mainly, her questions were about Katie. "Was Katie in his office twenty minutes ago? I just called and he's not answering," was something she always wanted to know.

Lauren loathed her time in his dysfunctional office. People hung out there wasting the day. Constituents were treated poorly. Lauren thought his chief of staff Jackie was sneaky and acted like had been elected to the seat. His assistant Katie was just plain rude.

Lauren found it difficult to even have a meeting with Collins who barely came in. When he did arrive, he would be in his office with his staff or in meetings with external parties for hours.

"I hope you are using condoms with him," Lauren said one night on a call with Amber who relayed the two of them had just returned from New Orleans.

"Yeah," she said unconvincingly knowing she was trying to get pregnant on purpose.

"Do you think he is messing with Katie, his assistant?" She asked.

"Maybe, I don't know. I rarely see him, but she does walk around there acting like she is his wife." Lauren debated whether to tell her how much time they were spending together. Or even the way they stared at one another when they thought no one was looking.

"While we were in NOLA, she was blowing up his phone," she said sounding pissed off. "She is the one who made the travel arrangements and booked some garbage hotel."

"Like the garbage bar I met him in?" Lauren asked.
"Are you sure it wasn't him?"

"No, he was embarrassed," she said. "We left, and he took me to another hotel."

"You think she did it on purpose?"

"Yeah, she did it. Fuckin'' bitch. She probably is around there sucking his dick. You know that's something he won't let me to do," she said.

How interesting Lauren thought. What man does not want a woman to give him head?

"Just call her the swallower," Lauren joked.

"I find that weird as fuck," she said. "Yeah, she probably is the headmaster."

They laughed.

"It's time for her to find another job. I've been trying to start. For some reason he will not fire her, so I can get her position," she said.

"You know Trent is gay right?" Lauren threw that out there letting her friend make her own justification about who the real headmaster was.

"Who is Trent?" She asked.

"The White guy. The head of constituent services. He's a cool dude though. I think he's from Dayton, Ohio. I can't believe all the times you've been in that office; you've never seen Trent? His office is in the back near the storage closet."

"I know the office, but no I've never seen him there. I've seen pictures online."

"That's interesting. I hope you are using condoms," Lauren repeated.

"In other matters," Amber said changing the subject. "Don't forget we will be out of here soon. By the time we get back from Turks & Caicos, she had better be gone," she said.

"Are you ready for our trip?"

"Sure am, a few days out of New York will do me good."

Lauren could not believe how naïve Amber was. The man was married. She was married. But she was more worried about who and what he was doing with another woman. How are you jealous of a relationship another woman's husband is having? Lauren wanted to ask her so badly.

CHAPTER 36

M onica encouraged Jeremy to grow a beard. She said it made him look more mature and dignified. Although he was not happy about all the gray that sprung up on his face, he loved the way it kept her scent on him throughout the day.

When her soft hands played with the hairs, he felt loved and cared for. Monica always took such good care of him.

This Sunday morning, they were spending it in bed. Sunday was their time. Sometimes they attended church, sometimes they took a long drive through New York's scenic upstate countryside. Monica always had something planned. They would turn off their phones for hours to escape into one another.

Today, Monica had hired a personal chef to come and cook them a buffet breakfast. Jeremy awoke to the smell of steak and eggs drifting through the house. Gospel music played over the speakers that he quickly changed to smooth jazz.

They dined outside in their small backyard with fresh air and nothing but smiles for one another. They caught up about one another's week and what was planned for the next.

After breakfast, Monica prepared them a warm bath filled with eucalyptus oil. They bathed sipping on Mimosas and tenderly washed one another.

Jeremy enjoyed sexual encounters, but he always knew the best acts of love he had always were with his wife. It was just something different.

Now they were lounging in bed and watching the Sunday morning political shows. When he saw his face on the screen, he turned up the volume.

One of the panelists, Brian Garcia, the chief correspondence for the *Political Times* relayed, "This will likely be the last time a Black person will be a senator representing Harlem. Senator Collins is finishing his second year out of four. Term limits prevent him from running again."

"That's true," conservative pundit Alan Shaffer agreed. "I'm not sure anyone is on deck yet, but Whites are moving into Harlem in record numbers. I suspect someone will be stepping up soon. I just hope it's from the GOP," he remarked.

"What a cocky asshole," Jeremy yelled.

The only female panelist, Melissa Garbing, added, "Don't be so sure. Remember Lasailla Adams was a formidable candidate against him in 2008. She's smart, progressive and has been helping residents in Harlem for a long time. It's time for a woman Senator. I think we are going to be surprised in a few years."

Jeremy switched off the television. *Well, for sure, I won't be there.*

"Wow! They are already talking about your replacement. That's crazy," Monica said.

"Yeah, well they can have it. Two more years to go baby, just two more."

Any thoughts about the con she had were immediately erased as he started kissing her, enticing her for round four.

For the first time in his life, Jeremy was intimate with a woman who had taught him how to make slow passionate love instead of just getting a quick nut which is what he did with Amber. Him and Amber's relationship was like the old chocolate candy commercial jingle. "Sometimes you feel like a nut, sometimes you don't."

With Monica he used his tongue as a sexual organ to please her. Sexually, he lived to please her.

"You will call me Madam Ernestine. Never mom, mommy or mother, she said while she placed her hands in his pants. She would rub him softly at first before getting vigorously harder.

Come to Mama Ernestine she would say.

The glass was always cold. Always with a cherry in it. Here drink this. Her special drink for him.

Then he would get drowsy, but he was still awake. He could not speak or move his body.

She would get on top of his penis and move up and down like she was in a trance. She moved fast until wetness would come out. Liquid that was not urine. Then she would get off him and make him leave.

Jeremy knew he was a sexual deviant.

Sadly, he knew why.

CHAPTER 37

Lauren grew tired of hearing about Amber's sordid love affairs. It just wasn't right. None of it.

Amber was her friend, and she cared about her, but everyone is judged by the company they keep. Her and Jeremy were taking the phrase "politics makes strange bedfellows" to an entire other level.

Lauren was planning her exit from working with him and the daily conversations surrounding Amber's love life. Lauren did not want to ruin her own reputation and was tired of being used by a man she thought was as phony as canned vegetables. They looked real but tasted like plastic.

"Did Jeremy give you the money he owes you?" Amber asked one day over dinner with all their kids at Lauren's house.

Lauren shook her head no.

"Don't worry he will pay you or he will be sorry" she said. "I would fuck his life up if he does not pay you. You know I know people who know how to edit videos."

She was referring to the tons of audio and video footage she had been secretly recording of her and Jeremy. Something else Lauren had no interest in knowing.

Lauren felt like she had been reeled into some sort of matrix. Her friend was deep under Jeremy, she was ready to divorce her husband. Lauren knew she was just a piece of ass to him and he had no respect for her.

One day, Lauren overheard Jeremy joking with his friends in his office about Amber.

"I'm telling you, she likes those golden showers," he said referencing people who like others to urinate on them during sex.

"Man stop lying," Orrin said. "Damn, you got a nasty one."

"Yeah that shit is just gross," Mark said.

"Seriously though, when I can meet Amber?" Orrin asked with a sly grin.

"No, this one is reserved for the top dog," Jeremy replied. "She's not allowed to fuck my friends."

"But I bet you can fuck hers," Orrin said laughing. "You already know," Jeremy said giving him a fist bump.

"Roof, roof," they chanted.

Lauren was horrified to think her friend, or any other woman for that matter, would stoop that low.

Either way, Lauren lost all respect for Collins that day and knew he was a fraud. A soulless man who had no clue what kiss and don't tell meant.

Publicly, he represented the community like a saint. Behind closed doors he was a cheat and evidentially, a real lowlife. It was sad women fell for such foolishness. Even sadder he had almost everyone fooled.

His wife had been so nice, Lauren thought from the few times she had spoken with her on the phone. As much time as him and Amber spent together, who was now showing up at public events with him, she had to know about their affair. That was if she was paying attention. Whatever they were doing it was none of Lauren's business.

Lauren did know this, as much drama that was going on in relationships, she was happily single.

CHAPTER 38

Katie glared at the woman walking through their office as if she owned the place. She had whisked by "Dolly the Dingie" receptionist, as Katie referred to her, before going straight into Jeremy's office and shutting the door.

Katie sprang into action and went to his office door only to find it locked. Jeremy rarely locked the door. Staff could walk in at their leisure, especially Katie. She knocked and waited.

The mystery woman opened it.

"Hi, can I help you?" She asked as if Katie was a salesperson knocking on the door to her house.

Katie ignored her and barged in.

Jeremy was sitting on his couch with the remote in his hand flicking channels.

"What is it Katie?" he paused. "Are you high?"

Katie was surprised he would say something like that aloud, and in front a woman she did not know. A woman who had on a dress up to her ass with black patent leather high heeled stilettos.

"Am I high?" She asked. "What kind of shit question is that? No. I just came in to see if YOU were okay," Katie said not hiding her pissed off attitude as mystery woman joined him comfortably on the couch and smiled.

"You know like, SHE is not on the calendar for a meeting," Katie said pointing at Amber.

"I'm good thanks," he answered.

The mystery woman interjected, "Don't worry Katie, I'm taking good care of him." Surprised she felt comfortable enough to call her by her name, Katie was turned red.

"And you are?" Katie asked.

"I'm a friend," she said as she rubbed on the back of Jeremy's neck which he allowed.

Katie wanted to wipe that smirk off her face.

"Hello friend," Katie said.

"Sir, shall I let Monica know you will be home late this evening?"

Just what Katie thought, his wife's name had turned her cheesy smile into a frown. That's how you throw shade when it's sunny outside, Katie thought.

"No," he answered giving her a snide look.

"Whatever," Katie said as she walked out the door smirking while tempted to throw up her middle finger at them.

"You see what I mean she has to go," Amber said as she locked the door. She was still upset because Jeremy had not fired her yet.

Jeremy laughed. *I am the man. Two jealous women ready to have a catfight over me.*

Before he could get rid of Katie, who had already proved her loyalty, he would need to make sure he could fully trust Amber 100%. Patience would truly be a virtue.

Meanwhile, it was time for Amber to do her show as he turned the station to the Atlanta satellite radio channel and turned up the volume.

Even though, Amber had a bad case of PMS, it was "Striptease Tuesday." Before she began, she went in the bathroom and made sure the camera was positioned properly in the side hole of her bag.

In the mirror she saw her reflection. Go make your man happy, she thought.

Back in his office, she drank down a large glass of Cîroc he left for her on the table. The liquor flowed down to her stomach like new oil in a car's engine.

Her aim was to please him totally.

Amber got down on her knees and let him put the pink dog collar on her neck. Then she slowly crawled across the cold office floor.

While she pretended to urinate like a dog, he released the leash and then sat to jerk off. Amber crawled over to him and let him cum all over her face, while he whispered, "lick the ice cream."

Amber had read somewhere sperm was good for a woman's skin and hair. If it were up to her, she would have preferred to suck him off, but he would not allow that. When he finished, she began
to dance as if she was on an imaginary pole in a strip club until he got hard again. Then he fucked her in her ass.

From time to time, they would have vaginal sex, but he always slid out. Her ass was better to take him he said because, "It is so much tighter than your pussy."

She did not mind. When she came, she would almost pass out.

Jeremy took her to ecstasy. It also kept her ass large and fat, which made men of all hues lust for her.

"My shit is natural. Good exercise and good eating," she would say.

Their looks would entice her. She would tease them, and give one or two a lucky night, but for the most part, Jeremy was the only man for her. If she could help it, she would be with him the rest of her life. He would be getting rid of Monica soon. She just knew it.

Knowing her period was coming was bittersweet. She wanted to get pregnant but had no idea why it was not happening.

However, without or without a little one, she made sure he knew she loved him with all of heart and soul.

These were the times she showed him as she began her slow dance to the song *Get Low* and then said, "I love you daddy."

**

Katie looked at the time. 4:03 pm. She would wait to see how long they would be in Jeremy's office. She put a glass up to the wall to try and hear through the thick concrete. All she heard was music. *Crunk music. Typical.*

She went online to try and find a digital footprint on Ms. Friend using her picture from the last event Katie saw her at.

Hello Amber, she said to herself as she discovered her Facebook account where she was standing with her husband and two boys, Katie assumed were her sons. *Damn she's a real cunt.*

While online, Katie decided to check her own bank account. It had almost $40,000—the amount she had earned since working with Jeremy. Petty funds she thought. She was ready for the big payoff, but something strange was going on.

For one, her and Jeremy had never actually had sex. They had only been staging sex scenes giving the impression they were. Was that going to be enough to sue him for millions?

Apart from the time in the car when he picked her up, he never touched her again. Her sex life had been on hold all year and she was tired of masturbating. She knew if she had sex with someone else that may work against the fact, she was going to tell the world she was Jeremy's love slave.

They had spent a lot of time together. They were working late nights and early mornings, but still nothing. She had introduced him to Xanax and Percocet. She enjoyed the nights they spent together when they were away on trips. They would get high and talk all night about everything under the sun.

Something was up. She had never met a man who would turn down her advances—especially when they saw her naked.

When he walked out of his office at 6:45 pm with Miss Friend and bid her a good night, Katie's stomach fluttered. Katie knew one thing for sure. She was in love with Jeremy and he had ditched her. She popped a Rexulti to control her depression before heading home.

CHAPTER 39

W hen are we going to go public?" Katie inquired as her and Jeremy rode the train to a conference in Philadelphia.

"What are you talking about?" he asked looking at her phone.

"It's not on," she assured him. "I think I have enough recordings for the lawsuit."

"Katie, you have me confused, I'm not sure what you're talking about," he said with a serious face.

Why is acting like he has amnesia? One lie is enough to question all truths.

"What's the game plan?" she said trying to control her temper.

"The staff in the office are complaining about you," he relayed.

"Then I guess it's a good thing, I'm not there for the staff," she responded sarcastically.

"They've said you have been coming to work high and drunk. That's not good."

She faced him and listened to the bullshit she felt he was spewing.

"Also, my schedule has been jacked up for weeks. Is something going on with you?" He said looking at her with glassy eyes.

She shot him a puzzled look

"I'm not sure if you are the right person for *the* job anymore," he said.

"I've been helping you all this time. Now you want to tell me I'm not the right person?" She had a thought about who her replacement was.

"Well actually, I've been thinking about aborting the plan. It just may not be worth it," he lied.

"Is that so? Well, I think differently. I still want my millions," she said looking directly in his eyes.

"What millions? We don't make that type of money," he laughed.

"Look at the comedian," she said.

"Well, I don't exactly need you, do I?" She said with conviction and letting him know she was not playing.

Jeremy had not thought she would consider moving forward without her. He had to admit she had just added something to the game.

"Stop it. You know I'm just joking," he said. "We need a little more time, thank you for being patient."

"Let's see, it's November now. Try and enjoy the holidays. Then you should go see my attorney in December. How does that sound?"

Like a bunch of lies.

"Sounds good," she said.

Jeremy turned her face towards him and began kissing her passionately on lips. He gently released her.

"I've been waiting for that," she said as she leaned her head on his shoulder and removed a piece of lint from his jacket. She too could play the game.

Jeremy stared out of the window hiding he was pissed off. The thought of Katie going public was not a risk he wanted to take. The staff would verify she drank and used drugs. Even an attorney fresh out of law school would slaughter her in a deposition. She would likely lose, but so would he.

No, he had to think of a way to get her out of his life.

CHAPTER 40

Lauren sat on balcony of the five-star hotel sipping a steaming cup of Hazelnut coffee. Each day you wake up is a blessing in and of itself she thought.

Some days, if you're lucky, God will awake you with a good spirit and a positive attitude to begin your day. Waking up on a picturesque island could almost guarantee it.

The ocean smelled good. She tilted her head back and let the warm sun rays engulf her.

Amber and Lauren were on their annual girl's getaway in Turks & Caicos.

Someone down here should be paying the actress Lisa Raye for all the free publicity she gave this place by marrying the former President. Now every Black woman wanted to visit the island, she thought.

Lauren smiled as she watched a young couple walking their toddler towards the water with a little bucket and shovel.

Then as if the devil notices you are awake drama appears.

Uninvited. Unannounced. Unwelcomed.

Amber was in her bedroom suite screaming.

"I'm serious. You will not see me anymore until she is gone." Silence.

"Would you want your daughter acting that way around a man?" She continued, "I don't want to hear she is innocent. When

I'm in your office, she always comes in and I don't like her attitude." Silence.

Lauren's knocked on her door.

Amber swung it open still yelling into her phone.

"Fire her by the time I get back or we are done."

Amber went to her bag and pulled out a water bottle and began drinking.

Lauren knew it contained alcohol. It seemed that Amber had been drinking heavily since she had met Jeremy.

Her teen son, Michael was complaining to his "Aunt Lauren" his mother was hardly spending any time at home. Lauren loved Michael like a real nephew but didn't know what to tell him. He told her he couldn't wait to turn 18, so he could leave for college.

"I'm never coming back," he had said. Lauren was going to miss him.

"What's going on? Lauren asked Amber concerned.

"He had better get rid of that bitch Katie or I'm bouncing."

"Don't you think it's too early to be drinking? Put that down and let's talk," Lauren said.

Amber ignored her.

"What?" she yelled as she answered her phone and drank some more.

Lauren went into her bathroom to get ready for the day.

Ever since they had left New York, Amber was on the phone nonstop. Texting or talking to Jeremy.

"How are you gonna disrespect me by cheating on me?" Lauren heard her yell before she turned on the shower.

Lauren knew Amber's emotional and mental health was unstable. The trip was supposed to be a relaxing break. Away from men, the kids, the jobs, everything.

Instead, Jeremy was not only on her mind but in her heart and, sadly in her attitude.

Lauren exited the bathroom and saw Amber crying on the couch.

"I'm tired of him and all these men. I can't even go to sleep at night without a drink or some pill."

Only a few months earlier Lauren had talked Amber out of committing suicide. Then she started seeing a shrink once a week. Yet, it seemed she was getting worse not better.

"Do you think he is going to really fire her?" She asked sniffling.

"Time will tell," Lauren told her.

"Dry those eyes and let's get out of this room. Let's go get something to eat and get our Turks & Caicos on."

Their trip only got worse.

In fact, it turned into a friendship nightmare.

Amber grew distant and curt with Lauren.

Jeremy had to be filling her head, Lauren thought. Amber had turned into Debbie Downer in a matter of hours.

Lauren tried to help, because friends do not let friends go off the deep end.

"Let me ask you something. Why are you allowing this man to affect you like this?" Lauren asked as they laid out on the beach getting a tan. Guys were walking by giving them looks, but Amber acted like she did not notice.

"Excuse me?" she answered sarcastically.

"What's the end game here? You can't even put the phone down long enough to take a swim. You're walking around with two phones."

Right on cue, her phone began vibrating.

"Go ahead and answer," Lauren said to her as if she needed her fix.

"No, he can wait," she said as she muted her phone. "But what I do with my man is my business."

"Your man? Seriously?" Lauren asked. "Your man, you know your husband, is at home in Riverdale, NY. This man, the one who can't stop calling is someone else's husband that you're trying to get advice on how to steal him," Lauren said hoping tough love would help her.

"That's another woman you are trying to hurt. You are a wife. I've been a wife. How would you feel?"

"First of all, a woman can't steal another woman's man. If he wants to leave than that is what he will do. I've even told him he should leave because he is so miserable at home. He should do it for himself not me," she said.

"Look at him," she said as pointed to her phone where the screen was illuminating to show a call was coming in. "He's in love with me. Poor thing can't live without me."

"Never confuse a man's attention with his attention," Lauren said.

"You know what, let me mind my business, you're a grown woman," Lauren said. "But I know he is doing his best to break up our friendship."

"He could never break up our friendship. Never. You're my girl, but why can't you believe he doesn't love his wife? She doesn't cook for him or even do his laundry. You see he eats out every day. I cook for him, I treat him out to dinner, I give him money," she said while adding, "He hasn't had sex with his so-called wife in a year and he sleeps in the guest bedroom."

Lauren could not believe what she had heard. It was time to go into mentor mode. She knew she had paid his car note once. He called it a loan, but now this was too much.

"There are two things a woman should never, ever, ever, ever do," she said emphasizing it.

Give a man cash and ass. Period.

"That is the definition of pimping."

"They are loans, he pays me back," she said.

"Good grief Charlie Brown, what type of elected official needs money from anyone?" Lauren said. "Please stop giving that man money and taking him out to eat. Cook for him, cool, pay a bill for someone's husband in a restaurant? No Bueno!"

"Well he treats me, so sometimes I treat him back," she said.

Lauren wanted to go and curse Jeremy out. Especially since he had been even undecided on whether he was going to buy Amber a Christmas present.

"I guess I should get her something right? He asked Lauren apprehensively one day in his office.

"Well, yes to that. Especially since you've been screwing her all year," Lauren responded.

"What do you think I should get her?"

"A fur," Lauren said so Amber would not have to borrow hers anymore.

"Yeah, that's true, I've never seen her in a fur," he replied.

"Always remember a woman always loves something from Tiffany's," Lauren added. "That blue box will get us every time."

Lauren stood quiet while Amber showed off her ring and matching necklace from Tiffany's. Lauren never told her where the idea came from as she bragged Jeremy had given it to her. Lauren let her have her moment and was happy for her. That is until she replaced her own husband's wedding ring with it on her left finger. *Girl gone.*

Jeremy and Lauren were from the same generation. She knew exactly what he was doing to a much younger Amber. The girl was falling for every trick in the Generation X playbook, but they say everyone gets to play the fool at least once in their lifetime.

"I'm miserable at home and I'm not sleeping with my wife." Classic tattletale of a cheating husband. Yet, they went home every night to them and got their trifling asses in the bed with their wives.

Jeremy went further and made sure he had Monica on his arm in public smiling. They both looked very much in love whenever Lauren saw them.

Monica Morton-Collins introduced herself as the First Lady of Harlem and was revered accordingly. They played Harlem royalty to a tee.

Jeremy also had no shame posting pictures of them together on social media with words of admiration for her.

Lauren knew Amber saw them because she was his Facebook stalker. She set up a fake account to spy. Lauren also knew this affair was not going to end well for her friend. Then again, maybe she just a part of an open marriage like comedian Mo'Nique had shared with the world.

"Just remember this and I'm not saying anymore," Lauren said after deciding she was going to the spa. "The same way you get a man, is the same way you will lose him. If you become his wife, just remember your position as the sidepiece will be vacant. Men like him never stop."

"I'm not worried," Amber said staring down at her phone.

"Are you mad because he owes you money?"

"Please don't think I'm mad. This is about saving my friend. A friend I've known before that knucklehead was even thought about. And trust he will pay me my money, or he will have problems," Lauren said pissed off.

"What kind of problems?" Amber inquired with an eyebrow raised.

"See that's exactly what I'm talking about. You're more worried about him than me." Incredible!" Lauren thought and knew right at that moment their friendship would never be repaired. Loyalty was the vital virtue in Lauren's life, and it was clear where Amber's loyalty now laid.

"It's all good though I can't help you," Lauren said shaking her head.

"Did I ask for your help?" Amber asked.

"No, I guess you didn't."

"Listen he is going to take care of me for the rest of my life or else," she said.

"Or else what Amber?" Lauren asked.

She ignored the question and just picked up her phone and began texting.

Lauren needed a drink and looked around for one of those fine hotel bartenders. She did not want to end their conversation on a sour note.

"Tonight's our last night. What do you want to do for dinner?"

"I'll let you know," Amber said as she continued texting.

Lauren went to dinner with a nice man she had met on the beach. No biggie. The next day they flew back to New York barely speaking except when Amber informed her, she would not be riding back into the city with her.

"Jeremy is coming to get me when we land. He misses me," she said. *Amber was like a moth to the flame burned by the fire.*

CHAPTER 41

J eremy greeted Amber with a passionate kiss as she got into his car.

"Hey beautiful, I've missed you so much," he said smiling. She had not noticed he did not help her with her luggage.

"How was your flight?" He asked checking out her legs before he pulled off.

"It was okay. Nice and quiet," she said while looking for the charger to plug in her phone. She was glad to be home and away from the bitch. Lauren ass was probably jealous of her. Somebody was always jealous, she thought. Jeremy had told her that too. After all, Lauren wasn't married or had a boyfriend. Yeah, that was it, Lauren needed her own man.

"Listen we have to talk. You were right about Katie. She is a liability," he said as the pulled off on the way to the dock.

"Well, I'm ready for the conversation," she snarled. "Did you fire her yet?"

"It's complicated," he said. "I'm working on it."

When they arrived at his boat, he asked, "Can I trust you?"

"You should already know the answer to that," she said.

"Get ready what I'm going to tell you. It's heavy duty," he said while picking up some of Monica's clothes off the table. Amber pretended not to notice.

Jeremy instructed her to turn off her phones.

"They're on silent," she said.

"No, turn them off," he requested.

"Did you know the microphones on the phone may still be on and could possibly be heard by others?"

"No, I didn't know that," she said as she shut them down.

"Now you and I are close," he began while she fixed them two cocktails from the bar.

"That's a good idea, I'll have some whisky straight—a double."

"What's wrong?" She asked curiously.

"Nothing's wrong, but what I'm getting ready to tell you is deep. Only one other person in the whole world knows. That other person is your friend Katie."

He had her full attention.

Jeremy spent the next thirty minutes sharing his plan.

"You see if I get rid of Katie, I will need someone to take her place." He waited for Amber to volunteer for the job.

"And you two in the office together is bad."

Amber could not believe her ears. She wanted in. Fifty million dollars and the chance to run away with Jeremy?

She wanted to scream yes, but she was cool.

"What would I have to do?" She questioned.

"For starters, I will hire you as my new executive assistant. Then you will begin recording us together while we are having sex."

"Wait a minute, were you having sex with Katie? I knew it!" She said ready to fight him.

"No, and you're missing the point. The recordings that Katie has are bogus and staged. It only looks like we are having sex. Then she has some phone conversations with us having sex talk and some texts."

"I see," Amber said believing him.

"The good news is she doesn't have anything that makes it look like I was harassing her. It was consensual and there is no law against me cheating on my wife."

Amber hated the way he said, "my wife."

"The worse that could happen is that you would be embarrassed," Amber said. "Also, if you fire her, she has grounds for a wrongful termination suit. Then when she shows you two were having an affair, it could add up."

"True. Which is why I need you to stop acting crazy around her."

"Say no more," Amber said. "You have to think what to do about her, so I can start working in the office. Or can you give me another position on a temporary basis?"

"You're saying you are in this for the full ride?" He asked while starting to undress.

"Yes! I'm in," Amber said looking around the beautiful trim on the boat wondering how much it cost. Jeremy was so lucky. A powerful man needed a powerful woman like her, she thought.

"Tell me, what happens after we do all this videotaping and shit?"

"We will get you a lawyer and you file the lawsuit against me for sexual harassment and go public," he said standing in his black silk boxers.

"Yes, and I've already researched some real sharks that have sued the government and won. I've also learned about quite a few that have lost, so we have to play this right," he continued.

"Wait, will I leak all of this to the press?" She asked.

Hold that thought, as he looked at the time. I must call Monica. She thinks I ran to the office. Excuse me for a second," he said as he went into the galley.

When he got back Amber was frowning.

"Why the look?" He asked.

"You're sitting here with me and you still call *her.*"

"Listen, I have to continue to play this off. I don't want her to get suspicious. You know I only love you."

"What happens to *her* when this gets out in the open?"

"I don't know, she will probably file for divorce or I will," he said. "It is what it is."

That's exactly what she had been waiting to hear.

"Then I'll resign from office. Fake depression or some shit and be forgotten about. Then you and I can get married and live somewhere like Cuba or Morocco."

"Dubai?" She asked.

"Dubai, it is. Come over here," he said.

"Why are you still dressed and so far away from me? You know I want to feel you all the time."

She went and sat on his lap on the couch.

"How will we move the money?" She asked while stroking his curly hair.

"I've got that covered as well. You will put the funds in offshore accounts under alias names. I already have the accounts. One is in the Cayman Islands, the other in the Bahamas. Now I'll research banks in Dubai."

"There's still one problem," he asked while rubbing on her thigh.

"How does a married woman get sexually harassed?"

"I had not thought about that, but we'll figure it out. Trust me. I want that money and my man," she said before she kissed him.

"I'm excited," She said.

"Let me ask you something. Did you fuck Lauren?'

"Hell no, where did that come from?" He asked putting his hand between her legs.

"I don't know she was acting funny on the trip," she said. "I'm tired of her. End her contract sooner than later."

"Anyway, I thought she was your friend," Jeremy said thinking his plan to get rid of Lauren's uppity ass worked better than he expected. Going to Turks and shit. Amber was his and she

no longer needed external influences. Her punk ass of a husband wanted a divorce and now the BFF was gone.

He smiled thinking how much Amber worshipped him. She had the top spot in the Cult of Jeremy. Not even Sha had been so weak minded.

"Friends come and go like seasons," she said coldly. "She'll be alright."

"Are you sure you want to do her like that? Plus, she knows about us. What if she talks?" he asked.

"Fuck her," Amber said leaning back and allowing him to put his hands in her panties.

"I've gotten all I need from her trust me."

"Well maybe we do something to make that more definitive." He stopped his hand from moving and stared at her.

"No, that would-be suicide. She has some treacherous people in her family. Real dark types," she said.

"They've nicknamed themselves Legit Mafia or some shit like that and there are a lot of them. Plus, she won't talk."

"Please I'm the law," he said with cockiness. "I can get the police just like that," he said as he snapped his finger.

"Ain't nobody messing with us. Mafia Legit, or whatever their name is."

"You know lawmakers get hit too, right?" She asked.

"You grew up away from the streets, but I'm not talking about some thug street justice shit. People in her family are judges, federal agents and cold killers I suspect. She doesn't share everything with me, but I have a feeling."

He listened intently, but Amber was making him nervous. He knew he did not have family or friends that would avenge him if anything went down.

"I'm telling you she will not snitch. Lauren would think that's too unprincipled and she is not worth the risk. Just terminate her contract and let her bounce."

Jeremy thought you never really know someone. "You know her better than me. Her contract is terminated effective this second. She was only there on the strength of you," he said.

"Baby fuck her, let's enjoy this time we together because I missed you too," she said. He smiled and then grabbed her by her neck which caused her to start moaning.

**

After Turks & Caicos, Lauren had not heard from Amber. She had no plans to reach out to her first.

Jeremy's chief of staff Jackie called Lauren to notify her that her contract had been terminated. What a punk, Lauren thought. He did not even have the balls to do it himself.

Jeremy liked playing with people's livelihood. Lauren chalked it up because his own life was so jacked up.

Jackie claimed to have no knowledge of the money owed on her contract. At the end of the day, Lauren knew Amber was behind it all. The same way she wanted him to get rid of Katie, she probably pushed him to do her the same.

The situation reminded Lauren of a quote by Kamand Kojouri.

"Some people are in such utter darkness that they will burn you just to see a light. Try not take it personally."

Lauren realized she should have not helped Amber, but it was good that her true colors emerged. Almost two decades of friendship ended for a manipulating man. Amber broke the girl code. Friends over men, always. Lauren should have known about Amber, she always talked about her other friends like dogs, but then posted how they were BFFs online.

Maya Angelou once wrote, "When someone shows you who they are, believe them the first time."

Good riddance to them both.

Lauren knew this for sure, karma knew their addresses.

CHAPTER 42

Katie was shocked to find a police officer and Jeremy waiting at her desk. The officer was sifting through a clear plastic bag filled with enough drugs to send someone to jail for twenty years. Katie was mortified when they claimed she was the owner.

"There's no way," she said knowing she had been set-up.

"I'm so disappointed in you Katie. How could you jeopardize my office in this manner?" Jeremy asked with the look of a father who had just found out his daughter lost her virginity.

Now, if she went public with the information of their affair, he would make her out to be a criminal.

Jeremy offered her a choice. Either resign or be arrested.

Katie turned beet red. He had used and tricked her.

"Sign this," he said as he handed her a pre-typed resignation letter in front of all the staff.

"You're such a son of bitch," she said snatching the paper.

"Jeremy, you have to know I would never do this. I would never jeopardize you, or us like this," she said.

Amber came out of his office and stood in the doorway. When Katie saw her, sadness turned to anger.

"You bitch. I should have known it was you," Katie said as she went to run towards her with the intent of hitting her.

"Come on. Let's go. I'm ready for that ass," Amber said balling up her fists.

Jeremy grabbed Katie.

"Ms. Romano, it's time for you to leave."

"Fine, I'll leave," Katie said furiously.

"You're a cunt, and you really think you're his wife. Your name is not Monica, but I bet you wish it was, don't you?" She looked at Amber who stared at her with vengeance in her eyes.

"Miss it's time for you to go," the officer. who was doing Jeremy a personal favor, said.

"You did this with her Jeremy? I'm going to get you for this. You both are going to be sorry," Katie said while knocking everything off her desk.

With revenge on her mind, Katie returned home to New Jersey. A lack of sleep plagued her. Most days, her mother could not convince her to leave her bed, let alone to eat. All she thought about was the number of ways she could catch and kill Jeremy.

A shotgun blast to the head which would splatter his brains all over his office wall. Two shots with a .45 in his groin. Some cyanide in his favorite bottle of liquor in his office, or a hit and run?

One night when insomnia called her name, she researched New Jersey's prison for women. She wondered about the accommodations. A pop-up ad greeted her.

"Meadow Banks, a place of peace welcomes you."

Peace. That is exactly she needed to erase the last year of her life and prevent her from possibly spending the rest of it behind bars she thought as she clicked on the ad.

CHAPTER 43

Jeremy's office was familiar territory. Amber settled in as if she had worked there for years. First executive assistant, next thing wife. Fuck anyone who did not believe it was going to happen.

She looked at Jackie sitting on the telephone in her junkyard of an office filled with stacks of files and papers all over her desk and floor. She laughed.

Look at the help she thought. That woman is working way too hard for what she is being paid and was too sneaky. Whenever Amber walked in her office, she was always turning over papers on her desk. Small stuff. Amber had no interest in whatever she was doing. She was lucky she had not made Jeremy fire her as well.

Amber had bigger fish to fry as she thought of the big payoff. Add to it that she would be with Jeremy and nothing else, besides her son, really mattered.

Now, it would be smooth sailing to the finish line. Monica and Richard would not know what hit them. Two spouses who did not even know one another. Life, she thought. You can't make it up.

Jeremy had hired Amber, but he was not sure he could trust her 100% yet. He needed more assurance, if there was such a thing.

Katie was enough of a liability and he wasted so much time with her.

Katie had walked into her own demise as far as he was concerned. Why did she have to get on Amber's bad side? Poor girl, he had really liked her.

Amber was like a real office wife. He would leave Monica each morning only to come and find Amber ready to serve.

"Hey baby, how are you doing today? Bright and early I see," Jeremy said as he walked into the office to find Amber already there.

"Yeah, I needed leave early today. I woke up to another mouse in my bedroom."

"Damn," Jeremy said. Until then, he never even thought about how she lived. Nor had she ever been to his house. They spent so much time together but had never seen each other's personal space.

Amber had suspected her husband was using rodents to scare her out of their house. A house he had purchased before they were married. A house he said her son could stay in until he graduated from high school. He had moved to the upstairs attic and since then, there were mice all over the rest.

"You want to go and sleep with another man. You go and live with him," he told her caring less about some mouse problem.

"Wait," he said. You can't go live with him because he already lives with another woman—that woman is his wife," he said shocking her one day.

"Yes, I know all about you two," he said as he threw some photos of Amber with Jeremy leaving a hotel at her. "Everyone says Collins is a player."

Amber could have cared less.

"Well, I'm no exterminator, but I can come by and plug up the holes for you with some steel wool. I saw some of our building superintendents doing that once," Jeremy volunteered.

Amber thought he was the sweetest man in the world, and it would save her some money from hiring a real exterminator.

"That's nice of you," she said.

"It's no biggie. Anything for my baby."

"Come by tonight at 7, he won't be home," she said.

"What about the kids?" He asked.

"I'll send them to the mall or something," she said. *Fuck and fuck his house. She would leave soon enough with a lot of money.*

"What's on the agenda today?" She asked.

"You," he said looking at the tight denim dress and leather boots she had on.

 "Let's go into my office."

"I'm not in the mood today," she said as a test.

"That's cool, let's just watch some TV," he said. Her turning him down for sex was really no biggie. He could take it or leave it. After all, he had a wife at home who was always ready, willing and able.

**

Jeremy glanced around Amber's sparsely furnished house. It was decent enough, but it felt cold and gloomy. He guessed she was right; love was not living there anymore.

Along with a ton of steel wool in some holes, he left two video recording devices--one in her bedroom and one in her kitchen.

At this stage, he trusted no one. Besides it would be a great way to test her loyalty and to learn what was really going on between her and her husband. As far as he knew, she could have been sent to him as a set-up.

When he finished, they went for a walk around her neighborhood.

"I've got some bad news," he told her.

"What is it?" She asked.

"Katie has been sending me threating messages," he said worried.

"Ignore her. This may be a sign we have to hit first and go public now," she said.

"It's only been few months since you've been working in the office." He said. "We're taking a huge risk if we shoot too early.

"I think we can do this now. Let me go and speak with the attorney. I'll ask about timing. Then we will know for sure."

"That's a good idea. I'll get you the information tomorrow."

"Just be ready," she said.

"I've been ready for three years," He replied.

CHAPTER 44

Monica knew something was up. She pretended not to mind the nights Jeremy had been coming home late or those early morning jogs where he would go straight to his office instead of returning home.

Weekends were worse. He had skipped the past three Sundays with her claiming he was working in Albany. Her distrust of him was growing. She tried to talk to him, but she felt all he was giving her were lies. She also noticed he had two phones, one in which she did not know the number.

What if he had only married her to use her for his sordid plan? Him and Katie had not gone public yet. Whenever she asked, he brushed her off.

"Listen big sis, if you really are having marital problems, either you let it go and put it in God's hands or you start searching through his stuff like he stole something from you," her little brother Patrick advised her via Facetime.

"Do you need me to hack into his email or his phones? Say the word: one, two, three and done."

"No, mom didn't sacrifice for you to attend MIT, so you could be a hacker."

"What do you think we did when we got back to our dorms after class?" Patrick laughed.

"I'm kidding, but personally I never liked the guy. He has always been a little weird with his pretty self. I always thought you would marry a rugged man. Someone who worked with his hands. Not some pencil pusher, behind the desk type of guy. But if he is doing my sister wrong you can count me in on whatever."

"I've always liked the suit and tie guys over the ones who wear Timberlands," she told him. "Don't ask me why."

"Besides, what does he actually do for the people of New York? How does he get work done when he is always traveling somewhere?"

Patrick was right. Jeremy had been taking a lot of trips lately. He told her he was in various cities. When she looked at his passport, she saw stamps from Cuba, the Cayman Islands, and he had taken another trip back to the Bahamas.

"Listen, little brother, I will keep you posted," she said as she tried to hurry him off the phone. Her nerves were bothering her. She wanted to go and take a run before dark.

Patrick put his face close to camera, so it could cover her screen, "Don't be scared, don't let nobody take your cornbread!" They both laughed at the reference to the line from their favorite movie, *Life* with Eddie Murphy and Martin Lawrence.

"Look and ye shall find," Patrick said.

"Love you little brother."

"Good luck! Keep me posted on Operation Asshole Husband."

**

Monica had convinced herself it was not really spying if she was worried. Maybe him and Katie had fallen in love, she thought.

Something was amiss in their relationship and she was mad at herself for believing he was having fake sex with someone. She patiently waited until a weekend when Jeremy was out of town to begin searching.

Her first stop, his man cave in the basement. She began at the bar. A shot tequila and a piece of lime. Then she did a 360 degree check around the impressively decorated room full of the latest in media entertainment that doubled as Jeremy's home office.

"Where would I hide something?" She thought.

The first place she checked was under the toilet. She had saw that in some movie. Behold she found a revolver taped under the toilet seat. I guess that was a good place to hide a gun. Who wants to be unguarded while taking a shit? she surmised. It was strange he had not mentioned it to her.

The bedroom was next. She removed all the pictures off the walls. Under one, was their safe. Sometimes things were hidden in plain sight, she thought. No luck, the regular stuff was in there—emergency cash, another gun, and their passports.

Next, she went to his walk-in closet. Her woman's intuition told her something was amiss.

"Think," she said aloud.

The winter clothes were missing. They are down in the basement. She had totally forgotten about his closet down there.

For the first time she noticed Jeremy had probably had more clothes than her as she looked in the wall-to-wall jam-packed closet.

In his basement closet, she found something new.

It was a portable vinyl closet. It was opened and filled with clothes which looked like he had just tossed inside. Maybe they were too small, and he was going to donate them to the Salvation Army or something? She started feeling through them and then the closet stated moving. It had wheels.

She slid it out and behind it there was a door with a latch.

What the fuck.

Where had it come from? Where did it lead to? Not outside because it would have a stronger lock. She got nervous.

What would she find on the other side?

She felt around the door frame for alarm wires.

Monica ran back upstairs and put the gun it in her waistband thinking no one was going to hurt her in her own home—well at least not easily.

On her way back, she grabbed a pair of the disposable gloves she used at work. Why would she be worried about leaving fingerprints in her own house? She had no clue. Why would her husband have a hidden room in their basement?

When she opened the door, she gasped.

There was another door. The top half was sealed with the words "Sophia's Son" written in blue spray paint.

Who the hell is Sophia? His mother's name was Ernestine.

The bottom had an opening, like the kind you put on a backdoor for a pet. She had to get on her knees to crawl inside. It was such a small space for such a tall man like Jeremy, she thought.

Once inside of the pitch-black room, she felt around for a light switch.

When she turned on the light, she found herself in some type of underground bunker. It was the size of a small bedroom and painted blue as well. It felt like a tomb and the air inside smelled like stale marijuana.

She put a box under the doorway and checked the signal strength on her phone in case she got trapped.

She walked over to a ton of shelves holding pictures of his children, trinkets from his worldwide travels, and pictures of unfamiliar women. Lots of pictures. Some in expensive frames, some taped up on the walls with dates. Women of all races and ethnicities; some clothed, some naked. The display reminded her of the type serial killers kept, or the type law enforcement kept when working on a case.

Do I run right now and keep going?

There was an urn with a Latino woman holding a baby, who looked like Jeremy taped to it.

Who are they?

Monica took out her phone and took pictures of the room from various angles. She had to be sure to put everything back in its place.

A file cabinet held various folders filled with documents. In the first file, there were welcome letters from the Cayman National Bank, the Bank of Dubai and the First National Bank of the Bahamas under unfamiliar names, Gabriel Montrell and Carla

Prince. There were account numbers and instructions on how to make account passwords.

That's why he stopped in the bank and has been traveling to the Bahamas?

In another file, she found adoption papers for a baby named Gabriel Montrell with the same birthday as Jeremy?

This shit is crazy. She took pictures of them all.

Two large plasma screens attached to the wall took her attention away. Below them was a table filled with surveillance equipment like they had upstairs for their security cameras. Tons of green and red lights were blinking. Monica turned on the monitors.

One monitor was Jeremy's district office. Six screens covering every inch of the office, including his own, where shockingly, he was sitting on the phone.

Again, he lied and said he was in Albany. Yet there he was sitting on his couch, in his underwear watching TV less than a mile away from home.

The other monitor was of someone's bedroom and kitchen, where two men were standing making some type of crate with wood. Monica looked closer.

That shit looks like a coffin.

Who are these people? Whose house is this?

She put on the headphones and turned up the volume. She had hoped to hear the sound from Jeremy's office, but it was the two men.

"There is an American saying, how does it go?" Man, number one yelled above the sound of a drill. "I got it! You must not turn a housewife back from a hoe."

Man, number two: "No, dad, it's you can't turn a hoe into a housewife."

Man, number one: "Besides your mother always wanted you to marry a nice West Indian girl like her. But no, you had to go and get an American girl, a poor classless one at that. You know she just wanted you for this house."

Man, number two: "She's still Black."

Why was Jeremy eavesdropping on these people?

**

Richard knew he was done with Amber. She was used goods.

He had spent years paying private investigators to follow her who would report back with pictures and more than enough proof of her adulterous ways. His wife was not only a whore, she was an alcoholic whore.

"Give her sip and she was on your tip," one of the investigators reported. Richard almost broke his hand when he punched him straight in the mouth for saying that. She was still his wife.

He thanked his lucky stars; they had never had children together. Although that was not entirely up to him, as she already had two abortions—well at least the terminations that he knew of. Now, he could not even be sure those were even his.

He had tried everything to make their marriage work. Counseling, talks with a priest, loving her despite it all. Nothing worked. He had to face she was beautiful on the outside, but her insides were sick and would likely never be repaired. There had to be something in her childhood that made her so promiscuous, he believed.

Most of the men she dealt probably did not even know she was married. But the latest one, he was a bold one. Prancing her around town, knowing full well she had a husband. He was so bold he even showed up one night at one of his restaurants. Yes, he had tried his patience.

Senator Jeremy Collins.

He was screwing his wife. Richard was planning to take him back to the old school.

"Everything will be alright," man number one said.

"You know what must be done."

Monica looked over at Jeremy in awe.

What have you done?

Those men looked like they were plotting to kill him. She was planning to get in the car and go warn him.

Just as she was about to leave, a woman walked into Jeremy's office and went to the bathroom. When she came out, she had on a French maid's uniform, heels and she held a cleaning duster.

Monica watched Jeremy summon the woman to him.

Who is she? Her picture was not on any of the shelves.

Monica stared in horror as she watched them.

Slowly, she walked over to him. Monica watched her lips moving. She assumed she was pretending to be the maid that had caught a hotel guest in a room she had come to clean.

Jeremy stared up at her and played along as if he had no interest in her. She turned around and bent over a little pretending to dust off his bookcase.

He rose and joined her from behind with his penis pointing directly at her ass. Then he pushed her against the wall while she backed into him.

Jeremy grabbed her neck and said something into her ear, before letting her go and backing up.

She turned around and Monica took a picture of her on the screen ensuring she had a close-up of her face.

As Jeremy removed his underwear, Monica felt a tear.

Jeremy put some saliva on his hand and inserted two fingers in her asshole. She stuck out her ass more as he thrust harder.

Monica felt her own ass tighten up. *Damn.*

Jeremy took his fingers out and abruptly inserted his hard penis in her ass.

OMG, he did not put on a condom.

The woman took every inch like a trooper while her face reeked of pleasure.

No bed. No soft sheets. Just doing it on a wall in his office.

Monica believed Jeremy looked like he was a German shepherd who had gotten a hold of a poodle as he fucked her vigorously.

Monica felt the sweat on her forehead and nose. She wiped her face before she put her phone in video mode to record them.

When Jeremy was done, he had not even pulled out. He had to have cum inside of her she thought. She could see them smiling at one another.

Monica was furious and angry. She felt the gun in her waistband and debated long and hard whether to join their little party. She could be there in 15 minutes.

Killing them both seemed like a sweet proposition.

Monica was beyond hurt. She was also feeling remorse. She asked herself, "If I would have done the things this woman was doing, would my husband be with her?"

She Facetimed Patrick.

"Can you come to the house right now?" She said crying.

I found something. She turned the camera to show Jeremy holding the woman on the couch. They were talking.

"I'm jumping in the car right now!" Patrick said as he saw the gun sticking out of his sister's waistband.

"Just be easy, don't move. I'll be right there."

Monica wiped her tears and called Jeremy. She watched him ignore her call.

She dialed him again and hung up quickly. She waited a few seconds and dialed again. He would think it was an emergency. She would dial until he answered.

"Yes, babe," he said when he finally picked up.

Monica watched them. The woman sat up with a disgusted look.

"How's Albany? I could not sleep."

"Hey, it's all good," he said as he motioned the woman to go into the bathroom.

"What cha doing?" Monica said playfully although the rage inside was overtaking her.

"I just came back from the hotel gym. I was working out, so I can keep this body tight for you," he said.

"Why are you whispering?" Monica asked as she watched the mystery lady return and sit down beside him. She started checking her phone.

Jeremy cleared his throat and spoke louder. "I'm not whispering."

"Anything else planned for tonight?" Monica asked.

"No, I'm heading back to the room. I'm exhausted. I have an early day tomorrow. A committee meeting at 10."

"Why do you have to work on a Saturday?" Monica asked.

"You know the state never closes," he said casually.

"Can you come home tomorrow? I really want to spend some time with you. We haven't had a romantic night in like forever, and I miss you," she asked.

"Well in that case, I'll come home tonight. It will only take me a few hours."

Mystery lady threw her hands up. He gave her a stern look and put his finger over his mouth signaling her to stay quiet.

"No silly handle your business. Besides I'm sitting here waiting for Patrick to come over. He wants to crash for the night. Something is on his mind and he wants to talk. Something to do with his new girlfriend. He thinks she is cheating on him with someone from work."

She watched Jeremy stand up. "Really?"

"Yes, but you know how he is. Always imagining things that aren't really there."

Jeremy walked into the bathroom, likely knowing he would have to say I love you at the end of their call.

"Well, there is nothing wrong with a little brother sister time. Tell him I said what's up."

Monica heard him take a leak.

"Yes, okay I will. I was just checking in. See you tomorrow?"

"Yes, meeting first and then I'm on the next train back."

"I'll pick you up from Penn Station and we can go grab something to eat. Just call me when you board the train," she said.

"Jeremy, I love you."

"I love you too baby have a good night," he said before walking out of the bathroom.

Mystery woman was getting dressed. He gestured her to stop. They laid on the couch together.

Monica called again.

"Jeremy, I love you," she said.

"I thought you just said that," he replied.

"Say it again please. You know I love your voice. But say it like Barry White this time."

"I love you wifey." He said as deep as he could. Mystery woman did not budge.

Bitch.

By the time Patrick arrived, Monica was outside with the bottle of Tequila. Patrick tried to pry it out of her hands.

"It's not fair. I waited for love for so long. I knew at my age most men were probably taken. When God sent me a single man, I really thought he heard my pleas," she said.

"Come, let's go in the house sis. Your neighbors do not need to hear your business," he said noticing a light went at the next house.

"It was the devil playing tricks on me," she said weeping.

"Come on, you need a tissue. Come inside sis please." Patrick begged.

She never wanted to go back in that house, but she had to show Patrick what she had found.

"Before you touch anything put these on," she said as she handed him some gloves.

"Damn sis, it's like that? You didn't kill him, did you?"

"No, he's not here. I just want to protect you," she said.

She pointed to the monitors.

Patrick saw Jeremy and a woman asleep.

"Where is that?" Patrick asked.

"His office up the street."

"Let's go," Patrick was ready to take off Jeremy's head.

Monica shook her head no.

"Who is that with him?"

"I don't know."

"Can you rewind while it still records live?" Monica asked.

"Yes, how far back do you want to go?" Patrick asked.

"Let's do his office first."

Monica, nor Patrick, were prepared for what they saw. For about an hour they watched Jeremy having sex with the mystery woman various times, day and night. Even while staff and visitors were outside the office.

"Our government dollars at work," Patrick said. "She visits too much to be a hooker."

Monica fell to her knees when she saw Trent on his knees giving Jeremy head.

So that's why you don't want a woman to suck it. You like it from men.

"Oh my God. He's gay too?"

"Bi-sexual sis," he said as he helped her up.

"Whatever, he's on the low down," Monica cried.

"Why me? Why me?" She bellowed throwing up her hands.

"Why would he record this sis? What is really going on?" Patrick asked.

Monica was tempted to tell Patrick about the case, but she was already embarrassed enough.

"Do the other one now, I want to see whose house that is. Earlier, there were some men there looking like they were making a coffin."

"This is crazy," Patrick said while rewinding the video and looking at the stuff on the walls. This is surreal he thought.

"Sis, are you sure you want to know anymore? We can just pack your stuff and leave."

"No, I need to know as much as I can find out. I'm married to a monster!"

"Wait, stop right there. Can you zoom in?"

"Oh shit," Patrick said looking over at the woman with Jeremy and the one who walked into the kitchen with groceries and gave man number two a big kiss.

"It's the same woman."

"It sure is and that has to be her husband," Monica said. "He was talking about her earlier.

"Yep. He has on a ring. What the fuck Monica? I'm telling you we need to go over there right now. I will fuck him up."

Monica knew Patrick would hurt Jeremy. He a former Golden Gloves boxing champion.

"No, there are other ways to skin a cat," Monica told him.

"Always remember you can't play someone without playing yourself," Patrick sympathized with Monica. She didn't deserve this.

**

Patrick stayed the night. In the morning he made her some eggs and toast that she would not eat.

"Let me tell you a story," he said as watched her sitting at the table while staring into space.

"I had this friend once who needed a place to stay. Her friend and her husband let her in. How did she repay her?" He said, as he put eggs on the plate in front of her.

"By getting pregnant from her husband."

"Figures," Monica said.

"You know you're not supposed to bring another woman in your house around your man—not even family."

"No, this one took a different turn. You didn't let me finish, but at least I got you talking," he said handing her a fork.

"The wife ended up killing them both. Shot them both dead and didn't do a day in prison. The jury called it a crime of passion."

"No shit," Monica perked up thinking perhaps she would do that the next time she caught them. Sadly, she knew in her heart there would be a next time.

"I'm telling you this because folks are sneaking around with people's spouses like it's nothing."

"Yeah, it's probably those damn reality shows or all these songs talking about hoes," Monica said. Got people going clinically insane. It's such a useless emotional tactic—the reality is people are getting hurt and our kids are growing up heartless."

"This hoe culture has gone to another level sis. People doing so much dirt, it's hard to figure out what's clean. I don't even think real love is still alive."

"Does anyone care about vows anymore?" Monica asked.

"To think we now live in a world where a wife needs condoms for her own husband is beyond crazy to me," she said refusing to shed another tear.

"I should have stayed single and celibate."

"Listen, keep your head up," he said raising her chin. "Come on eat," he said. "He's not worth it."

"I should write a book for the ladies. Call it how to end a side chick 101?" He laughed.

"What you would advise?" She asked picking at the eggs.

"Destroy her ass workwise, dog her credit, posters up where she lives, works and plays. And if need be, whip her ass. Another dog can't come in my yard. Trust and believe."

"Now there's a thought," Monica said.

"I like it, but you know what? I don't know jack about her. Who has the energy? I married Jeremy, not her."

"The wife rarely ever knows," Patrick said. "You were too busy living your own life for such deceit."

"You know what to do for Jeremy's ass?" Patrick asked but it was more like a suggestion.

"Men hate when you mess with our money and our cars. Make Jeremy learn through his wallet. Take his credit cards, his cash and sell his car. If he chooses to stay or go, it's whatever, but he would be a broke man walking."

Monica laughed.

"See there. A laugh."

"And let's not even discuss how these hoes are a reason why herpes and shit are running rampant through America like a new brand," Patrick said.

"Sis, you will come out on the other side of this madness. Mark my words but be careful."

Monica knew her marriage was over. Jeremy was playing her for a fool. No matter what she knew the first thing she had to do was get to the GYN doctor and get tested. For his sake, she prayed she did not have a disease, or she would kill him.

CHAPTER 45

Had he heard correctly? Did someone just announce on the news that New York Senator Jeremy Collins was being sued for sexual harassment? Detective Klowsky stopped brushing his teeth to run in the other room to catch it. The running water had distorted the sound. He had to go and find the story online.

He read the headline, *"Female staffer sues Senator Jeremy Collins for $50 million dollars."*

How coincidental. Senator Collins' name related to two cases in one year.

He clicked the video.

"Staffer Amber Williams has filed a $50 million-dollar lawsuit charging State Senator Jeremy Collins of sexual harassment. Williams alleges the senator made her his love slave and, on several occasions, forced her to have orgies with him and other male staffers.

Allegedly her proof includes tape recordings, both audio and visual of their sexual escapades, in various locations including his government offices in Harlem and Albany.

The married father of two spoke through his attorney, Elena Harris-Davis.

'Clearly, this is a scorned employee. We plan to diligently defend these allegations against Senator Collins.'

Williams, a former social worker with the state university says she was lured in by Senator Collins' charm. The suit states the Senator used his position of power and privilege to exploit her for his own sexual gratification with threats of termination and bodily harm."

What an ass, Klowsky thought. Was Meadow Banks linked in there somehow? He was still trying to find out how the woman who died there over a decade ago, the same way as Romano was connected.

When Klowsky arrived at this office, he retrieved the file and looked over the case notes. No one had even questioned Senator Collins. However, he knew when you went after someone with power, you had better be sure you had facts and evidence. There was nothing to tie Senator Collins to Romano's death except she had worked in his office and was terminated.

Although her official cause of death was suicide, they had never found what was used to cut her wrists. It was a critical missing piece of the puzzle.

It was unfortunate the staff had compromised the scene by leaving the room unattended. Anyone could have gone in and picked it up, he thought.

Today's announcement made Klowsky feel there was something more. Something told him to keep searching and he knew that would make Dr. Andelman happy.

Even a broken clock tells the right time at least twice a day.

CHAPTER 46

Lauren played with a straw in her rum punch until her cousin Regina returned to the living room. She was visiting to tell her about the Amber and Collins triangle she had gotten herself involved in.

"Now about you, I can't believe what you've shared, and they are all over the news," Regina said as she carried out a blender with more drinks.

"You know as a judge; I don't like the public attention and neither does the family. So honestly tell me are you involved in any way with their saga?"

"No. But his ass owes me money for my services," Lauren said. "I need an attorney from the family council."

"Negative, let it go," Regina replied.

"This is definitely going to be on the next meeting's agenda and others are aware. They did you wrong, that I can agree. But how many times have we told you, that you can't trust anyone but family?"

"You have a big heart, so you are always going to be a target for evil people. That's why the family protects you. Even at times when you don't even know it."

Lauren was not surprised. She thought about several people who had taken her kindness for weakness and how she always repaid them. People tended to forget the devil was once an angel.

"Keep it moving. Neither of them really knows you, or any of us," Regina warned. "We'll see what Rodney thinks when he gets here."

"OMG, you called Smooth?" Lauren yelled referring to their cousin who hung out with Cubans so much, they thought he was from Cuba.

"Had too," she said while filling up Lauren's glass making sure she got buzzed. "No secrets."

They paused their conversation catching up about family, when Murphy, her German Shephard, began barking to alert to them someone was at her door.

"Hush, it's just Rodney," Regina said as she petted him.

"Hey there Rodney, how was your flight?" The family had nicknamed him Smooth because he handled certain matters smoothly.

"It was quick. I came from Miami."

"Miami? I thought you were coming in from Bermuda?" Regina questioned.

"No, I've been down there for about three months now taking care of some things," he said.

"Is Lauren here yet?" he asked looking around.

"Yes, we're in the living room having some drinks."

Lauren got up and gave Smooth a hug. "What's up cuzzo!" She felt his gun bulging on his side.

"Don't cuzzo me. You should have known better. How are the kids? Good?" he asked checking.

"Cuz, I'm going to ask you some simple questions as they sat down on the couch. Just answer them directly. He pulled out a small writing pad out of his jacket.

"Yes," she said nodding her head.

"Who are the primary principals? I want their names and tell me about them, including their family ties, children, people who work with them, etc."

Lauren shared what she knew.

"Do you have something that would end their careers? Jeopardize their money?"

"All I know is about two cheating people. People do it every day. I'm not thinking about them."

"Yes, but that doesn't mean they aren't thinking about you."

"Have either of them threatened you? Wait let me say that another way, because if they would have threatened you, we would not even be having this conversation."

"No, and I ain't scared," Lauren answered.

"Whatever happens, let me say don't involve their kids. They're innocent and no one better mess with mines."

"If anyone comes for your kids, their entire DNA would be wiped out," Smooth said nonchalantly.

"Your wishes are respected. I doubt it will get to that or they would have made a move already. I'm only here for fact checking," he assured her. "But you will let me know if anything changes. I want to know if you even get a parking ticket or the police pull you over for bullshit."

"If you want, we can send some new pussy and some new dick their way. They seem sexually gullible. It's easy to send volunteers to get close to an elected official. There are all kinds of ways this could go, if it gets to that," Smooth said a bit too excited Lauren thought.

Regina interjected, "I want you both to keep in mind, there are cameras everywhere, even in places you would not believe. I get a monthly report on them. Two, remember the wise words of Aunt Doris. She used to say, 'Do not press a desperate foe too hard. The wise warrior avoids the battle.'

Together they said, "*The Art of War.*"

"So, tell me little cousin," Smooth said. "Because I'm intrigued as fuck. What's the story? A politician and a social worker walk into a bar..."

CHAPTER 47

Breaking News: Senator Jeremy Collins has resigned from his position after the state has agreed to settle a lawsuit filed by former staffer Amber Williams for an undisclosed amount.

Calls to Senator Collin's office were unreturned.

A representative from the Governor's office announced a special run-off election will be held in three weeks for Collins' successor.

**

The strong pineapple scent in the care was making Jeremy sneeze. The driver must have been in love with Hawaii or something, Jeremy thought. His shirt had a ton of flowers on it including some purple lilacs. It made him think of Mama Ernestine. It felt like she was with him for some reason as he looked for his handkerchief.

Jeremy cracked the window and let in the cool breeze.

His stomach churned from the hamburger and fries he had for lunch he knew he had no business eating. He looked out the window and enjoyed the sights of NYC's most diverse urban borough as he rode on the Van Wyck Expressway.

In a few hours, he would be an official millionaire relaxing in a hotel suite on a tropical island.

Thanks to Amber the state had settled for $20 million dollars out of the fifty she had sued for. Take the first offer he told her. Millions were still millions.

Amber, like the good girl she always was, had safely deposited the money in several bank accounts across the world.

Her confessing she was once molested as a child by one of her uncles, along with the fact that she claimed she had feared for her life, garnered her sympathy from everyone from the state attorney general's office to the insurance company.

The girl could lie.

Women created hashtags calling him #CollinstheCunt. His favorite was #JusticeforAmber, which took the story viral.

They had been brilliant in their execution he thought to himself as he watched a plane disappear into the clouds from JFK.

Almost there.

The ding on his second phone alerted him he was receiving a text. It was Amber. The poor girl had risked it all for his love and attention. Her father must have jacked her up when she was younger. Clearly, she had daddy issues. Now she was waiting for her new daddy ready to begin a new life.

"Hi babe. On the way to Dubai. See you soon. Travel safe. I love you," she texted.

Jeremy tossed the phone out the window and watched an 18-wheeler truck smash it. No more evidence.

A few moments later, NYPD police lights and sirens were summoning his car over.

Mr. Hawaii said, "I have to pull over."

What in the hell, Jeremy thought.

A police officer asked the driver to step out of the car.

Jeremy heard a tap on his window and a man flashed a gold shield.

"Jeremy Collins?" The burly looking man asked, sounding more like a confirmation.

"Yes, I'm Jeremy Collins," he said annoyed.

"I'm Detective Cohen with the NYPD. Can you please exit the vehicle?" he commanded over the sounds of cars and trucks speeding by.

"What is this about?" Jeremy asked.

"Sir, please exit the vehicle."

"I will not. Not until you tell me what this is about. Is there some emergency? Is my wife okay?"

Detective Cohen said sarcastically, "Is your wife okay? Sir, I think you know this is not about your wife. Please step out of the vehicle," he requested again.

A female officer with a stern look stood about 15 feet away. Her hand was on top of her holstered Glock 9mm. Because of Amber's case every woman in New York City likely hated him. She had told a vivid tale. The officer's facial expression looked as if she was hoping he made a wrong move, so she could blast him all over the busy highway.

"Listen officer, I have a plane to catch," Jeremy said as he stepped out of the car.

"You're a lot taller than I expected," Cohen said looking up at Jeremy.

"Sir do you have any weapons on you?"

"No," Jeremy said. "I told you I was on my way to the airport."

"Well you know some people can travel with their weapons. Didn't you help make that law for the state?" He asked sarcastically.

What the fuck is this?

"We have two warrants for your arrest," he said as he pulled out some papers and gave them to Jeremy.

Blood rushed to Jeremy's head as he read the charges.

"Accessory to murder of Katie Romano?" He said aloud.

The other one was from a New Jersey court. Another signed by a New York judge for embezzlement from a government entity.

"How did she die?" He asked sadly.

How is Katie dead? No one was supposed to get hurt.

"We will explain that to you downtown. Please come this way," Cohen said as he led him to the patrol car. He noticed Jeremy was scared and he looked like he wanted to crap in his pants.

Cohen was a little surprised at his response. He really did not seem to know Romano was dead. He also knew, as human nature, when you tell someone that someone has died, their first question is usually, "How?"

In his line of work, the ones who asked anything else, or said nothing usually already knew. That made them an instant person of interest. There was a strong possibility he was telling the truth.

Collins was a politician, with a psychology degree, so lying likely probably came easy to him, Cohen believed. Either way, he would need to take a lie detector test. Plus, Cohen knew he had pulled off a con against the state, so he was not exactly innocent.

"Mr. Collins place your hands-on top of the hood.

Cohen read Collins his Miranda Rights. "You have the right to remain silent."

"I know my rights," Jeremy said.

"I won't need this will I?" he asked showing him a pair of handcuffs.

"No," Jeremy answered devastated.

On the ride, he thought back to the day he had picked Katie up at Port Authority. *Who would want to kill her?*

After what seemed to be the longest ride of his life, they pulled up to a media circus outside of the Midtown South Precinct.

Photographers took pictures of him in the back seat. Reporters bombarded and screamed at Jeremy as he stepped out of the squad car. The police did not even refrain them. One even pretended to accidentally drop something forcing Jeremy to stop during the already humiliating perp walk.

Bystanders used their phones to record and take pictures. Microphones came out of everywhere.

"Mr. Collins, did you help kill Katie Romano?"

"Mr. Collins were you Katie Romano's lover?"

"Is there any truth that you stole state funds?"

Jeremy pictured people boarding his flight as they led him with his head down into the station.

He had been so close he thought.

Jeremy's arrest was breaking news.

Monica was in her office when her assistant ran in and showed her the live coverage from her tablet.

Jeremy has been arrested?

Monica was shocked.

Someone had killed Katie, the news reporter said.

Jeremy was arrested on his way to the airport. Then they announced something about embezzlement.

Airport?

Jeremy deserved punishment, but this was not what she had expected.

Inside the station, Jeremy was led to an interrogation room and left alone.

He glanced around the room and thought it was a lot dirtier than he had seen on television shows. It smelled like a dead mouse, or a few, were rotting in the walls. The odor of sour milk made him want to throw up.

I'll never survive in prison.

"Please, I need to use the bathroom," he yelled staring into the glass he assumed was a two-way mirror. He wondered whether anyone was on the other side looking at him.

"Look at him in there," Klowsky said who came all the way from New Jersey to see this.

"Let him out to use the bathroom," Cohen directed to an awaiting uniformed officer. "When he is done, I'll go inside and see I can get a confession."

"Hey, afterwards let's grab a beer, since I'm visiting from out of town," Klowsky laughed.

"Sure, let's see how many a good ole N Jay copper can hold down," Cohen said.

When Jeremy returned from letting his lunch out of his stomach and his mouth, Cohen entered the room and sat across from him.

"Do you need anything to drink? I can get you some coffee or water."

"Yes, water please," Jeremy said feeling like he suddenly needed a shower.

"Why am I here?" he asked.

"Which one do you want first? The one that is going to give you fifty years, or the one that is going to give you fifty and a half years?"

"Do you know who I am?" Jeremy asked.

"Yes, you're Jeremy Collins. We met on the highway."

"I'm a former senator, not some common thug you have pulled off the street."

"Let me ask you again detective, why am I here?" he asked with anger.

"Let me get right to it then. I will begin with the New York charges since that is within my jurisdiction. A New Jersey detective is outside awaiting to speak with you next.

"Look just tell me, New York, New Jersey, federal, state. I want to know what the hell is going on?"

"You're a suspect in the murder of Katie Romano and you, along with your chief of staff, Jackie Potter who is sitting in cuffs two doors down, are being charged with embezzling $1.4 million dollars from your office funds."

"Get the fuck out of here. I have never stolen or mismanaged a dime and I damn sure did not kill anyone," he said while slamming his hand on the dirty table. "This is obviously a set-up which I do not find humorous at all."

"I can assure you this is not a joke and you're not being punked. There are no are no TV cameras around," Cohen said.

"This is real life and a woman is dead. It's crazy because if the New Jersey cops were not snooping around Miss Romano's death, we would not even be here," he told Jeremy.

"You two would have gotten away with all that money."

Jeremy wanted to know how that bitch Jackie had managed to steal over a million dollars without his knowledge.

As the elected official, they would never believe he was not a part of it. He thought back to the day she had him write his signature.

"We're buying a stamp pad, so you don't have sign every letter we need for constituents," she had said.

Shit. They are messing with my mind, my money and my freedom.

"Now would you like to hear about the murder?"

332

"I would much rather know why you all THINK I murdered her. Like what's your evidence, facts, you know things like that?"

"Hey, no need for an attitude," Cohen said hinting he should calm down.

"Sir, you would have an attitude as well if you were arrested for something you did not do, and especially before you were going on vacation.

"So again, I ask what makes you think I murdered anyone?"

"The actual charges are accessory to murder."

"Okay, so you don't believe I actually killed her, just helped?" Jeremy asked with a puzzled look.

Cohen started clicking his pen while staring at Jeremy. He was trying to decide how he would break that cocky attitude. The sound annoyed Jeremy.

"Can you please stop clicking the pen?"

"My wife gets on me about this all the time," he said as he placed the pen on the table.

There was an awkward silence. Both men were staring at each other like they were at a Mexican stand-off minus the guns drawn.

"We believe Katie Romano was murdered by the woman who just charged you with sexual harassment and won a hell of a lot of money in a settlement."

Amber killed Katie? No way.

"This woman, Amber Williams was your lover. We believe you two conspired together to murder Katie who threatened to reveal your sexual harassment suit was a fraud," he said.

"There is a quote I would like to share with you because they say politics makes strange bedfellows. Are you listening?" he asked Jeremy who was staring at the two-way mirror.

Journalist P.J. O'Rourke says, 'A man should never be unfaithful to a lover, except with your wife.'

We believe Williams got so jealous of your affair with Ms. Romano that she killed her. She was also protecting your money. Money, we suspect you were on your way out of the country to get."

There's the motive.

"Whoa, wait a minute," he said as pushed the chair back and made a gesture like he was going to stand up.

"Sit back down or I'll cuff you," Cohen said.

Jeremy did as he was told.

This is some serious shit.

"All I'm trying to say is that I'm innocent. It's tragic that Katie is gone, but I can assure you I have nothing to do with her death."

"We have texts and messages showing you two were conspiring together to fire her from your office. Once you did, Williams took her job," Cohen said.

"Fire her yes, kill her no. Hell no. I liked Katie. She was a great young woman," Jeremy said.

Jeremy knew they had absolutely no proof. It was impossible he thought. The bank accounts were held under the name he was born with. The documents with the names he had already sent to his hotel.

The only one who could get to the money was Amber. He put his hands on his face and said aloud, "Damn!"

"I'm sorry did you say something?" Cohen inquired.

Fuckin' bitch, he thought. She had done all of this and ran off with the money herself. He had to give it to her, she was clever. Crazy as hell, but clever. And that last text saying she was waiting for him in Dubai was a nice touch. But even still, he thought, he did not know about any murder and how could they prove anything? He destroyed all the tapes and everything from his house. No Amber was the one who was in trouble, not him.

Jeremy knew she was always jealous of the relationship him and Katie had, but enough to kill her? He was filled with regret. Nothing was worth his freedom.

"Hello Collins, are you still with me?" Cohen asked waving his hand in front of Jeremy's face.

"Yes, I'm here," Jeremy said looking around at the chipped paint on the walls. He had heard enough.

"I want to speak with my attorney, and I want my phone call," he requested.

Cohen hated when a suspect said those words, but he respected the process.

"Fine, Mr. Collins, but you're making this harder than it has to be," he said as he rose from the table.

Twenty minutes later, another officer came into the room and said, "Follow me."

She led him through the station. Officers were staring and mumbling under their breath. Some shook their heads in disdain for him.

"You can use the phone in here," she said as she led him into an empty private office.

"I live in your district and I voted for you," she said before she closed the door and stood watch.

Jeremy called Monica.

"Listen, I've been arrested. I'm in jail at the midtown south precinct on 35th Street. I don't have a lot time to talk," he said. "Don't believe anything you hear. I did not kill Katie, nor did I help have her killed."

"I believe you. Are you okay?" She asked sounding concerned.

"No, I'm not okay. My stomach is in knots," he said wondering who the last occupant of the office was he was in.

"What are they saying about you? Did you embezzle money from your office?" Monica asked knowing he did have a lot of cash they had never reported on their tax returns. He would likely not give her an honest answer because he was calling from a police station.

"This is the first I'm hearing of it in here. You must believe me. I don't know shit about what Jackie was doing. I gave her full autonomy over the funding. All I did was sign," he answered regrettably.

The officer peeked in signaling him to hurry.

"Listen, I need you to call Elena. Tell her what happened and tell her to get here asap. I need to get out of here."

"Why did you leave your car home?" Monica asked hoping for once he would tell the truth.

"Long story. Please get in touch with Elena and call Chad. I have to go now," he said as the officer came in and summoned him to hang up.

"Okay, I will. I should be there soon," she responded.

"Thank you, Monica. I love you," he said.

"Yes, I love you too. Jeremy don't worry, we will get through this," she assured him.

Jeremy was then taken to a room where he was ordered to strip his clothes. When he had to bend over so his anal cavity could be searched was the lowest point in his life.

"No, wait I need those," he said referring to his glasses an officer was placing in a plastic bag.

"You're on suicide watch," the officer said reading from a clipboard.

Jeremy grew fearful. Would he be killed, and they reported he had done himself in? No, no one would believe that he thought. Or would they?

"I'm not gonna kill myself. I can't see a thing without my glasses," he pleaded.

Ignoring Jeremy, the officer said, "Come with me," as he led him to a holding cell.

Jeremy jumped at the sound of the metal bars closing. The two other men inside started laughing.

"First time here?" a man who smelled like rotten eggs asked while the other, who looked like King Kong, stared at Jeremy like he was going to be his new bitch for the night.

Shit. Shit. Shit.

**

Elena arrived at the police station and was told there were strict orders that no one could see Jeremy yet.

"Who gave such an order? I am his attorney. He has the right to speak to his attorney," Elena told the desk sergeant.

"Please miss have a seat, I'll find out what's going on," he responded.

Two hours later she was still waiting.

Where is Monica? Elena thought. Her calls to her went straight to voicemail.

She would wait another hour before she tried to reach her friends who were high up the NYPD chain of command and owed her a favor, or she would owe them one. The least she could do was make sure Jeremy stayed safe and comfortable.

"Jeremy Collins," an officer yelled as he opened the cell.

"That's me," he said thankful it was time to go.

"Come this way," he said as he handcuffed his hands and led him outside to a white van.

Jeremy squinted to read the letters on the side of the van: "CORRECTION: New York City."

"He's all yours," the police officer said before going back inside and slamming the door, which made Jeremy jump again.

"Wait. Where am I going?" Jeremy asked.

"To the island," a correction officer said while he held the door open for Jeremy.

"Riker's Island?" Jeremy asked confused.

"I'm supposed to see my attorney. I have not even seen a judge yet. You can't take me to Riker's now."

"Listen buddy, we have an order that says Jeremy Collins is going to Riker's. Get in and shut up NOW!" the officer said looking around to see if anyone else was in the alley.

"Right this way Mr. wink," he said while pointing to the inside of the van.

"Wait, what. What did you call me?" Jeremy asked.

"Get in the van inmate," he yelled.

"Inmate? Hold on someone is making a big mistake here." Jeremy said noticing he was the only one in the van besides the driver at the wheel.

"Well if it's a mistake, we will drive you back. But for now, get your tall ass in the seat and be quiet," he said as he shackled him in the van.

"Sit back and relax. It's going to be a nice scenic 35-minute ride through the magnificent countryside of New York City before arriving at the beautiful island of Rikers. A place where everyone is waiting to greet a pretty gentleman such as yourself. You'll have a choice between WINKING at Helen or her nice brother Hakeem."

339

The officer's both started laughing while Jeremy stared straight ahead.

Ain't none of this shit funny.

"How many times are you gonna tell that joke Morrellio?" The driver asked as he slammed the door.

Morrellio?

"My brother does all this law enforcement stuff. Right now, he's a correction officer at Riker's. Kevin Morrellio, have you heard of him?"

"Kevin Morrellio?" Jeremy asked fearing the worse, but he knew it was Katie's brother.

"At your service, you piece of shit," he said before he gave him a wink and banged him upside his head with the brass knuckles on his hand.

"Wait!" Jeremy yelled while he threw up his hands trying the stop the next blow while he felt the van pull off.

CHAPTER 48

Detective Clarissa Genova felt like she had been in a sardine can. She anticipated the airplane's door opening as if she was running out the gate at a marathon. The NYPD doesn't pay me enough, as she thought about her two years of service left before retirement.

"That was a long ass flight," she told her partner, Detective Nelson Monfleury, as he grabbed their suitcases from the overhead compartment.

"Fourteen hours. I'm almost positive it was the longest flight I have ever taken," Monfleury said.

Genova was grumpy as hell and wanted nothing but a cup of the strongest Middle Eastern coffee she could find.

"It's gonna be alright. We'll do what we have to do and go sightseeing on the city's dime," he said as they walked into the terminal and sighted the Dubai police officer waiting to meet them.

"Welcome to Dubai. I'm Brigadier Manar Yasmin of the Dubai Police," he said in perfect English. "The woman we believe you are looking for is over there," he said pointing.

**

Amber patiently awaited Flight 489 from JFK to land at the Dubai International Airport.

Although her Emirates flight had arrived late, being able to take a shower as a first-class passenger on the airplane was excellent. Flying coach was now a memory.

She knew she looked stunning with her middle eastern attire. She smiled knowing it was all for the man she was going to spend the rest of her life with. Her own flight delay prevented her from leaving the airport, so she just hung around. Jeremy would be surprised.

Getting the man and the money was a prize. She always knew she was his one and only true love.

I bet that no cooking, no sex having wife of his, is going to be shocked as a fuck when she realizes he won't be coming home tonight.

One by one the passengers exited the plane, but there was no Jeremy. Maybe he went to use restroom at the last minute? She thought as two men and a woman approached her.

"Amber Williams?"

"Yes?"

"We are with the NYPD. I'm Detective Genova and this is my partner Detective Monfleury," she said as they flashed their badges. "And this is Brigadier Yasmin of the Dubai Police."

"Can we speak with you for a moment?" Genova asked realizing the freezing terminal gave her an instant buzz and woke her up.

"Yes, okay sure," Amber responded.

"Please have a seat," she motioned to Amber.

"Collins won't be joining you today," Monfleury said as he sat down and saw her staring at the gate door.

"Who?" Amber asked. Monfleury gave his partner a look of disbelief.

"Jeremy Collins, you know the man you just sued," Genova said sarcastically while preferring to stand.

"A little humor," Amber laughed.

"I know him, but what makes you think I'm waiting for him?" She asked.

Genova was ready to throw the handcuffs on her. Her smug attitude was not appreciated.

"Listen young lady you are in a lot of trouble back in the states. We have come a long way to speak with you," he said hoping she would take them serious.

"Why is that?" Amber asked.

"You are a person of interest in the murder of Katie Romano," Monfleury said.

"Murder of Katie Romano? That's ridiculous," she said. *They have nothing.*

"Yes, murder," Genova blurted out wanting to add the word bitch.

To her, Amber was the most gullible woman in the world. Not only was she a married woman, but she was also cheating with a married man. A married man the police suspected she had committed fraud with and murdered a young woman.

All for what? Many cases had confused her, but this was the most bizarre she had come across.

Williams had reminded her of the time she caught her own husband with some floozie. Her thoughts of revenge were halted when she deemed her children and the career, she worked countless hours to build, were more important. She ended up getting hers when someone stole her ex-husband from her. What goes around comes around she knew for a fact.

Whatever happened to the sisterhood women share? Genova thought. Times sure had changed. Amber would have a lot of time to think about that when they gave her life in prison.

"Katie Romano died ironically, six months ago today, at the Meadow Banks Psychiatric Hospital," Monfleury read from his notepad.

"I heard Katie committed suicide," she said as she shifted in her seat.

"Initially, that was the coroner's report, but we have reopened the case. We are from the homicide division and are working with the New Jersey police to capture her killer which is you," Monfleury continued.

"You should know whomever gave you up were really good. Dare I say, they either loved Katie a lot or they hated you more."

"Hated you more." Genova said.

Amber sat quietly. She knew silence was golden as she looked at the Dubai police officer staring intently at her.

"Do you remember the razor?" Monfleury asked.

Amber sat expressionless. *They were fishing. If they had something concrete, I would not have been allowed to leave the United States. Fish on.*

"At first, we could not understand how you did it. How you could get inside the hospital, kill Miss Romano and leave undetected?" Monfleury said.

"Of course, good detective works means connecting the dots," he continued. "Unfortunately, as in most murders you slipped up."

Amber attempted to reach into her bag.

"Easy now," Genova said watching Amber's hands.

"I can't go in my bag? No worries detective just pulling out a little bottle. See?"

Amber pulled out a miniature Jack Daniels bottle she had saved from her flight.

"No alcohol in a public space. It's against the law to drink in public in Dubai. Put that away or I will arrest you," Brigadier Yasmin warned her.

"I'm very sorry" she said smiling at Brigadier Yasmin who smiled back. *I need a drink badly.*

"Funny thing Mrs. Williams, we found out a woman named Rita Shreveport died the exact same way at Meadow Banks fifteen years ago. The same way as our victim--sleeping pills and her wrists slashed," he purposely stopped to see her reaction which was sullen.

"That woman was your mother."

A look of anger came over Amber's face.

"Fuck my mother. She always hated me."

Now, we're getting somewhere Monfleury thought.

"That's how you knew the layout of the hospital. It was genius of you to fake being a member of the staff while most of them were busy getting the killer Terrence Shane admitted. Most of the security guards were monitoring that situation. All except one. *Yeah, that was brilliant and easy she thought.*

"Do you remember the patient Randolph?"

Yeah, the fuckin' retard.

"Well, he had the razor. We found it in a box in his room. It matches a box you purchased from your neighborhood Walgreen's only two days before Ms. Romano died."

"You have quite a story detective. You know this is merely a coincidence. My mother's death was a suicide. A suicide for an evil life," she said growing impatient.

Where the fuck is Jeremy?

"You have nothing on me."

Genova shook her head. Let her have it, she thought.

"We have overwhelming evidence and witness reports that places you at Meadow Banks the day Ms. Romano was killed— even photos. Photos which were mailed to us anonymously with the words "smooth sailing" written on the back.

"Photos of you leaving the building, walking to the woods and getting into a rental car." He pulled out several 8x11 photographs of Amber and handed them to her. She let them fall to the floor.

"Now that was just rude," Genova said while she picked them up.

Amber smirked at her.

"You really should look at the pictures, especially this one here," he said as he held it up in front of her face.

"This one is of you at the Enterprise counter at LaGuardia Airport getting the car." He laughed. "Someone, we don't know who, was following your every move."

Who could it have been Amber thought? Was Jeremy following her? No. He loved her. *Why wasn't he here then? Where is he?*

"Did you also know Collins had surveillance cameras in your house? Someone also sent us that footage."

"Let her listen," Genova said.

"The guys got such a kick out of one your conversations. They recorded it and sent it to me while we were on the plane. It's the conversation you two had about him firing Ms. Romano and your friend Lauren, is it?" He asked.

Genova was happy to see Amber cringe.

"Collins was a creative guy. You fell for his bullshit, don't take the rap for him," he said as he pulled out his phone and played the voicemail.

"Your pussy is so good; you have the power to hire and fire. Katie and Lauren are both gone, are you happy now?"

"That's a good one for the jury," Genova said.

Amber wanted to cry. He had a camera in her house? How could he betray her like this? No, she would not believe these two strangers. She had to be strong.

Just get your money and wait for Jeremy. He's coming.

"This is all circumstantial," Amber said watching an airline agent closed the gate door.

"Your jealously got the best of you and that's so unfortunate. Ms. Romano was an innocent young woman caught up in a bizarre game. You should have just settled for the money. Collins played you both and now you both lose."

Jeremy call me.

"Whatever he promised you, as we said he will not be joining you today. Right now, he is with *his wife.*" Genova emphasized.

That statement hit Amber to the core.

Time to go.

"Am I under arrest?" she asked.

No bitch, but I would drag your ass back if I knew it would not mess up my pension and you would get to go free on a technicality. Genova thought.

"No, you are not under arrest," Monfleury said.

"Since this is Dubai, we do not have the authority and the United States does not have an extradition treaty here."

Amber looked at Brigadier Yasmin and asked, "Am I under arrest?"

"No," he said.

Amber stood up to leave.

"If you're innocent, you have nothing to worry about." Monfleury said.

"You should know your son and husband's passport have been revoked. Yours has been tagged as well. Several authorities will be monitoring your movements.

Not a problem, Amber thought. I know many people who can make fake documents.

"If you do not come back with us you will be on the FBI's Top Ten wanted list as a fugitive from America." Monfleury stated.

Amber laughed relieved that she was on safe soil.

"That's not going to happen," she said.

"If I were you, I would probably not leave Dubai." Monfleury said. "The Dubai police are watching you as you can see."

"You all have a great day," Amber said before getting up and quickly walking away.

Amber dashed to the first ladies' room she found. She dialed both of Jeremy's phones. They both went straight to voicemail.

Monica's hands shook as she nervously dialed the Bank of Dubai.

Her scream of, "No, you bastard" echoed throughout the airport terminal as she listened to the automated bank recording announce, "Your account balance is zero."

CHAPTER 49

Amber called Jeremy nonstop leaving him voicemails and texts while concluding he had stolen her money. He could be anywhere in the world she thought. Broke and heartbroken was too much to bear.

Where did she go wrong? It had been the perfect plan.

She had risked it all and now everything was gone. She phoned her son and told him she loved him. Richard would not come to the phone.

After sipping on cocktails at the rooftop bar of the JW Marriott Marquis Hotel, Amber casually walked to the ledge of the 77-floor tower. She waved to the police officer who had been following her before leaping to her death.

**

"Former Senator Collins violated the public's trust on two occasions in two states," Caroline Vintage, the US Attorney for the Southern District of New York announced. "He has been charged with accessory to murder for the death of 29-year old Katlin Romano, two counts of embezzlement, fraud, misuse of the public trust, mail fraud, and three counts of wire fraud. If convicted, he faces up to 40 years in prison."

**

"Is there anything else I can help you with?" The waiter asked the gentlemen sitting in the restaurant of the Ritz-Carlton in the Cayman Islands.

"Yes, can you bring me another drink please? Also, we're going to need a glass of cherries for my friend."

Trent glanced at the time on his phone and looked up at the picturesque sunset.

We are going to have such a great night, he thought.

EPILOGUE

Monica asked, "Can I put on my headphones now?"
"In one second Madame Prince," the sexy looking French anesthesiologist said as he prepared the needle for her arm.

"I have a few questions for you to answer first."

Monica glanced around the immaculately sterile state-of-the-art operating room and smiled.

In few hours she would look ten years younger and her new name, Carla Prince, would do just fine. She was leaving everything Collins behind. Everything, except his money. That and proof that would help exonerate him in Katie's murder which included hours of their telephone conversations, none of which spoke of killing Katie. She knew Jeremy was trifling, but he wasn't a murderer. He did not have the heart.

He had been lucky she had one.

She thought about how gracious the bank executive had been that morning when he transferred all that money into her new Swiss bank account.

After the attorney was paid, Jeremy and mystery video woman, she now knew as Amber Williams, had walked away with $7.5 million dollars each. Monica was disappointed he never told her he had gotten the money.

No honor among thieves, she surmised.

Why would they Amber kill Katie?

No honor among hoes either, she guessed.

She wondered how Amber's husband felt when he found out there was a million dollars in an offshore bank under his name.

He would likely think it was a joke, so she included a note and video footage of their spouses.

Yes, it was only right that he received compensation for what his wife had done. Maybe someday, she would have a chance to ask him whether the coffin he was building that day was for Jeremy or Amber?

Jeremy would be likely be sent to prison for the other crimes. Amber was likely somewhere trying to find out where her money went.

"Is there an emergency contact we can list Mrs. Prince?" The anesthesiologist asked.

"Miss Prince," she corrected.

"My apologies, I thought you were married," he said looking at her wedding ring she had forgotten to take off.

"No, it's okay. Maybe someday," she answered.

"Yes, marriage is a good thing. I love my wife, he said. "You can put on your headphones now."

"Don't ever cheat on her," she said.

"Never. She would kill me."

"Something like that," she said smiling

"Never forget. Karma has no deadline," she said while hitting play to listen to her favorite artist, Mary J. Blige.

S.R. CHASE

AUTHOR INFORMATION

The Chase Is On!

S.R. Chase is a native New Yorker who has a passion for prose.

Thank You for Reading!

PRIVATE BETRAYAL!

Stay Tuned for the next Chase!

Coming in Spring 2018

www.srchase.com

@SRChaseAuthor | SRChaseAuthor@gmail.com

PRIVATE BETRAYAL